CW01656328

SHADOWS ON THE FENS

SHADOWS ON THE FENS

EAST ANGLIAN TALES OF TERROR

EDITED BY WAYNE ADRIAN DREW

Shadows on the Fens: East Anglian Tales of Terror
Edited by Wayne Adrian Drew

ISBN: 978-1-908041-13-5

Published by IndieBooks
4 Staple Inn, London, WC1V 7QH

www.indiebooks.co.uk

This edition © IndieBooks 2016

Set in Adobe Hebrew

Printed by TJ International, Padstow, Cornwall

To B.V.T.

We are very grateful to those who helped in our efforts to identify the rights-holders for those works that remain in copyright, and apologise for any we have been unable to trace. We would particularly thank The Reverent Jonathan Boston for the inclusion of his father's story Lot 629, and the advice of Rosemary Pardoe, editor of 'Ghosts and Scholars', Richard Dalby, and Jason Hall of gladysmitchell.com. 'The Bure at Midnight' is reproduced by kind permission of Gregory and Company. 'Black Shuck the Devil's Dog', 'The Lantern Men', 'Shadows on the Fens' and 'The Guide' are reproduced by kind permission of the authors.

CONTENTS

INTRODUCTION

Conjuring Ghosts:
An East Anglian Literary Tradition

On All Hallows Eve 2013, at our cottage in the Norfolk countryside, I first began work on this collection of strange tales, all set in remote East Anglia – a region that, for the last twenty years, I've called my home. My aim? To provide a selection of the finest supernatural literature this ancient and secluded realm has inspired, from times long past up to the present day.

In the last century an abundance of chilling stories were written, firmly rooted in the eastern counties' stark and atmospheric landscape that brought a pleasing terror – if sometimes sleepless nights – to readers young and old. Yet today, very few are easily found, to be enjoyed before a roaring winter's fire, or summer's night beneath a gibbous, witch's moon. So, my first task was to search them out and select the very best.

The wind was howling, the oak beams creaked, and a true sense of expectancy was in the air as I turned the yellowing pages of many rare and much-prized tomes, deciding on which stories my anthology should include. Our cottage dates from the 15th century and many claim we have a ghost whose dim outline can appear on such late autumn nights, when flames burn blue inside the smouldering hearth, and the gale shouts loudly in the tall old chimney stack.

On one side of our inglenook a solitary candle flickered, while at a mullioned window a fresh-carved pumpkin grinned out at the stormy dark, defying those unwelcome spirits said to roam at such a time. For Hallowe'en, in the district hereabout, remains the moment when the veil between this world and the next is lifted – so they say. An occasion to be celebrated, yes, but feared as well.

A time not just of apple bobbing, and predicting what's to come, but of story-telling too – as anecdotes of witchcraft, ghosts and ghastly creatures from the fens are passed from one generation to the next; when, with nervous eyes, the young – and old, who still take fright when graveyards yawn – peer deep into the corners of the room, dreading what might hide within the dusky shadows lurking there.

From the misty fenlands to the storm-lashed coast, it comes as no surprise that, over centuries, Norfolk, Suffolk, Cambridgeshire, and that wild country to the west as far as Peterborough, have inspired so many writers to produce their tales of terror. For the ghost story is central to this far-off corner of England, rich in its folklore, myth and remembered grim events. Here witchcraft, occult practices and traditions (quaint, strange and sometimes most obscure) survive right to the present day in isolated villages far removed from city life; rich remnants of a rural legacy some may challenge, others mock or even fear, but many prize and celebrate.

For natives, such as me, the cry of Old Black Shuck, the 'devil dog' will always echo on the wind. He's part of our romantic heritage – but woe betide the poor soul who meets him on a stormy autumn night. Darker still, the vile crimes of Matthew Hopkins – known as the Witchfinder-General – resonate in those places where he undertook his cruel trade. The scent of smoke from his burning pyres lingers even now upon the evening breeze; as does the creak of swinging gallows' ropes, and cries of dark plumed crows that feasted on his victims hanging there.

At the stately halls of Blickling, Rainham, Felbrigg, and great Oxburgh, it's claimed ghosts walk not only at the midnight hour, but also in the midday sun. For, just in Norfolk alone, there exist almost two hundred sites where things claimed paranormal, or unexplained at least, have taken place. As for the adjoining counties? The list is endless and the events there equally bizarre and terrifying.

So, as the spectral and macabre have always played a central part in this area's dark folk culture, it's hardly a coincidence that they emerge in its literature as well. For exist or not, these phantoms evidently fulfill some deeply-rooted human need and tales of their horrifying deeds plainly fascinate as much today as they always did.

The anthology I finally devised brings together a broad selection of some of the most powerful supernatural stories inspired by this land of myth and magic. Alongside such masters as M. R. James and E. F. Benson, I have included other works from books by lesser known, but similarly evocative, authors from the past. They are mostly out of print, but even when these rare editions can be found, they may fetch prices difficult to believe.

Then, added to my witches' brew are new 'ingredients' too, from modern writers who themselves are genuine keepers of the gothic flame. In their subjects, atmosphere, and ability to enthrall, they clearly show this region's proud tradition of the ghostly tale is not only resonant and ongoing, but as potent as ever in its power to chill even the most sceptical of minds.

The locations of many of these haunted tales can be discovered with some diligent research and all may be visited by the curious and brave. M. R. James' Fenstanton – from his unfinished story *The Fenstanton Witch* – is a real village, but very different now to that of the author's day, let alone the period in which his tale is set. Seaburgh is unquestionably Aldeburgh, in his *A Warning to the Curious*, and Burnstow, in *O Whistle And I'll Come to You, My Lad*, is Felixstowe. Though, as time has considerably changed these actual places, they no longer prove conducive to producers adapting James' stories for film or television, and more atmospheric sites have understandably won out.

E. F. Benson, in *The Face*, may have had that most evocative of villages, Dunwich, in mind for the fearful conclusion of his story, but the shack, still visible on Blakeney Spit, is certainly the site of *The Tale of the Empty House*. The Blakeney Hotel, where Benson took refuge during a torrential thunderstorm as recounted in the story, still looks out from its prime spot on the old quay on to the endless marshes and the grim old house itself standing ominously, next land, sea and sky, on its far distant promontory.

Blakeney Spit is also *Stivinghoe Bank*, in R. H. Malden's memorable tale. For those with energy enough, a demanding two hour each-way trek, along its pebble path, next to shallow hummocks (that in summer are rich with multi-coloured sea blooms but in winter forbidding, harsh and bleak) will take you to Benson's 'Empty House' itself. Piers Warren (the winner of the ghost story competition run in conjunction with this publication) had that precise location in mind too, when relating the horrid antics of the wicked Black Shuck, in his tale *The Devil Dog*. A wildlife photographer and film-maker, for several years Piers lived close to Norfolk's endless northern beaches, and the great marshlands that teem with bird and animal life. So surely, as he walked that lonely path to the far reaches of austere Blakeney Point, the same dark thoughts must have occurred to him about the vicious Hound of Hell, as they had once to me, when amid the fierce wind and sound of crashing waves, I visited that secluded spot. Though, unlike the narrator in Coleridge's *Ancient Mariner*, as I travelled down the 'lonesome road' I did look back, if not exactly 'in fear and dread', but with a definite degree of anxiety, to see, what, if anything, might be following.

What unfolds in *Lot 62* by Noel Boston (coincidentally, the father of our local priest) also originates in an unspecified great house near Blakeney. A mansion, very similar, can be found just outside the village on the way to Cley. There, garden produce is now sold, an art gallery displays some local artwork, and accommodation is available as well. O tempora! O mores!

Then further along the sea road to the east, 'the seventeenth hole at Duncaster', in R. H. Wakefield's tale of the same name, can most probably be played on the large golf course close to Sheringham – for an appropriate fee. The Poppy Line that runs nearby, equipped with steam trains and period costumed staff, offers a spectacular ride along the coast to Weybourne and then to the Georgian town of Holt, and is used in period dramas that sometimes have a supernatural theme. Its sister line, the Walsingham and Wells Light Railway, also runs throughout the year and it was most probably that which brought the victim (played by Michael Horden) to his fateful destination, in Jonathan Miller's classic adaptation of James' *O Whistle and I'll Come to You, My Lad.*

At Wells was filmed *A Warning to the Curious*, the famous installment of the BBC's series *A Ghost Story at Christmas.* The reasons for the choice are clear enough and virtually all the locations they included in that adaptation still remain within the quaint old town. While just outside there are the marshes where the central character sees the frightening William Ager prior to their terrifying final confrontation – an event recorded, for the episode, at the pine-clad dunes near Holkham beach.

The benighted spot for Ramsay Campbell's contemporary tale, *The Guide*, is nearby as well. It's somewhere between Cromer and Hunstanton, the narrative claims, where both an old inn and ancient church are said to stand. I've spotted ruins that might just fit the bill to the north of Cley. There, a path leads towards the distant remnants of a small, seemingly religious building, and the cold North Sea. Perhaps one day you'll venture down that track yourself? I didn't have the courage, I'm afraid.

The section I have included from *Wraiths and Changelings*, Gladys Mitchell's rare story of ghost hunting and murder, provides a much less speculative destination – it's misty Wroxham Broad (a spot greatly loved by the author). Indeed, her novel is related with such geographical precision, readers can easily chart the exact location of all the eerie incidents that take place on that fateful trip.

The occurrences in *The Everlasting Club* by Arthur Gray all happen at Jesus College, Cambridge (in a chamber near a staircase with the idiosyncratic name of 'Cow Lane,' although that's where all humour ends in the tale!); while those in *Bone to His Bone* by E. G. Swain take place just a little further north in Stanground (termed Stoneground by the writer). That village, on the borders of the Fens, now lacks the charm a reader might expect from Swain's delightful stories of 'ghosthunter extraordinaire' the Reverend Rowland Batchel, but the church in which he served can still be found.

There is a conscious indefiniteness about the locations of most of the other fenland tales I have included. We are simply told that Hetty Pegler's Christmas celebrations take place in 'her small flint cottage on the edge of the Fens,' in Celia Dale's rush-lit yarn.

R. H. Malden in *A Collector's Tale* deliberately withholds the village in question, only saying that it was about 'twenty-five miles from Cambridge – I don't think I will tell you in what direction.' While the horrific happenings in his *Between Sunset and Moonrise* occur 'off a drove' near the fictional village of Yaxholme, positioned to the north of Cambridge. We've no idea where – but judging from what takes place there, it's probably best avoided too. Similarly, James Humphreys' *The Lantern Men* inhabit some vague and desolate spot between Wisbech and Cambridge, and *Shadows on the Fens*, the title story, unfolds in a frozen purgatory between Revesby and Boston. But as for Bullen's mill 'where poor little Euphrosyne got her fright' in R. H. Mottram's *The Headless Hound*, its whereabouts are anyone's guess, I'm afraid!

Still, Witches at Hallowe'en, from W. H. Barrett's delightfully anecdotal *Tales from the Fens*, is a true account of an autumn evening spent at a very real Welney, when the narrator's fearful belief in local myths and legends suddenly materialise in a decidedly unexpected way. While at Bungay, much further to the south, Black Shuck appears again, in Abraham Fleming's authoritative and seemingly authenticated, *A Strange and Terrible Wunder*. The text of his pamphlet, written in 1577, provides a frighteningly 'true' account of the demon dog's misdeeds (and is one of the sources of the *Hound of the Baskervilles*, which Conan Doyle reportedly began while staying at a hotel in Cromer). Could such an event really have taken place? And if not, what accounts for the great deep claw marks that remain to this day on the door of Bungay church?

For where truth begins and folklore ends is not easy to unravel in the Eastern Counties – and with that rests their profound mystery and enduring fascination.

So, as the nights draw in, the wind rattles the casement windows, shadows flicker and autumn's withered leaves flurry before the late October moon, why not settle down, next to a blazing fire of apple-wood, and sample this selection of strange and ghostly tales I've here compiled for you? You won't be disappointed by then. More likely chilled; chilled to your very bone…

Wayne Adrian Drew
October 31st 2015

BETWEEN SUNSET AND MOONRISE

R. H. Malden

During the early part of last year it fell to me to act as executor for an old friend. We had not seen much of each other of late, as he had been living in the west of England, and my own time had been fully occupied elsewhere. The time of our intimacy had been when he was vicar of a large parish not very far from Cambridge. I will call it Yaxholme, though that is not its name.

The place had seemed to suit him thoroughly. He had been on the best of terms with his parishioners, and with the few gentry of the neighbourhood. The church demanded a custodian of antiquarian knowledge and artistic perception, and in these respects too my friend was particularly well qualified for his position. But a sudden nervous breakdown had compelled him to resign. The cause of it had always been a mystery to his friends, for he was barely middle-aged when it took place, and had been a man of robust health. His parish was neither particularly laborious nor harassing; and, as far as was known, he had no special private anxieties of any kind. But the collapse came with startling suddenness, and was so severe that, for a time, his reason seemed to be in danger. Two years of rest and travel enabled him to lead a normal life again, but he was never the man he had been. He never revisited his old parish, or any of his friends in the county; and seemed to be ill at ease if conversation turned upon the part of England in which it lay. It was perhaps not unnatural that he should dislike the place which had cost him so much. But his friends could not but regard as childish the length to which he carried his aversion.

He had had a distinguished career at the University, and had kept up his intellectual interests in later life. But, except for an occasional succès d'estime in a learned periodical, he had published nothing. I was not without hope of finding something completed among his papers which would secure for him a permanent place in the world of learning. But in this I was disappointed. His literary remains were copious, and a striking testimony to the vigour and range of his intellect. But they were very fragmentary. There was nothing which could be made fit for publication, except one document which I should have preferred to suppress. But he had left particular instructions in his will that it was to be published when he had been dead for a year. Accordingly I subjoin it exactly as it left his hand. It was dated two years after he had left Yaxholme, and nearly five before his death. For reasons which will be apparent to the reader I make no comment of any kind upon it.

The solicitude which my friends have displayed during my illness has placed me under obligations which I cannot hope to repay. But I feel that I owe it to them to explain the real cause of my breakdown. I have never spoken of it to anyone, for, had I done so, it would have been impossible to avoid questions which I should not wish to be able to answer. Though I have only just reached middle-age I am sure that I have not many more years to live. And I am therefore confident that most of my friends will survive me, and be able to hear my explanation after my death. Nothing but a lively sense of what I owe to them could have enabled me to undergo the pain of recalling the experience which I am now about to set down.

Yaxholme lies, as they will remember, upon the extreme edge of the Fen district. In shape it is a long oval, with a main line of railway cutting one end. The church and vicarage were close to the station, and round them lay a village containing nearly five-sixths of the entire population of the parish. On the other side of the line the Fen proper began, and stretched for many miles. Though it is now fertile corn land, much of it had been permanently under water within living memory, and would soon revert to its original condition if it were not for the pumping stations. In spite of these it is not unusual to see several hundred acres flooded in winter.

My own parish ran for nearly six miles, and I had therefore several scattered farms and cottages so far from the village that a visit to one of them took up the whole of a long afternoon. Most of them were not on any road, and could only be reached by means of droves. For the benefit of those who are not acquainted with the Fen I may explain that a drove is a very imperfect sketch of the idea of a road. It is bounded by hedges or dykes, so that the traveller cannot actually lose his way, but it offers no further assistance to his progress. The middle is simply a grass track, and as cattle have to be driven along it the mud is sometimes literally knee-deep in winter. In summer the light peaty soil rises in clouds of sable dust. In fact I seldom went down one without recalling Hesiod's unpatriotic description of his native village in Boeotia. 'Bad in winter; intolerable in summer; good at no time.'

At the far end of one of these lay a straggling group of half a dozen cottages, of which the most remote was inhabited by an old woman whom I will call Mrs Vries. In some ways she was the most interesting of all my parishioners, and she was certainly the most perplexing. She was not a native, but had come to live there some twenty years before, and it was hard to see what had tempted a stranger to so unattractive a spot. It was the last house in the parish: her nearest neighbour was a quarter of a mile away, and she was fully three miles from a hard road or a shop. The house itself was not at all a good one. It had been unoccupied, I was told, for some years before she came to it, and she had found it in a semi-ruinous condition. Yet she had not been driven to seek a very cheap dwelling by poverty, as she had a good supply of furniture of very good quality, and, apparently, as much money as she required. She never gave the slightest hint as to where she had come from, or what her previous history had been. As far as was known she never wrote or received any letters. She must have been between fifty and sixty when she came. Her appearance was striking, as she was tall and thin, with an aquiline nose, and a pair of very brilliant dark eyes, and a quantity of hair – snow-white by the time I knew her. At one time she must have been handsome; but she had grown rather forbidding, and I used to think that, a couple of centuries before, she might have had some difficulty in proving that she was not a witch. Though her neighbours, not unnaturally, fought rather shy of her, her conversation showed that she was a clever woman who had at some time received a good deal of education, and had lived in cultivated surroundings. I used to think that she must have been an upper servant – most probably lady's maid – in a good house, and, despite the ring on her finger, suspected that the 'Mrs' was brevet rank.

One New Year's Eve I thought it my duty to visit her. I had not seen her for some months, and a few days of frost had made the drove more passable than it had been for several weeks. But, in spite of her interesting personality, I always found that it required a considerable moral effort to call at her cottage. She was always civil, and expressed herself pleased to see me. But I could never get rid of the idea that she regarded civility to me in the light of an insurance, which might be claimed elsewhere. I always told myself that such thoughts were unfounded and unworthy, but I could never repress them altogether, and whenever I left her cottage it was with a strong feeling that I had no desire to see her again. I used, however, to say to myself that that was really due to personal pique (because I could never discover that she had any religion, nor could I instil any into her), and that the fault was therefore more mine than hers.

On this particular afternoon the prospect of seeing her seemed more than usually distasteful, and my disinclination increased curiously as I made my way along the drove. So strong did it become that if any reasonable excuse for turning back had presented itself I am afraid I should have seized it. However, none did: so I held on, comforting myself with the thought that I should begin the New Year with a comfortable sense of having discharged the most unpleasant of my regular duties in a conscientious fashion.

When I reached the cottage I was a little surprised at having to knock three times, and by hearing the sound of bolts cautiously drawn back. Presently the door opened and Mrs Vries peered out. As soon as she saw who it was she made me very welcome as usual. But it was impossible not to feel that she had been more or less expecting some other visitor, whom she was not anxious to see. However, she volunteered no statement, and I thought it better to pretend to have noticed nothing unusual. On a table in the middle of the room lay a large book in which she had obviously been reading. I was surprised to see that it was a Bible, and that it lay open at the Book of Tobit. Seeing that I had noticed it Mrs Vries told me – with a little hesitation, I thought – that she had been reading the story of Sarah and the fiend Asmodeus. Then – the ice once broken – she plied me almost fiercely with questions. 'To what cause did I attribute Sarah's obsession, in the first instance?' Did the efficacy of Tobias' remedy depend upon the fact that it had been prescribed by an angel?' and much more to the same effect. Naturally my answers were rather vague, and her good manners could not conceal her disappointment. She sat silent for a minute or two, while I looked at her – not, I must confess, without some alarm, for her manner had been very strange – and then said abruptly, 'Well, will you have a cup of tea with me?' I assented gladly, for it was nearly half-past four, and it would take me nearly an hour and a half to get home. She took some time over the preparations and during the meal talked with even more fluency than usual. I could not help thinking that she was trying to make it last as long as possible.

Finally, at about half-past five, I got up and said that I must go, as I had a good many odds and ends awaiting me at home. I held out my hand, and as she took it said, 'You must let me wish you a very happy New Year.'

She stared at me for a moment, and then broke into a harsh

laugh, and said, 'If wishes were horses beggars might ride. Still, I thank you for your good will. Goodbye.' About thirty yards from her house there was an elbow in the drove. When I reached it I looked back and saw that she was still standing in her doorway, with her figure sharply silhouetted against the red glow of the kitchen fire. For one instant the play of shadow made it look as if there were another, taller, figure behind her, but the illusion passed directly. I waved my hand to her and turned the corner.

It was a fine, still, starlight night. I reflected that the moon would be up before I reached home, and my walk would not be unpleasant. I had naturally been rather puzzled by Mrs Vries' behaviour, and decided that I must see her again before long, to ascertain whether, as seemed possible, her mind were giving way.

When I had passed the other cottages of the group I noticed that the stars were disappearing, and a thick white mist was rolling up. This did not trouble me. The drove now ran straight until it joined the high-road, and there was no turn into it on either side. I had therefore no chance of losing my way, and anyone who lives in the Fens is accustomed to fogs. It soon grew very thick, and I was conscious of the slightly creepy feeling which a thick fog very commonly inspires. I had been thinking of a variety of things, in somewhat desultory fashion, when suddenly – almost as if it had been whispered into my ear – a passage from the Book of Wisdom came into my mind and refused to be dislodged. My nerves were good then, and I had often walked up a lonely drove in a fog before; but still just at that moment I should have preferred to have recalled almost anything else. For this was the extract with which my memory was pleased to present me. 'For neither did the dark recesses that held them guard them from fears, but sounds rushing down rang around them; and phantoms appeared, cheerless with unsmiling faces. And no force of fire prevailed to give them light, neither were the brightest flames of the stars strong enough to illumine that gloomy night. And in terror they deemed the things which they saw to be worse than that sight on which they could not gaze. And they lay helpless, made the sport of magic art.' (*Wisdom* xvii. 4-6).

Suddenly I heard a loud snort, as of a beast, apparently at my elbow. Naturally I jumped and stood still for a moment to avoid blundering into a stray cow, but there was nothing there. The next moment I heard what sounded exactly like a low chuckle. This was more disconcerting: but common sense soon came to my aid. I told myself that the cow must have been on the other side of the hedge and not really so close as it had seemed to be. What I had taken for a chuckle must have been the squelching of her feet in a soft place. But I must confess that I did not find this explanation as convincing as I could have wished.

I plodded on, but soon began to feel unaccountably tired. I say 'unaccountably' because I was a good walker and often covered much more ground than I had done that day.

I slackened my pace, but, as I was not out of breath, that did not relieve me. I felt as if I were wading through water up to my middle, or through very deep soft snow, and at last was fairly compelled to stop. By this time I was thoroughly uneasy, wondering what could be the matter with me. But as I had still nearly two miles to go there was nothing for it but to push on as best I might.

When I started again I saw that the fog seemed to be beginning to clear, though I could not feel a breath of air. But instead of thinning in the ordinary way it merely rolled back a little on either hand, producing an effect which I had never seen before. Along the sides of the drove lay two solid banks of white, with a narrow passage clear between them. This passage seemed to stretch for an interminable distance, and at the far end I 'perceived' a number of figures. I say advisedly 'perceived,' rather than 'saw,' for I do not know whether I saw them in the ordinary sense of the word or not. That is to say – I did not know then, and have never been able to determine since, whether it was still dark. I only know that my power of vision seemed to be independent of light or darkness. I perceived the figures, as one sees the creatures of a dream, or the mental pictures which sometimes come when one is neither quite asleep nor awake.

They were advancing rapidly in orderly fashion, almost like a body of troops. The scene recalled very vividly a picture of the Israelites marching across the Red Sea between two perpendicular walls of water, in a set of Bible pictures which I had had as a child. I suppose that I had not thought of that picture for more than thirty years, but now it leapt into my mind, and I found myself saying aloud, 'Yes: of course it must have been exactly like that. How glad I am to have seen it.'

I suppose it was the interest of making the comparison that kept me from feeling the surprise which would otherwise have been occasioned by meeting a large number of people marching down a lonely drove after dark on a raw December evening.

At first I should have said there were thirty or forty in the party, but when they had drawn a little nearer they seemed to be not more than ten or a dozen strong. A moment later I saw to my surprise that they were reduced to five or six. The advancing figures seemed to be melting into one another, something after the fashion of dissolving views. Their speed and stature increased as their numbers diminished, suggesting that the survivors had, in some horrible fashion, absorbed the personality of their companions. Now there appeared to be only three, then one solitary figure of gigantic stature rushing down the drove towards me at a fearful pace, without a sound. As he came the mist closed behind him, so that his dark figure was thrown up against a solid background of white: much as mountain climbers are said sometimes to see their own shadows upon a bank of cloud. On and on he came, until at last he towered above me and I saw his face. It has come to me once or twice since in troubled dreams, and may come again. But I am thankful that I have never had any clear picture of it in my waking moments. If I had I should be afraid for my reason. I know that the impression which it produced upon me was that of intense malignity long baffled, and now at last within reach of its desire. I believe I screamed aloud. Then after a pause, which seemed to last for hours, he broke over me like a wave. There was a rushing and a streaming all round me, and I struck out with my hands as if I were swimming. The sensation was not unlike that of rising from a deep dive: there was the same feeling of pressure and suffocation, but in this case coupled with the most intense physical loathing. The only comparison which I can suggest is that I felt as a man might feel if he were buried under a heap of worms or toads.

Suddenly I seemed to be clear, and fell forward on my face. I am not sure whether I fainted or not, but I must have lain there for some minutes. When I picked myself up, I felt a light breeze upon my forehead and the mist was clearing away as quickly as it had come. I saw the rim of the moon above the horizon, and my mysterious fatigue had disappeared. I hurried forward as quickly as I could without venturing to look behind me. I only wanted to get out of that abominable drove on to the high-road, where there were lights and other human beings. For I knew that what I had seen was a creature of darkness and waste places, and that among my fellows I should be safe. When I reached home my housekeeper looked at me oddly. Of course my clothes were muddy and disarranged, but I suspect that there was something else unusual in my appearance. I merely said that I had had a fall coming up a drove in the dark, and was not feeling particularly well. I avoided the looking-glass when I went to my room to change.

Coming downstairs I heard through the open kitchen door some scraps of conversation – or rather of a monologue delivered by my housekeeper – to the effect that no one ought to be about the droves after dark as much as I was, and that it was a providence that things were no worse. Her own mother's uncle had – it appeared – been down just such another drove on just such another night, forty-two years ago come next Christmas Eve. 'They brought 'im 'ome on a barrow with both 'is eyes drawed down, and every drop of blood in 'is body turned. But 'e never would speak to what 'e see, and wild cats couldn't ha' scratched it out of him.'

An inaudible remark from one of the maids was met with a long sniff, and the statement: 'Girls seem to think they know everything nowadays.' I spent the next day in bed, as besides the shock which I had received I had caught a bad cold. When I got up on the second I was not surprised to hear that Mrs Vries had been found dead on the previous afternoon. I had hardly finished breakfast when I was told that the policeman, whose name was Winter, would be glad to see me.

It appeared that on New Year's morning a half-witted boy of seventeen, who lived at one of the other cottages down the drove, had come to him and said that Mrs Vries was dead, and that he must come and enter her house. He declined to explain how he had come by the information: so at first Mr. Winter contented himself with pointing out that it was the first of January not of April. But the boy was so insistent that finally he went. When repeated knockings at Mrs Vries' cottage produced no result he had felt justified in forcing the back-door. She was sitting in a large wooden armchair quite dead. She was leaning forward a little and her hands were clasping the arms so tightly that it proved to be a matter of some difficulty to unloose her fingers. In front of her was another chair, so close that if anyone had been sitting in it his knees must have touched those of the dead woman. The seat cushions were flattened down as if it had been occupied recently by a solid personage. The tea-things had not been cleared away, but the kitchen was perfectly clean and tidy. There was no suspicion of foul play, as all the doors and windows were securely fastened on the inside. Winter added that her face made him feel 'quite sickish like,' and that the house smelt very bad for all that it was so clean.

A post-mortem examination of the body showed that her heart was in a very bad state, and enabled the coroner's jury to return a verdict of 'Death from Natural Causes.' But the doctor told me privately that she must have had a shock of some kind. ' In fact,' he said, if anyone ever died of fright, she did. But goodness knows what can have frightened her in her own kitchen unless it was her own conscience. But that is more in your line than mine.'

He added that he had found the examination of the body peculiarly trying: though he could not, or would not, say why.

As I was the last person who had seen her alive, I attended the inquest, but gave only formal evidence of an unimportant character. I did not mention that the second armchair had stood in a corner of the room during my visit, and that I had not occupied it.

The boy was of course called and asked how he knew she was dead. But nothing satisfactory could be got from him. He said that there was right houses and there was wrong houses – not to say persons – and that 'they 'had been after her for a long time. When asked whom he meant by 'they' he declined to explain, merely adding as a general statement that he could see further into a milestone than what some people could, for all they thought themselves so clever. His own family deposed that he had been absolutely silent, contrary to his usual custom, from tea-time on New Year's Eve to breakfast-time next day. Then he had suddenly announced that Mrs Vries was dead; and ran out of the house before they could say anything to him. Accordingly he was dismissed, with a warning to the effect that persons who were disrespectful to Constituted Authorities always came to a bad end.

It naturally fell to me to conduct the funeral, as I could have given no reason for refusing her Christian burial. The coffin was not particularly weighty, but as it was being lowered into the grave the ropes supporting it parted, and it fell several feet with a thud. The shock dislodged a quantity of soil from the sides of the cavity, so that the coffin was completely covered before I had had time to say 'Earth to earth: Ashes to ashes: Dust to dust.'

Afterwards the sexton spoke to me apologetically about the occurrence. 'I'm fair put about, Sir, about them ropes,' he said. 'Nothing o' that sort ever 'appened afore in my time. They was pretty nigh new too, and I thought they'd a done us for years. But just look 'ere, Sir.' Here he showed two extraordinarily ravelled ends. 'I never see a rope part like that afore. Almost looks as if it 'ad been scratted through by a big cat or somethink.'

That night I was taken ill. When I was better my doctor said that rest and change of scene were imperative. I knew that I could never go down a drove alone by night again, so tendered my resignation to my Bishop. I hope that I have still a few years of usefulness before me: but I know that I can never be as if I had not seen what I have seen. Whether I met with my adventure through any fault of my own I cannot tell. But of one thing I am sure. There are powers of darkness which walk abroad in waste places: and that man is happy who has never had to face them.

If anyone who reads this should ever have a similar experience and should feel tempted to try to investigate it further, I commend to him the counsel of Jesus-ben-Sira.

'My son, seek not things that are too hard for thee: and search not out things that are above thy strength.'

HETTY PEGLER'S CHRISTMAS

Celia Dale

Once the Fens were a world apart, a land of water and peaty bogs dotted with islands' A misty and mysterious land peopled by fishermen, fowlers and reed-cutters who walked on stilts when the water rose. Even after the Fens were drained, the region remained apart – a flat, peat-black landscape, criss-crossed by dykes and embankments, with scattered villages and isolated cottages, just like Hetty Pegler's in Celia Dale's ghostly Christmas tale.

The small flint cottage on the edge of the Fens was mellow with the light of innumerable rush dips. From the open windows came the heart-warming scent of roasting meat. The windows had to be open in spite of the choking mist that crept damply in, so that Hetty Pegler would know when her guests were arriving.

Along one wall of the living-room was a trestle table with mugs and tankards; some of earthenware or crude glass, and others of pewter. Old Hetty hobbled round leaning on a stick, her bright black eyes taking in all the details to see her friends would be comfortable.

Drawing her shawl close around her shoulders she looked at the white scrubbed table in the middle of the room. Yes, it would do. Pewter plates for the favoured; wooden platters for the rest.

Sniffing appreciatively she went towards the back kitchen

which was divided from the other room so that Hetty could entertain certain special and private friends away from the prying eyes of her two serving girls, who were now preparing the Christmas meal.

'You're doing well,' she said to Tamsin and Armine, the buxom girls perspiring and striving over the spit and lifting lids from the heavy saucepans on the fire. Tamsin wiped her forehead with the corner of her apron.

'Plenty of mulled ale, mind,' warned Hetty, going forward and putting on the crisp fat of the meat a finger which she licked. 'Lovely,' she said, closing her eyes, 'That'll suit ol' Mo' to a T. Open the window wider, gals,' although she knew the rush lights would flicker in the draught.

'It'll cool it all down, ma'am,' said Armine.

'Ne'er mind. No matter,' replied Hetty, her cheeks red from the fire and the agitation of old age. 'I want to hear when they all come. There must be a Christmas welcome for'em.'

'What hour d'you reckon it is?' asked Armine of Tamsin, who peered closely at the new-fangled clock on the wall.

'As I can see, it's near ten of the clock. Time for'em to start comin'.'

'Ave-aye,' sighed Hetty, limping away. She opened wide the front door, which groaned and complained on its hinges.

The soft wreathing mist came in like an eager guest. As she stood in the damp silence there came the calls of marsh birds talking in their sleep.

She became aware of the liquid sound of a boat on the water. Presently, the shipping of oars made her even more alert. With a great deal of grunting and swearing a male figure emerged. She could hear his heavy boots squelching in the mud. As he stumbled towards the light she called out.

'Come you in, me old tiger. It's bin a long time.'

'How are ye, me flower,' he answered. He held out his arms and in their brief embrace he seemed taller and younger and in his eyes she resembled one of the delicate flowers of the Fen.

They went into the cottage and he sat in a stout wooden chair by the fire. Hardly had he begun to drink the spicy ale put into his hand by Armine, than the sound of another boat was heard.

Again the shipping of oars. A giant of a man appeared in the doorway, kicking off his boots and smoothing the damp from his hair with a huge hand. Hetty went to greet him.

'Sam me old love, come in. There's mulled ale by, the gallon to warm you.' A cavernous grin showed above his beard. Then Mo, sitting by the fire, got to his feet and with a great show turned back his sleeves.

'Now then,' he growled. Sam took a defensive stance.

Tempers were high.

'Now then, let each other be. It's all gone and finished this many a year,' persuaded Hetty and she signed to Armine to bring a brimming measure of ale for Sam. Shamefacedly both men sank into chairs and stared at their feet.

Then small pattering steps sounded on the cobbles outside, shrill laughter and a shy tap on the door. With a glory in her face Hetty let in two little girls of about six years old, who, a little hampered by their long skirts, almost tripped over the threshold into her arms.

Kneeling down Hetty hugged them to her. 'Me loves, me doves. How've you bin?'

'All right, mother. The time goes so quick.'

'A posset for the babes,' she called. 'A milk posset. No ale for them.'

Happy and laughing, they sat on low stools in the inglenook and played with the cats dozing in the warmth. Mo put out a hand to fondle the children's bright curls. Tamsin looked in, tousled and flushed. 'Roast's done, ma'am, and the pudding likely to boil dry.'

'There's just two we're waiting on, gal. They won't be long. Get on with the serving. They'll not be late.'

Someone was coming, singing a little hoarsely. Nearer and nearer came the song until it stopped outside the door. Hetty opened it to a tall, wild-looking young woman with tousled hair and frightened eyes. 'Come in, Pernel. We were waitin' on you.'

The newcomer stepped into the misty hot fug of the room.

'Is this all?' asked Mo. 'For if it is, shet that door.'

'Yes, all but,' soothed Hetty, going to fetch a hot drink for Pernel, who smiled after sipping, and said it was comforting to her poor throat which still hurt after all that time. 'Ne'er mind,' whispered Hetty. 'S'all over these dunnamany years.'

'I got a hunger on me heavier nor a guv'ment man's staff,' grumbled Sam. 'Don' we have no vittles?

Hetty went to the door and listened. The marsh birds murmured in their dreams again and that was all. 'Reckon he ain't comin',' she said sadly, turning back into the room.

Gathering mugs and tankards she went into the kitchen, where, with all the activity going on, there was scarcely room for her to refill the drinking vessels for her guests. 'Get on, Mo, and you, Sam, and put chairs up to the table and set you down,' she called.

It took her some time to carry in the heavy mugs and tankards one by one, while Tamsin brought in the plates.

Hetty smiled at the two little girls who sat with their noses at table level as there were no cushions. When all was served a small plate was brought, full of meat for the cats and a tinier one for the tame rats who scurried from under a large oak chest.

'E'n't Alice a going to come? I'd a thought she'd a come with you,' Hetty said to Pernel.

'She tried, but they kept dragging her back. But she'll get here somehow.'

One of the children looked up with a scream. A white object was bobbing at the window. Had the moon fallen from the skies? Hetty followed the children's gaze, then screeched back her chair on the scrubbed flag floor and went with lame speed to the door. It was Alice who came in amid scarves of mist.

'Good evenin' to you all,' she said, her hands to her throat, which was badly bruised.

'How are ye?' asked Sam, sopping up gravy with a hunk of bread. 'It's all of a year since we met.'

'Seems longer than that,' answered Alice, 'what with me neck always paining.'

Pernel looked up. 'You still complainin'? Mine's nearly as

bad and I'm not always croakin'.'

'You went quicker,' Alice reminded her.

'Best meal I've had for a year,' said Mo', loosening his belt.

'Me too,' added Sam, massaging his paunch.

'Best meal for a year. That's good,' and Hetty laughed shrilly.

As Armine and Tamsin cleared away she reminded them to save the scraps for you-know-who.

'Who's that?' piped up one of the children.

'I told you last Christmas we mustn't say 'is name. It might bring evil on us so you couldn't come next year.' As a diversion the second little girl said she felt sick. Hetty gave a tender smile. 'Your eyes always were bigger nor your belly,' she said. 'Go sit in the chimney corner and play with the cats.'

It was not until the pudding was being enjoyed that a scratching and whining was heard at the door. Heavy thuds came on the stout wood. When Hetty opened the door there stood a large black dog, almost as big as a donkey. The cats jumped on to high shelves and the rats scrambled under the safety of the chest. The dog came in and Armine rushed to bring in a large dish of scraps. The huge dog assuaged its hunger.

Hetty went to look at the clock. Midnight was not far off. She told Tamsin they'd all have one last sup of ale, and settled herself in a chair between Pernel and Alice. The large black dog sat with its chin on her knee.

A silence so deep had fallen on the little group that they started when the clock wheezed and the weights slowly fell as it struck twelve. 'Well, me dears' It's come,' Hetty said. Then getting up she straightened herself proudly, holding on to the back of Mo's chair.

All raised their heads to listen as she intoned:

Alive or dead
You've all been fed.
Do not grieve,
But take your leave.

Sam and Mo' were the first to get up. 'Goodbye, me beauties,' said Hetty, kissing them. 'I always loved you both.'

They bade farewell to the rest, before going out into the mist. A few seconds later there came loud quarrelling voices and the sounds of fists on flesh. There were cries as the men fell into the water. Arms threshed, legs flailed, as the two of them gurgled to their death for the love of Hetty.

The next to go were Pernel and Alice. 'Til next Christmas,' they said as they left the cottage, their feet slipping on the wet cobbles. Hetty listened expectantly. Then it came. The screams of the women, protestations of innocence and last of all strangled curses before the final gasps.

She turned back into the warm, food-scented room and gazed at the two little girls lying in each other's arms in the inglenook, their faces pale, eyes closed. Just as they had lain all those years ago when she had unwittingly killed them by an overdose of opium when they had ague. She leaned over them.

'My pretties she said softly. 'You'd a bin women grown by now with babes of your own.' And even as she looked at their soft innocence they became misty wraiths and disappeared.

'Ah ha,' sighed Hetty, sinking into a chair, and the great dog went to her, putting a sympathetic paw on to her lap. She thought of the friends who spent two hours of each Christmas with her. 'Twas a pity,' she mused, thinking of Alice and Pernel who were hanged as witches when they were young. It was fortunate that Hetty herself, an even more skilful witch, had remained undetected, for by her incantations and the burning of herbs she was able once a year to bring her friends together again. The only condition being that when they left after the Yule-tide feast they did so in the manner in which they died. Sighing, she patted the dog's head. At least she always had Black Shuck for company.

THE LANTERN MEN

James Humphreys

The road ran dead straight to the horizon. To one side lay a wide drainage ditch, carrying a vast mass of water high above the surrounding land towards the distant sea; on the other, a drop of twenty feet to fields of dark earth. From time to time a clump of low-lying willows or a distant farm building broke the flat geometry of fields and drains, but he could not find any landmark to plot their progress. The dying day had taken on a feeling of unreality: the strange reconnaissance they were embarked upon, the alien surroundings, and the presence of Ella in the passenger seat. The horizon was no more than a slight change in the shade of the grey where the land and sky met; both hazed by the moisture drifting down from the low cloud. The road ran dead straight, and the car crawled across the empty landscape like an insect across a spider's web.

Ten years ago, at university, he had longed for Ella hopelessly, ineffectually and against his own better instincts. He had hardly seen her since, until they had been seated together at a dinner party a few days befoee. He had found her as desirable and as unpleasant as ever. She had hardly spoken to him all evening, favouring the man on her left who had made appreciative noises about her latest article for one of the Sunday papers. She might have said no more except that, it being the weekend before Halloween, talk had turned to the supernatural. Each guest in turn had told conventional tales: something glimpsed in a churchyard; a family curse; flickering lights that would lure the unwary to fortune or to their death. And this talk of mysterious lights amid the marshes, the Will-o-the-Wisp or the Lantern Men, prompted him to tell his own story.

One evening in the previous autumn he had been returning to Cambridge across the Fens after visiting a friend in Wisbech. He'd taken a short cut and, predictably given the maze of side roads, drains and ditches, he'd lost his way. After a while, he had noticed a bright light away to the left and he'd headed towards it like a moth, down a private road paved in concrete. Soon he could see a fire blazing against the dark. He passed a barn, then the road turned to cross one of the wide drains. And there were two men standing on the bridge, lanterns in their hands, as if waiting for him.

'What were they doing?' Even if he had lost the other end of the table, he'd still had Ella's full attention.

'Just standing there. So I pulled up and leaned out and said: Is there anything I can do? Have you phoned the fire brigade? Or something like that. Anyway, the man said nothing. He just stared at me. So I said: The fire: is everything OK? Still no response.'

'What did they look like?' she had asked.

'I only really saw one of them. He was thickset, in a green anorak and waterproof trousers. And wellingtons, of course, and one of those round knitted hats. The other looked much the same, I think. Perhaps taller. Then the one I'd spoken to came over and said something like: You want to be turning round. And he pointed back the way I'd come. So I did. It was really scary. I don't know what was going on, or what was burning. I never got close enough to see, but I'm fairly sure it wasn't a building, and it certainly wasn't stubble-burning. It came only from one point. Not a whole field. But the whole thing was really, really weird.'

'Did you go back later to see what it was?' his host had asked.

'No. I can't explain why, except there was a real atmosphere to the whole thing.'

With that lame conclusion, the talk had moved on and Ella had barely noticed his leaving soon after. So her message that morning had come as a complete surprise:

> SO INTERESTED IN STORY ABOUT FIRE. WILL BE ON THE 1620 FROM LIVERPOOL STREET ARRIVING ELY AT 1805. MEET ME. LOVE EL.

It rankled, this blithe assumption that he would drop everything for her. He knew she had no interest in him; and would laugh off any fumbling approach he might make. But of course, he had been there to watch her walk down the platform, her lithe assurance filling him with hateful desire.

They had set off, saying little: he mired in frustration, she concentrating on the maps she had brought. An hour passed, but after several false starts and sighs of annoyance from Ella, he had eventually recognised the turning where he had first gone astray. After a mile or so she asked him to pull over, and the sudden silence was complete, save for an erratic tick from the engine as it cooled. The emptiness was broken only by the latticework of ditches, drains and cuts that kept the water from reclaiming the land. It was a man-made landscape; yet also empty and inhuman.

Ella studied the map, ringlets of hair falling over her face. Then she looked up, not at him but away towards the west, where the slight rise he had seen most likely lay. He noted quite pitilessly her defects; the habitual, sullen pout, the slight fattiness under the chin that came from self-indulgence. Yet all this was submerged by his desires. He took some moments to surface when she turned to him, and he sensed a mocking awareness in her glance.

'Shall we go on? I think I've found the place. About two miles further.'

He nodded, and started the engine. Then Ella touched his arm.

'I'll drive. You look out for the turning.'

She slipped into the driving seat as he walked round the back of the car. A fine rain was now falling from the leaden sky. He shivered and polished the moisture from his glasses.

As Ella drove, he let his eyes play over her. There had been many such furtive glances in college days; he had considered them as payment for the hurts and snubs she had inflicted on him. Perhaps she had done so too, for as if aware of his scrutiny, she shifted in her seat and lifted her head back, like a cat arching its back in satisfaction.

They came to another of the long tracks paved with crude concrete slabs which ran from the road towards distant farms, or barns, or sometimes nothing visible at all. She stopped the car while he peered at the map.

'I don't think this road is marked,' he said, half-apologetically.

'We'll take this one.'

Before he could reply she swung the car into the side-road and had switched off the headlights. The car rattled over the ruts and potholes as it dropped to the level of the surrounding fields. After a half-mile or so of coasting on the side-lights he recognised the barn, ghostly in the dark.

'We'll leave the car here,' she said. 'Any closer and they'd see us.'

The front of the barn was open, and inside were bales of straw arranged with wide aisles for loading and unloading. These would just be wide enough to take the car, and already Ella had pulled a few yards beyond before neatly reversing in. Hidden at the back, it was very unlikely anyone would see it. Without speaking, she eased herself out of the car, closing the door after her silently. He joined her, less deftly, and they walked cautiously to the open end of the barn and then on to the edge of the bank. Just opposite, a pipe crossed the drain, carrying water or gas towards the distant farm buildings. About two hundred yards further down, the road turned sharply and climbed up to the bridge where he had met the men a year before. It was deserted now.

They lay side by side on the bank, watching for five minutes or so, before Ella slid backwards down the slope and led him back to the car.

'I guess we've got an hour or so before anything happens,' she said as she rummaged through her bag. 'You stay by the bridge and try to get pictures of anyone coming or going. Try to brace the camera on something. If it shakes, nothing will come out in this light. OK? I'll go along one of the ditches towards the buildings to see what's going on.'

He was surprised by the extent of Ella's preparations.

'Do you really think there's something behind this?'

'Of course. Would I be here if I didn't?'

He made no reply, grateful that the dark would mask the hurt her words had caused.

'Think of the dates,' she went on. 'And it's a full moon. You see—'

She broke off, listening. After a moment a Landrover swept past and up the road. They looked at each other for a moment, then she moved quickly back to the door. The Landrover had stopped by the bridge, but no-one got out.

'We'd better go back.'

'We're here now. Anyway, it proves there's something going on.'

'But they've blocked the road. How can we get across the bridge?'

'I'll climb across by that pipe.' Then Ella's voice hardened. 'Don't worry. You'll be safe enough here.'

They waited another half-hour, hardly saying a word, until she judged it was dark enough. She was twitching with tension as she paced up and down, and his eyes followed her cat-like movement, half-seen, half-imagined in the faint moonlight. Then she turned to look at him, and then walked over to stand unexpectedly close.

'If there's any trouble, don't let me down.'

She ran one hand lightly down his chest, then was gone. He stood in surprise for a moment, then followed her as if to say something; but she had already slipped across the road and climbed onto the wide iron pipe that spanned the drain. She crossed with assurance, unafraid of the sluggish waters below, and was soon on the far bank, lost to sight. He went back to the car and tried to work out how long she would be. He was so impatient to see her again, could still feel her touch. Working through the ditch, watching the men on the bridge, reaching the farmhouse, looking around, and then returning: at least two hours, perhaps longer. And then? He would have proved himself to her; and perhaps, just perhaps, she would reward him.

An hour passed. Once or twice he crept back to the opening, but there was nothing to be seen.

Then came the scream.

It sliced through the night, shockingly loud; then was cut off to leave only muffled and confused noises. He saw lights by the bridge, shadowy forms struggling near the darker mass of the Landrover. He hesitated, unsure of the situation, of himself; then ran back to the car. He fumbled with the keys, but got it started and drove straight out of the barn towards the bridge. In a few seconds the figures were caught in the headlights: one man holding Ella's arms as she struggled, with another two looking on.

One held a rifle: raised not to fire but to cover his eyes. The others froze in the glare almost until he reached them, then jumped aside. Ella broke free and start to run as he sped past. The car hit the verge, bucked, the twin bands of light played into the rain-streaked sky. Then it slid through a wire fence and into a ditch, throwing him hard against the steering wheel.

Sickened and dazed, he listened to the chuckle and gurgle of water flowing past the bonnet, to the footsteps and voices above him, but took none of it in. He gazed instead on the instrument panel, the sweep of the second hand on the clock.

Then he was bundled out of the car and dragged back up the side of the dyke. There were two of them, one on each arm, ignoring his feeble kicking. He was pulled along the road a few yards to the bridge, then dropped to the ground by the parapet. The shorter and stockier of the two bent over him, reaching underneath to pass a loop of rope around him. He recoiled from the smell of spirits and stale sweat, tried to struggle, but the man kicked him in his side, leaving him winded and gasping, while the other finished the task.

They left him after that, and eventually the cold began to revive him; but he knew he could not run or fight. At least she had escaped. He wondered how long would it take for her to bring help. She couldn't just go to the nearest house: how would she know who was part of this thing, this group, whatever it was?

Then the Landrover returned, a man with a rifle in hand jumped out, and for a moment he was back in his childhood, back in the Scottish Highlands, at the hotel where he had once stayed. Men in boots and rifles, and the gamekeeper opening up the back of a Landrover to reveal the carcass of a deer. It had been so alive, so glossy and sleek, that he had half-expected it to leap to its feet and make off. But from the way it had lain, its limbs awry and abandoned, he had known, with a sickening certainty, that it was dead.

Ella's body lay with that same carelessness where it had been slung onto the floor of the vehicle. One of the men jumped into the back and manhandled her body to the edge, then used his boot to push it out. The body fell and rolled over, quite limp. Under the moonlight it had the same sleek sheen as the deer, but the eyes stared blankly and unmoving into the night sky.

One of the men fetched a rope and the other followed carrying in each hand a lump of concrete with an iron ring set on the top. In a moment they had tied one end of the rope to his legs and the other end to one of the concrete blocks. This they then heaved on to the parapet of the bridge. It stood only a foot or so away from his face, and although he knew it was for effect, to try to break his resolve, he was scared. It would only take a slip, a misjudgement, a moment of carelessness, and the block would fall into the thick black waters of the drain, dragging him down with it.

He began to tell them why he was there, to explain it was all Ella's idea, to assure them he knew nothing and would say nothing; the words pouring out in a hopeless, fearful jumble. But they ignored him while they tied a rope around her body and lifted it onto the parapet, ready for disposal; all quite methodical; practised. He felt nothing for her now; except a kind of pity, thinking how much she would have hated dying without knowing why.

One of his captors opened the door of the Landrover and started the engine. The other two looked at each other.

'You?'

The other nodded, and time began to slow as he realised what was to happen. They were not going to interrogate him. They were going to kill him, with no more ceremony than drowning an unwanted kitten.

He shouted and screamed. Strands of thought ran in tangles of fear and pleading, while a cold voice inside him working out how many seconds left he had of life.

The man reached the concrete block, then looked down at him. He could see nothing in the other man's eyes, for there was nothing to see.

The block turned over. There was pain, unbelievable pain, and a mad, gut-wrenching flight before the shock of the water. Darkness closed in, and the waters flowed on without a ripple towards the sea.

WITCHES AT HALLOWE'EN

W. H. Barrett

This is a story told by William Kemp, who died, aged ninety-one, in 1906. His home was near Welney. Superstitious Fen people certainly believed that witches could change into animals: owls, snakes, hares and mice were particularly feared as witches in disguise. 'Putting the white mice on people' is a recorded expression for spell-casting in the Norfolk Fens, while 'tuddled' means bewitched.

I reckon I was a lad of about seven or eight when, because Mother was expecting another little one to join our already crowded house, I was sent to stay with an old aunt in one of the loneliest parts of the Fens. She had a big family, this aunt, though most of them were grown-up by then, except for a boy of fifteen and a girl of twelve. Although there wasn't another house within a mile, that didn't bother them; the farm was run by the family and for most of the year they went to bed when it got dark and got up at daybreak.

While I was there, Hallowe'en came round. In the afternoon everyone was busy putting osier twigs in front of all the doors and windows, the pig-styes, stables and cow-house. Uncle killed one of his black hens and hung it on the chicken house door after he'd pulled out two of its wing feathers and tied them on the yard dog's collar; then he caught the cats and shut them up in the barn. From all the talk going on I found out that this was the night when the witches went round the Fen, meeting each other and then, at the chiming of midnight, coming to some spot they'd chosen and casting spells over all the folks and animals nearby. That was why the peeled osier rods were put at all the ways into the house because no witch dared cross over them, neither would they go near black chicken feathers.

As the evening went by we all sat round the big open hearth. Aunt didn't put peat on the fire that night because witches could smell peat smoke for miles away, she said; instead, huge logs of oak were blazing away. The candles had been blown out so the only light we had came from the fire as we sat and listened to Aunt's stories of what witches could get up to. After supper, a plate of thick slices of ham and half of a loaf bread were stood outside on the door-stone so that, if a witch called, she wouldn't have to go away hungry because, if she did, she might start casting her spells on us. Then I was given a glass of ginger wine while my aunt and uncle and the others drank a lot of home-made botanic beer. After a while Uncle stood up and said to me:

'Come along, it's time we were up and doing.'

He told me it was the custom, this night, for the oldest man and the youngest boy in the house to go round the farm an hour before midnight; so we set off. It was very queer padding along behind Uncle as he carried the lantern. All the animals seemed restless and Uncle said they were like that because they could see and hear things that we couldn't, and they all knew what was going on.

After we'd been round the farmyard we had to visit the bees. As we went into the orchard an owl swooped over us with a loud screech, just above Uncle's head. I was scared, but Uncle got a firm grip of the thick stick he was carrying and, when the owl turned to fly over us again, he caught it such a clout that it fell down to the ground, fluttered its wings a bit and then lay stilt. My uncle bent down, turned it over and said:

'Well, there's one old witch who won't go home tonight.'

When we got to the bee-hive we went close up and listened to the noise going on inside; it was just like the hum of a threshing tackle on a frosty morning.

'Bor,' said Uncle, 'they're all worked up because they're a lot wiser than we are'; then, after tapping the hive with his stick, he bent right down to the entrance and said:

'Well done, my old beauties; I got one just now and, by the sound of it, you've got another; push her outside when you've done with her.'

When we were back indoors we all sat round the fire again while Uncle told my aunt and the others what had happened while we were out.

'It looks as though some of us will be tudded for sure before morning,' said Aunt, 'if we're not careful. There's nothing, after all, to stop one of those old witches coming down the chimney and casting a spell on us.'

I saw everyone backing away from the fire, and I did so too. Then Aunt got up, went over to the cupboard in the corner and came back with a big brown paper bag.

'Whatever any old hag turns herself into,' she said, 'I promise I'll make her cough before she gets to the hearth. This ought to make her sneeze a bit first,' and she took a handful of flowers of sulphur out of the bag and threw them on the fire. Bright blue flames and yellow smoke roared up the chimney. Aunt did this several times even though Uncle told her not to forget that the roof was thatch and if we were burnt out it wasn't going to be any good blaming it on any witches; but she only told to be quiet, she knew what she was doing. This started a lot of arguing, everybody joining in till it seemed to me that the witches had been forgotten and that I was in the middle of a good old family row. Anyway, Aunt got in such a temper that she threw the whole bag on to the fire and the yellow smoke came pouring out into the room worse than ever, making us all splutter and choke.

Uncle said that two could play at that game and he went over to the cupboard and fetched out a linen bag full of the black gunpowder he used in his muzzle loader. He'd no sooner hurled it at the back of the fire than there was a hell of a bang and we were all smothered in soot from head to foot. Well, that cooled everybody's temper and when the smoke had cleared away a bit Uncle said:

'Well, I'll be damned,' because lying on Auntie's lap was a jackdaw, just kicking out his last gasp. And just then the old grandfather clock struck midnight.

After we all ate a lot of thick ham sandwiches and the others drank some more botanic beer and I had another glass of ginger wine. Then Uncle said to me:

'Come on, bor, we've got to make another round.'

It was still very dark when we got outside but all the animals were quiet and settled down. When we got to the orchard we found the bees quiet, too, but on the flight board, believe it or not, was a dead mouse, still warm. Uncle picked it up then went back to fetch the owl which he'd killed the time we were out before. When we were back in the house he threw the owl, the mouse and the jackdaw on the fire and said:

'Three witches on one Hallowe'en isn't a bad bag. Now, all of you get up to bed and sleep well, you won't have to worry about any witches for another twelvemonth.'

Now if you want to know where all this happened then just walk a couple of miles from Littleport till you come to Crouchmoor Drove[1]. Go along the drove for three miles till you come to the place called Coldharbour and by the side of the drove you'll see a corner of a field all grown up with wild plum and nettles. That's where the farm was where I spent that Hallowe'en, and that was over seventy years ago.

1 Part of the Fenland between the New Bedford River and the Ouse.

THE FENSTANTON WITCH

M. R. James

Nicholas Hardman and Stephen Ashe were two Fellows of the King's College in Cambridge: they had come like all their contemporaries from the sister College at Eton where they had spent their lives from about the age of six to that of sixteen, and at the time when we encounter them, they were both men of about thirty years old. Hardman was the son of a Lincolnshire parson, living at Thorganby-on-the-Wolds, while Ashe's father was a yeoman-farmer of Ospringe in Kent.

Hardman was black, dour and saturnine with a rasping voice and a strong Lincolnshire accent which cannot be reproduced here. Ashe had the sturdy and somewhat slow intelligence of his Kentish ancestors; the phrase 'a good friend and a bad enemy' represents the opinion which the men of his year held of him. Both were in priests' orders, and each, we might suppose, looked forward in the fullness of time to occupying College livings, marrying and bringing up a son or two: one most likely to reproduce his father's career; another, perhaps, to go on the land and become a reputable farmer in a small way.

I say we might suppose their aspirations to have been of this nature: for such was the programme of a majority of Fellows of Colleges at that time. But there is an entry in the book called Harwood's Alumni which shows that they entertained ideas of a very different sort; and it has occurred to me that it may be worthwhile to tell the story of what they adventured and what came of it.

I have alluded more than once to 'their times' but I have not yet told you when they lived. Anne was filling the throne of England, Scotland, Ireland and France, and Dr James Roderick was Provost of the College, having been elected by the Fellows in preference to Sir Isaac Newton, whom the Prince of Orange, King William the Third of blessed memory, would have intruded into that pasture. The Fellows of King's had vindicated their right of election and the Lower Master of Eton occupied the Lodge – he was known as one of the 'four Smoaking Heads' – while Sir Isaac lived in the Observatory over Trinity Great Gate, and, according to popular legends, gently remonstrated with his dog Diamond, or cut holes in his door to admit his cat and kitten. The University was a happy, sleepy place in those days, one is apt to think; but after all, what with the Church in danger and the excitement of depriving Dr Richard Bentley, then Master of Trinity, of his degrees, there was probably no lack of sport to be had within the precincts. And certainly just outside them there was more than there is now. Snipe were shot on Parker's Piece, and the dreary expanse of undrained fen was the haunt of many a strange fowl, not to speak of other inhabitants of whom I may one day find an occasion to tell.

But it is time to leave generalities. The two sheep to whom we must return – and I am afraid they were black ones – were very close friends; but few men in the University, or indeed in the King's College itself, could boast of more than a speaking acquaintance with either. They occupied one room in the Old School of King's, north of the Chapel, which room was always locked when they were out. And these were not days when Fellows, nor still less Scholars, were in the habit of dropping into each other's abodes to partake of casual hospitality in the way of tobacco or whiskey and water. The common life, such as it was, was confined to Chapel, Hall and the Fellows' Parlour.

All that was known of Hardman and Ashe's way of employing 'their leisure' was that they went for long walks together and smoked apparently very bad tobacco when they came back.

It was a fine afternoon in October when these events began, or to speak more truly, came to a head, which served to show what manner of men were Nicholas Hardman and Stephen Ashe. Chapel service, we may be sure, was at three, and both of our friends were there, staring at each other from opposite stalls. The reedy and pedalless organ helped the rather infirm and jaded choir through a new verse anthem by Dr Blow during which the snoring of Provost Roderick was not doubtfully heard. At near four, Dr Tudway, the organist, played out the scant congregation with a march of his own composition. The choirmen hurried off to go through a similar performance at Trinity. The boys rushed off to whatever haunts in the town they had emerged from. The Provost strolled to his Lodge, then at the eastern end of the Chapel, and the Fellows and Scholars made their way across the strip of ground on the north side, holding on their caps - for a strong west wind was blowing the yellow leaves about - and so into the Old Court, and to dine in Hall. A coarse meal, I expect it was, and a silent one. The Vice Provost and three or four Seniors occupied one table on the dais; the Masters of Arts - among whom were Hardman and Ashe - filled a second along with the Fellow-Commoners; and the Bachelors and Undergraduate Fellows and Scholars, two more. There may have been fifty people in the room. Not much passed at dinner, which lasted about forty minutes; but afterwards the Fellows returned to the parlour and the Scholars to their rooms. With these last we are not concerned, but we may as well follow the Seniors. They are sitting at a large table, cloth-less, with some decanters of wine (I don't know whether port or claret: much depends upon the date of Lord Methuen's treaty with Portugal), and something like conversation has broken out.

'Where did ye ride today, Mr Bates?' said Mr Glynne.

'Only so far as Fenstanton.'

'Fenstanton. Ah — is that where the witch was ducked last week? Lord Blandford was riding by at the time' (this was the Duke of Marlboro's son and heir who died shortly afterwards and was now a Fellow-Commoner), 'and his Lordship made some hot-headed show at rescuing the old creature. Has there been any stir made? Dodgson of Magdalene has this living, but I doubt, if he hath not moved, no one will. 'Tis a lost place, Fenstanton, for all it be on the Huntingdon road.' Thus far Mr Glynne, who had rather a knack of monopolising conversation.

'Well, to tell truth,' says Bates, 'I had not heard of the matter, but the bell was tolling for a burying as I rode through, and I happened to meet Dodgson coming from his beer and pipe, as I judge, to the churchyard. He did let fall something which could fit with what you say. Pray, did you hear the name, Glynne, Galpin or Gibson; some word with a 'G' in it?'

'Gibson! Mother Gibson! That was the name for a guinea! So that ducking has finished the poor creature,' said good-natured Glynne. 'These fen-rustics are little but brutes. I vow the coroner should have sat, and there should have been a dozen strung up at the Assizes, and in any but Dodgson's parish there would have been. But Lord! the man thinks of nothing but his tithes and his beer.'

'Matthews had the parsonage before Dodgson,' said Bates, 'and in his time there were four attempts at swimming that old woman. Not a boy nor man in the parish, he told me, but was ready to swear she had signed herself away. But Matthews threatened to call in the sheriff, and he would have done it too, so they kept mum in his time.'

'For all that,' said Glynne, 'I remember his saying in this parlour that when he looked at her he was half in a mind to believe the tale. He pointed her out to me one day, and it is sure that she might have sat for a portrait of the Enemy as far as her eyes were concerned: they were as red as blood and the pupils like a goat's.' With which Mr Glynne was silent and shuddered slightly.

'Did they bury her in the churchyard, Bates?' said Dr Morell, the Vice Provost.

'Yes, Mr Vice Provost. I noticed a grave dug on the north side, which I take it was for her.'

'All this talk about burying witches puts me in mind of William of Malmesbury's tale, that Dr Gale printed not so long back.' This was from a new contributor to the conversation, Mr

Newborough, afterwards Head Master of Eton, who was more bookishly inclined than many of his compeers. 'Do you know it, Mr Glynne? You should look at Malmesbury': and he proceeded to tell the story which Southey has put into rhyme under the name of the 'Old Woman of Berkeley'. After that came a short discussion of the Witch of Endor; then the conversation drifted to Dr Hody's book on the Versions of the Bible, then by a not uncommon fate to Dr Bentley's last enormities, and thence back to the familiar question of College livings and probable vacancies.

In the midst of this, Hardman and Ashe made their bow to the Vice Provost and went out. They had neither of them made any remark since dinner but Dr Morell, an observant man, noticed that they had taken a very considerable interest in the early part of the conversation.

'Two dull dogs gone,' said Dr Glynne, when the door closed behind them: 'I pity their wives if ever they marry and their parishes if ever they take 'em.'

'Quiet enough if they are dull,' said Newborough.

'I don't know that, Newborough,' said Morell. 'The man that has chambers under theirs doesn't always sleep best. What can keep those two men treading about the whole night, as I am told they do, and what have they on their minds that makes them sigh and moan like two sick owls, as Burton says? You know everyone in College, Glynne; tell us, pray, were you ever in Hardman's and Ashe's chambers?'

'Not I,' said Glynne. 'I knocked at their door one day, I recollect, last year. Such a clatter as they made before they opened it, I vow I never heard, but all I can tell of the matter is that Hardman was as pale as a ghost when he opened to me, and that the place smelt as sweet as a bonfire of old rags and bones. Hardman made shift to ask my business, and then shut the door in my face!'

'Well,' said the Vice Provost, 'he might have spared himself the question, Glynne. I never knew you have any business in this life yet. Never matter! 'Tis time to turn unto the coffeehouse, Gentlemen. I have told Dr Cotes we should be there before eight, and the clocks are going the quarter now.'

The company adjourned therefore to a coffeehouse on the Market Place, and smoked clay pipes till ten with Dr Roger Cotes and some other gentlemen from Trinity, Queens' and Bene't Colleges.

ii

The curfew bell was ringing and it was a fine night when Hardman and Ashe, each with a packet and a stick, emerged from the gates of King's College and told the porter – a fuddling old ruffian, as were most College servants of that day – that they were not like to be returning that night. Neither said any word until they were clear of the town and on the Huntingdon road. Then said Nicholas Hardman, 'If all goes as it should tonight, Ashe, we shall know a matter worth knowing.'

'Yes, Nick, and there will be a matter worth having in one of these bundles,' said Ashe: 'I dare swear though that there will be some disappointment. Newborough's tale of the old witch set me a-thinking. You have the book upon you, Nick?'

'Book, what book? Dr Gales' print of Malmesbury, I suppose? A fat folio of a stone weight. It is likely?'

'No, not Malmesbury. Our book, the book, I mean.'

'Call me fool if you like, Stephen, but don't ask such another question: have I come forth without my head? That is as likely as it would be for me to leave the book in my chambers. But why, pray, does that ass Newborough's old story set you thinking?'

'Why, only, that if the same gentry that came for their friend in that story were thinking of waiting upon our friend at Fenstanton tonight, it is like we may see trouble.'

Hardman gave a snort. 'And if they did, do you think a circle is broken so easily? Have I nothing here that avails to make them give back? Still, you are right in a way, Stephen, as you have been before. If we are later in the field than they, there may be trouble, even danger. But what we would have is not what they want. If we get the three locks of hair and the winding sheet, we are masters of the Elementals. The others want the soul.'

It was a thought that seemed to dash both of them for a

moment, and they were silent. So the clouds flew across the moon, and the wind blew over the bare fields, and the bells of Cambridge came more faintly to the ear, as they walked quietly on towards the sleeping village of Fenstanton.

iii

Those who remember the road between Cambridge and Fenstanton will bear me out when I say that it is eleven miles long, and presents few features of interest. There is an occasional wayside inn, a few farms lie a little off the road, and on a clear day we may see the lantern and western tower of Ely, and a good many nearer church towers. The church that lies nearest to the road is that of Lolworth, on the left hand, some five or six miles out. There was something doing at Lolworth when Hardman and Ashe passed it. The bell was going, and the windows lighted. Nocturnal funerals were almost the rule in Queen Anne's time for anyone who claimed to be a magnate, so that it did not surprise the lookers-on when they saw two lines of torches working their way slowly through the trees near the church, and when they saw a figure in white flit out of the south porch to meet the cortège, they knew that it must be the parson. Yet a few moments, and the procession was in the church: then they walked on again, for they had paused a moment.

The turning out of the main road towards Lolworth church lay some little distance ahead, and down the lane were coming a group of figures at a great pace. They reached the road and turned down it towards the travellers: who were a little daunted thereby, because they did not wish to be recognised as Cambridge parsons at that hour of the night. There appeared to be seven people clustering round one in the midst, and their action and gait was like that of watchmen who had taken a prisoner. The party came on, and it seemed as if this conjecture might fit the situation, for the person in the midst was plainly reluctant, and as plainly was being hurried on by the rest. Hardman and Ashe drew toward the hedge to let these men pass, and their eyes were riveted upon the face of the captured man. It was not lightly to be forgotten, for it is not often that any one beholds the face of a man who has lost all hope, and yet has room in his brain for an unspeakable fear. This is the sight which those two ill-starred priests were now looking upon: and they saw moreover that, in spite of his terror and desperation, the captive could look nowhere save straight in front of him, for anything seemed tolerable rather than to see the faces of the seven who were about him. When they pictured the scene to themselves thereafter, they realised that his was the only face of which they had caught sight at all; nay, it even seemed to them that there was no other face for their eyes to catch.

The thing was passed; it passed quite silently, and for many moments these two men stayed breathless to within an ace of sudden flight or swooning. They knew that they had seen that which no mourner at that funeral had seen, and it was in their minds that it is not always well for those whose eyes are opened. It may happen to some to see the mountains full of bones and chariots of fire, but to others are shown very different sights from that. Yet the natures of both were so obstinate and dogged that neither would broach to the other the thought of returning, and giving up the dismal project they had in their minds. They went on.

Soon they sighted Fenstanton spire, and half a mile further they left the road and made their way across the fields to the side where the churchyard was accessible away from the street. It was not a difficult wall to climb, yet they were unnerved and took several minutes to get over it. Then they proceeded to go through the sinister rites and ceremonies which were to safeguard them against those powers with whom they supposed themselves to be leagued, for they are treacherous allies, as those tell us who claim to know the heart of the matter. On the north side of the dark church, even in its shadow, and not more than ten yards from a new-made grave – the only one on that side of the building – they picked out a space where the grass was shortest, and drew two large circles, one within the other. And in the space between the circles they marked out with some pains the symbols of the planets and a few Hebrew letters which were meant to indicate names of angels and of the Great Power, whose aid, by one of the strange contradictions of art magic, they promised themselves they would gain for the work they were at. When their defence was completed they stopped, and Ashe looked at his time-piece. The hour was something short of a quarter to twelve, so they must wait till the middle of night was reached.

And now – what was it that these two educated clergymen proposed to themselves? And how came it that they were on an enterprise which one associates, not always correctly, with the darkest mediaevalism and the most defective civilisation?

You have guessed that they were earnest and credulous students of art magic: how came such men to be in Cambridge in the reign of Queen Anne? I can only answer that in that day there were many such men in Germany, and that the instinct which prompts men to seek intercourse with the unseen peoples of the air is one that may come to the surface in any civilisation and in any century. Many have a sneaking idea that the intercourse has been sometimes gained, but that is little to the point.

That which Hardman and Ashe were determined upon was the obtaining of an ingredient for future spells, which should end in making them able to command the forces of nature to a degree which they believed many to have attained before them. They meant on this night – and they were confident of accomplishing it – to go through certain forms of words which would have power to make the corpse of the old woman buried that day to arise out of the grave and come to them, and give them – it is horrid to think of – the portion of the grave-clothes and the locks of hair of which Hardman spoke when they were on the road. Then should the body return to the earth as it was, and the soil be replaced above it. They were to go back to their College the next day; and in seven days' time, who so rich and powerful as Nicholas Hardman and Stephen Ashe, Esquires?

It was with a strange kind of exaltation that, as midnight came near, Hardman drew from his bosom a paper book, about a hundred years old, ill-written and full of diagrams like that which had just been drawn upon the ground, and within whose compass both of them were standing. He began to read, or intone, a Latin form of conjuration, a sinister kind of Church service, in which the most sacred of names were freely employed; and to this Ashe made the set appointed refrains. The night had been disturbed throughout and windy, but no rain had fallen and the thin clouds kept covering the moon, which was by this time low and near the horizon. The wind rattled in the louvres of the tower, and every now and then swung the tongue of a bell so that it sounded in a dim and far off fashion. Nicholas Hardman read on, and read faster and louder, and Ashe responded at short intervals. They had now entered upon the 91st Psalm: 'Qui Habitat', 'Whoso dwelleth', and they were just promising themselves deliverance from the terror that walks in darkness when a blacker cloud than usual left the moon's face and Stephen Ashe fell like an ox at the feet of Hardman. For it seems that it had been determined that these fools should be answered according to their folly.

I have said that the miserable and criminous old woman whom the fen-men had killed was buried a bare ten yards away from the two conjurors: and their eyes were often fixed upon her grave as upon the point to which their spells were directed. Looking over at the grave, Hardman beheld crouched upon it a shape which there was small likelihood of his ever forgetting. It was the figure, one would say, at first sight, of an enormous bat, with folded wings and hints of head approaching the human form. In a short moment, Hardman caught sight of the folds of wrinkled skin or hide that hung down from the cheeks, of the wide ears which shone transparent in the moonlight, and of the two lines of dusky red fire which marked the almost closed eyes. And further, he declared afterwards, he saw the earth heap upon which this being was crouched stir and wave beneath it. Not long was he allowed to remain a spectator, for this terrific appearance rose to its height and for a minute seemed to look about as if for a victim whom it knew to be near. Hardman, almost at the pitch of despair, yet trusted dimly in his charmed circle. But the creature on a sudden turned full in his direction and stepped swift and straight towards him, not flinching for an instant at angelic names or planetary symbols. In another moment, its talons were raised toward his face, and he knew no more.

It was Ashe who helped him back to Cambridge in the morning of the next day: and it was Ashe also who, for the twenty years that he survived, sheltered him in the parsonage of Willoughton and ministered to him, himself a stricken man. But Hardman never saw light again.

The College at large never learned the rights of the story. Two days after the catastrophe, Mr Glynne says to Mr Morell, being Vice Provost, 'What did you do at the Seniors' Meeting this morning, Mr Vice?'

'Sealed the presentation to Weedon Lois, and received a declaration, Glynne.'

'A royal declaration, or what?'

'No, Glynne; Mr Provost will tell you about it, maybe, if you ask him.'

So off goes Mr Glynne to the Lodge. But Provost Roderick is pale, which is not natural to him, and not smoking, which is decidedly unnatural, and disturbed and uncommunicative. And Mr Glynne can only learn that it is a matter which the Seniors have decided to keep private. During the next week, a barrowload of matters from one set of chambers in the King's College is wheeled off in the direction of Barton and does not come back: and most of the Seniors are very regular in their attendance in the Chapel for some months.

I cannot help connecting these events I have set down with that entry in the Protocollum book, which states that two gentlemen, being Fellows of the College, were permitted to register a solemn abjuration of all unlawful acts in the practicing of which they had grievously transgressed: and that it was agreed that the Provost and Seniors shall exercise their utmost discretion to the end that this matter be kept strictly private to the Seniority.

SHADOWS ON THE FENS

Wayne Adrian Drew

To be read aloud, before the Yuletide fire,
as the snow falls....

QUIST EST ISTE QUI VENIT.

Who is this who is coming?

He was the sort who passes by unnoticed. A man in middle-age – not remarkable in any way. His name and profession do not matter. All that signifies… is his story…

It was 5 o'clock on New Year's Eve and the new century was fast approaching. In the rime sifted windows of the lonely cottages he drove past, lamps were already lit and plumes of purple smoke, drew silent witness to fires of well-seasoned logs, piled high against the cruel cold.

Old Black Shuck was in the wind that bayed across the raw and frosted Fens. It stripped the last few shriveled leaves – tenacious traces of the autumn past – and skated them along the murky mirrors of the frozen dykes. It threatened rot-weakened fences. Quivered, till they cracked, the pan-tiles on the wrinkled earth-red roofs. And where it could, made mockery of gardens, prized for their proud tidiness in summer's kinder months.

Then, as the traveller drove on, soon signs of habitation vanished too, as the countryside grew more deserted still – 'till neither towering pylons, nor stunted telegraph poles, remained to bare witness to man's coarse intrusion on the natural world.

As the sky darkened, snow began to fall. At first no more

than the occasional dry flake drifted across the windscreen of his car. But rapidly, like many wives in hopeless partnerships, it dismally clung on, resolute, determined things would change, until the landscape too, became as cold and desolate as a hapless marriage bed.

No! This was no night to travel. And most certainly not in deepest Fenland – that was clear. But he had accepted an invitation to stay with a relative in that little-populated region of South Lincolnshire, only sought by reclusive folk seeking solitude, total anonymity – or both in fact.

To be frank, although he had no wish to remain in London for the celebrations shortly to begin, the effort needed to reach sunnier climes had seemed too much for him – as initially indeed appeared the requirement to drive four hours to accept this invite too. However, his aged uncle, who normally was fiercely protective of the privacy afforded by his isolated location where he undertook his passion for antiquarian pursuits, felt, in the sad circumstances, he should lend his nephew some support, at what undoubtedly, would be for him, a difficult time. So the old man's dogged persistence, in ensuring his offer was accepted, finally achieved its desired result.

It was the first Christmas since her death, you see, and the thought of meeting the New Year alone in the smart, but increasingly cheerless house they'd shared just off the Cromwell Road, was not a pleasant one. But now, while he travelled far from there, as the distance lengthened so did his thoughts drift slowly too from the dark memories that occupied him day and night since she had gone. Yes, this invitation was exactly what was needed, he at last admitted to himself; if one he almost had declined.

Still, as he'd driven on, the road had passed from the places he knew well, to those of less familiarity, until finally it reached a strange terrain that seemed, he thought, more suited to enthusiasts of myth and folklore than the sensible and unimaginative man he'd most certainly become. But she had been both born and raised in this wild place and, though the daughter of a primitive preacher, whose fundamentalist beliefs had terrified her with his threats of hellfire and damnation, she'd loved her birth-land. Loved it with her very soul. The lure of its windswept grandeur, if harsh austerity, had never left her – and it was to here she always said she would return.

Yet, during the four brief years of their marriage, they had never visited her home. She'd asked him, pleaded with him really, to travel back with her, but he'd always said he was 'too busy' – and sometimes meant it too. How petty that excuse now seemed. So today, he was finally to make that journey through places she'd have known so well – but alone – and ironically, in order to forget.

Despite the forecast of an imminent cold spell, when he'd left the city earlier in the day, the weather had been good. There was a crisp but pleasant wind, pale azure skies, and strong clear winter sunlight to accompany his trip. It was the M11 that had proved troublesome – and very troublesome indeed. So the holiday traffic, and ceaseless roadworks, had persuaded him to try some less congested route.

The country roads had not made for the fastest of journeys but first, at least, a decidedly more interesting one. For the villages he passed through had a rustic charm – even at this depressing time of year. All went so well in fact that, just after Revesby, he took what promised to be a short cut down a narrow road across the Fens themselves.

It was only then, as resident of the crowded capital, he realised the true sense of space and timelessness embodied in this stark and ancient land. Extravagant vistas now encircled him, over-arched by melting ever-changing skies that, at the far horizons, resisted all perception of where the earth's crust ended and the heavens began.

The colours of the land itself then quickly changed as well. The green of winter crops was soon replaced by freshly ploughed black ground – so dark it looked unreal. But, as the day drew to its close, the ebony earth slowly vanished beneath a veil of mist, as cold air sucked warm moisture from the sodden soil. Then, with infinitely greater speed than it had arrived, that disappeared too, swept away beneath a blanket of harsh dry snow. The weather forecast had been right! Winter had finally come.

Within no time at all, the man realised, he was lost. Lost and alone – for he'd seen no other car for quite a while. The road ahead had faded now to little more than just a track, fast vanishing beneath the drifting snow. The last remaining echoes of a grim grey twilight were soon gone too as he drove onward through the savage curtain, that shimmered in the headlights of his car. Yes, he had plenty of petrol thank God, but his wipers were fast losing their battle with the falling snow. How much longer would they hold out? What would happen if they failed?

Twice he skidded. The second time so badly he was forced to crawl along the freezing surface of the road.

Slowly another worry came to him – then more still – until a throng of fears stampeded through his brain. What would happen if he was trapped here? Could he walk to safety? What chance a driver should appear to offer aid? Surely a house was nearby? There must be someone that could lend a hand?

No! There was no one – nothing anywhere… He was alone in the encroaching night. He tried his mobile – still no signal. There hadn't been one since he'd left the motorway. Technology was clearly a stranger to these parts! 'Those who live in the sticks, die there too! I wonder if that's true of visitors as well!" he said aloud and coldly laughed. Then wished he hadn't – for fate needed no further tempting in his life…

His bleak thoughts vanished! A blast of wind caught at the car and he swerved violently once more. Just through luck he kept on what appeared to be the road. Or was it? Before him lay a solid mass of white with just the faintest of clues to where the fields ended and his track began.

His body bathed itself in clichéd sweat as he grasped the full reality of his plight. Although his clothes were warm, he had no food or drink if forced to spend the night out there. How long would it take before hypothermia set in? Could he actually freeze to death? He'd read, with no real emotion, save incredulity, reports of men found dead in such a place. How could they've been so foolish? was his only thought before moving on to some more interesting piece – a man's lost life surpassed by trivial sport's reports, or tales of petty politicians new misdeeds. But now he fully understood the horror of such fates – understood it all too well – on such a night. It was a bitter lesson, in every sense of the word!

Suddenly he hit some ice. The skid was dramatic and intense! What advice was always given? Slam on the breaks? Turn with the—

Too late. The car spun through a mighty curve – then quickly came to a wrenching, violent stop, on what must surely be the verge – bringing with it a whiplash that stunned in its brutality.

But no – he seemed okay. His ribs weren't broken. His back and neck were fine. And yes – he could restart the engine too – thank God! Still, try as he might, the car just wouldn't budge. It was fixed fast, the wheels spinning in whirring mockery at his attempts to release them from the freezing drift. 'Dear Lord, what now?' he said aloud – his words formed dismal wreaths in the freezing air, as he called upon his non-existent deity.

Outside the dark was absolute. He looked at his watch. It was only seven o' clock but it might as well be the middle of the night. In futile hope he tried his phone once more. No signal, and the battery was running down as well. There was nothing left but to wait it out! Did he dare keep the heater going? If he drained the battery would he ever get away?

Quickly, he leant back, opened the small leather suitcase on the car's rear seat and pulled out clothing that could help against the cold. He found a sweater and, luck was clearly on his side, a pair of gloves he'd included as an afterthought. There was a thick pair of socks too, and very swiftly, he took off his shoes and pulled them over his freezing feet.

Then in the glove compartment he discovered a tired bar of chocolate, long since forgotten. He ate it ravenously, despite its faded colour and curious stale taste. Thus fed, cocooned in his warm extra layer of clothing, and much more confident, he committed himself to the long hours ahead – and within minutes, totally exhausted, fell asleep.

Shortly before eleven he woke again. His arms and legs were numb and now frost had formed on his coat and gloves, and even on the steering wheel. Not a promising sight! He banged the windscreen and a layer of white fell clean away. Things weren't all bad! For outside he saw, with great relief, the snow had finally stopped.

A full and brilliant winter's moon lit-up the night as it drifted between banks of thick dark clouds. But how foreign this scene was. It was like some strange Dutch painting. Its eerie beauty, fascinated him, but it frightened him as well. For what lay before the man in no way resembled the scene he so remembered from earlier in the day. What power the elements had to achieve such a transformation!

This new world glowed with a cold and fierce light. A light so pure that everything achieved a clarity both harsh and yes, unnatural too. So clear in fact, that, for an instant, the man thought he was able to see into the fabric of the snow itself and glimpse its structure, symmetrical – iridescent. A crystalline metaphor for divine order and hope too perhaps? No! Irony was clearly out of place.

But then there came a lowering cloud – the moment was over – and all was plunged into blackness yet again. A darkness that was total and complete… It caught at his throat and he felt like a diver who had descended into the far-most depths of the sea, down to a zone where light had never penetrated since the birth of time. A realm of monsters! And, with a child-like panic, he was gripped with a seminal terror of the unknown.

Then, with equal suddenness, the moon, like some terrible, if further clichéd eye, rushed out from behind the clouds and once again the land around was irradiated with a naked light. The effect was more astounding than before. For mile upon mile the flat and featureless fens stretched far into the distance – an icy sea – desolate – unknown – and terrifying too.

He opened the window of his car – the stillness shocked him more than the freezing air. For it was absolute. As total and complete as when he'd sat by her bed, smoothed her raven hair, and held her cold dead hand...

Then across the night he heard a sound – the tolling of a bell.

How could a bell be rung at this ungodly hour? Of course! It was New Years Eve. A service would be held to welcome in the coming year. I'll find salvation in the House of God, he grimly joked – as only a confirmed atheist could. Yes, as a country church was surely near at hand, with it would come sanctuary too!

The bell was clear – if leaden and funereal perhaps? No! Solemn was the word he forced himself to think! He'd dwell no more on thoughts of death! So, marshalling what further clothing he could find for protection against the cold, he set off in the direction of the sound, albeit grimly aware the distance might be greater than he'd wish – as, in the stillness, such resonance could travel far from its source of origin.

Although a bank of dark, thick clouds hovered oppressively in the east, the brilliance of the moonlight, and the solidity of the frozen snow, let him travel with more speed than he imagined possible. So after ten minutes, when he looked back, he saw his car had merged into the ice-infested night. But his tracks, shallow though they were, would indeed allow him to retrace his steps if needed? But Fear, his fellow traveller, shook his head, as it kept a steady pace beside him, always ready to conjure up some new and ominous threat to a man who hovered on the threshold of despair.

The bell tolled on and led him towards a grove of trees that, even at a distance, he could see must cover several acres. Could such woodlands of this kind exist in the fenland any more? Clearly the answer was yes, and this must be the remnant of a far earlier time. So the church he sought, and the village it must serve, most probably was hidden in its midst. Though even now he saw no signs of settlement or reassuring cottage lights.

On nearing twelve, he entered, first a thicket, that fast became a grove, and then a woodland dark and somewhat forbidding too. The clouds he'd seen, now conquered all the sky – blotting out the moon and any stars that dared to venture forth. A brisk wind rose – it whispered, shouted, and then screamed across the frozen fens – roaring and howling through the branches of the stunted oaks and then the denser pines. Yet, through the groaning of the ancient wood, the tolling bell seemed ever near – though just beyond his reach.

Blindly he struggled further still into the snow-encrusted trees in the direction of the sound. Ever more fiercely he pushed forward – penetrating deeper the blackness of the night – driven by a desperate need. Survival? Yes! But there was something more as well…

All feeling left his arms and legs. His face was numb and pinched with cold. His lungs ached as he breathed the biting frozen air. Then when he thought he was beyond all fear – true terror gripped him fast. The bell had stopped!

In panic he ran forward tripping over fallen branches – rushing madly amongst the mighty pines. Then all went black!

In his confusion his head had struck a low-hanging bough of a gnarled and massive oak. For some moments he lay stunned upon the frigid soil looking up at the canopy of branches beating wildly high above. The accident had calmed him down at least. And with composure came a sense of the inevitable as well. For when he'd touched his cheek and saw his hand was bloody from the oak's rough bark, the warm dark fluid had seemed a sign that he would die. Yes, he would die here, all alone in this benighted place. And – with exhausted resignation – he accepted what was sure to be his fate.

So it was with amazement, when he sat up, he first saw the church and then…the house. Why hadn't he seen those buildings earlier? Had panic blinded him to those as well?

He staggered to his feet and walked with overwhelming relief, towards the ancient manse. Could there be a God then, after all? It was clearly the parsonage of this lonely parish church set next to a grim and overgrown graveyard. An eldritch spot indeed, but to the man it meant safety – surely?

The snow began to fall once more with even greater force. A blizzard was impending he was sure, as icy shards of hail now stung his skin and, as he looked across the frozen churchyard, he saw them ricochet against the lichen covered gravestones like pellets from a keeper's gun.

It was then that he saw the shape: an outline, no more, drifting across the frozen earth between the worn and crumbling age-old headstones. Surely just a configuration of snow and light and icy flakes? No! It was a woman! A woman with black flowing hair.

Dear God. Could it? Could it be her?

And then he heard the sounds. No! Surely they were words? Yes! Words had drifted to him upon the icy wind? It was a woman's voice, high and strange, but at the same time curiously familiar too? A voice that echoed down long and best-forgotten corridors.

"He was wrong!" It said. And then again more softly, but without all warmth, or one small glimmer of humanity:

"He was so very wrong..."

No! It was the wind, he prayed. Just the icy wind.

And all at once the frozen mirage was no more. It had dissolved into the desolate night. A product of exhaustion and the accident he'd suffered? That was it, without a doubt. But his thoughts lacked the comfort of conviction. And he turned and ran towards the house, then climbed the wooden steps and hammered on the manse's studded door.

The noise was hollow and forbidding. Just like the sound... The sound the earth made as it fell...fell on her coffin. A resonance irrevocable and profound, that should have meant a chapter in their lives was past. As he thought it was – 'til now.

The door swung open and he walked inside.

The hallway – a dim void lit only by some flickering candles – now stretched before him.

'Hello? Is someone there?'

With a fearful crash, behind him the great door slammed shut – the wind had caught it, clearly. Its echoing violence emphasised still more, the silence deep within the shadow filled passageway.

To both his right and left were rows of doors – more doors, it seemed, than any house should surely have. Without a clear thought, an instinct took him first to that upon his right. He firmly grasped its large and tarnished handle and entered in the room.

It was a large chamber, a library in fact, of grand proportions. A fire smouldered in the hearth – its flames burned blue but scarce provided any warmth. The walls were lined with antique books and in the centre of the room there stood a carved oak table, where a five-branched candelabrum spluttered in the gloom next to a Parian head of Dante so it seemed. Here the silence was as profound as if he'd travelled down deep into the dark earth.

On the table lay a book, a massive bible, held open by a small brass clasp, fashioned in the shape of a hand – a woman's hand. Upon the page it held, he saw a passage, heavily scored, and moved closer to read the verses marked. The candle's fetid, friendless light, illumined clearly what was written there.

"The wages of sin are death", was underlined in thick black ink.

He swiftly turned! For surely, someone else had entered the room too? And as he did he sent the book and candles crashing to the floor. The molten wax that splattered both his hands bore no warmth at all – solidifying like ice, upon his skin, as the darkness grew.

'He was so very wrong.'

Right at his side, he heard the voice again.

He blundered forward, overturning the oak table – the Parian head exploding on the flagstone floor - then flailed helplessly in the Stygian gloom – smashing into chairs and bookcases too, whose contents readily crashed down – a literary avalanche of worm-eaten tomes!

Finally he staggered to the door and threw it open. The light from the bleak hallway was enough for him to see around the room. It was empty. She had gone.

But he knew he'd heard that voice. A voice, that once had seemed so loving… and seductive too... But now appeared lost... And lacking any hope... Still, it was her voice. And as Orpheus had found Eurydice, he must find her too. Find her once again – and soon. For it was the only way he ever could gain peace.

Beyond logic, beyond reason, driven by a force as powerful

as life itself, he ran along the hallway and climbed the great oak staircase at its end. For he knew where she would be.

The carpet had long since worn away and his footsteps echoed in the night, and even more so when he reached the bare boards that formed the first floor landing. As if guided by unseen hands, he opened the door directly to his left. It was a bedroom, large and once well-furnished too. But now, like the dried and faded rose lying on the dressing table, a place of withered reminiscence and memories long since decayed.

Quietly, he walked up to the large oak bed – its dusty counterpane was old and worn, but yes, familiar too. The same, in fact, as that on which she'd lain and where he'd stroked her hair and held her hand. Held her dead cold hand… and laughed!

Here the artic chill seemed even more intense. It was cruel, deep and yes, malignant too – a cold such as he had felt when first he'd found the truth about her lovers. Oh so many there had been! A cold that had destroyed his very soul – and only went away as he had placed the white lace pillow over her calm sleeping face – and smothered the lying breath from out her struggling body.

She entered silently and stood there at his side.

'He was so wrong. So very wrong'.

And as he turned to look at her, she smiled – a smile that said so much. Reflected in her midnight eyes he saw a car swerve in the snow and ram itself into a bank of unforgiving ice. And there inside, there was a man – a man whose life-blood streamed from out dead lips. A man with his own face!

She smiled again - her look – a terrifying mask – and bade him welcome to the home they'd now forever share.

'He was so wrong. My father, he was always wrong. There are no flames here. None at all. It's cold. So very cold... in hell.'

It was then he picked the pillow up once more…

A WARNING TO THE CURIOUS

M. R. James

The place on the east coast which the reader is asked to consider is Seaburgh. It is not very different now from what I remember it to have been when I was a child. Marshes intersected by dykes to the south, recalling the early chapters of *Great Expectations*; flat fields to the north, merging into heath; heath, fir woods, and, above all, gorse, inland. A long sea-front and a street: behind that a spacious church of flint, with a broad, solid western tower and a peal of six bells. How well I remember their sound on a hot Sunday in August, as our party went slowly up the white, dusty slope of road towards them, for the church stands at the top of a short, steep incline. They rang with a flat clacking sort of sound on those hot days, but when the air was softer they were mellower too. The railway ran down to its little terminus farther along the same road. There was a gay white windmill just before you came to the station, and another down near the shingle at the south end the town, and yet others on higher ground to the north. There were cottages of bright red brick with slate roofs... but why do I encumber you with these commonplace details? The fact is that they come crowding to the point of the pencil when it begins to write of Seaburgh. I should like to be sure that I had allowed the right ones to get on to the paper. But I forgot. I have not quite done with the word-painting business yet.

Walk away from the sea and the town, pass the station, and turn up the road on the right. It is a sandy road, parallel with the railway, and if you follow it, it climbs to somewhat higher ground. On your left (you are now going northward) is heath, on your right (the side towards the sea) is a belt of old firs, wind-beaten, thick at the top, with the slope that old seaside trees have; seen on the skyline from the train they would tell you in an instant, if you did not know it, that you were approaching a windy coast. Well, at the top of my little hill, a line of these firs strikes out and runs towards the sea, for there is a ridge that goes that way; and the ridge ends in a rather well-defined mound commanding the level fields of rough grass, and a little knot of fir trees crowns it. And here you may sit on a hot spring day, very well content to look at blue sea, white windmills, red cottages bright green grass, church tower, and distant martello tower on the south.

As I have said, I began to know Seaburgh as a child; but a gap of a good many years separates my early knowledge from that which is more recent. Still it keeps its place in my affections, and any tales of it that I pick up have an interest for me. One such tale is this: it came to me in a place very remote from Seaburgh, and quite accidentally, from a man whom I had been able to oblige – enough in his opinion to justify his making me his confidant to this extent.

I know all that country more or less (he said). I used to go to Seaburgh pretty regularly for golf in the spring. I generally put up at the 'Bear', with a friend – Henry Long it was, you knew him perhaps – ('Slightly,' I said) and we used to take a sitting-room and be very happy there. Since he died I haven't cared to go there. And I don't know that I should anyhow after the particular thing that happened on our last visit.

It was in April, 19—, we were there, and by some chance we were almost the only people in the hotel. So the ordinary public rooms were practically empty, and we were the more surprised when, after dinner, our sitting-room door opened, and a young man put his head in. We were aware of this young man. He was rather a rabbity anaemic subject – light hair and light eyes – but not unpleasing. So when he said: 'I beg your pardon, is this a private room?' we did not growl and say: 'Yes, it is,' but Long said, or I did – no matter which: 'Please come in.' Oh, may I?' he said, and seemed relieved. Of course it was obvious that he wanted company; and as he was a reasonable kind of person – not the sort to bestow his whole family history on you – we urged him to make himself at home. 'I dare say you find the other rooms rather bleak,' I said. Yes, he did: but it was really too good of us, and so on. That being got over, he made some pretence of reading a book. Long was playing Patience, I was writing. It became plain to me after a few minutes that this visitor of ours was in rather a state of fidgets or nerves, which communicated itself to me, and so I put away my writing and turned to at engaging him in talk.

After some remarks, which I forget, he became rather confidential. 'You'll think it very odd of me' (this was the sort of way he began), 'but the fact is I've had something of a shock.' Well, I recommended a drink of some cheering kind, and we had it. The waiter coming in made an interruption (and I thought our young man seemed very jumpy when the door opened), but after a while he got back to his woes again. There was nobody he knew in the place, and he did happen to know who we both were (it turned out there was some common acquaintance in town), and really he did want a word of advice, if we didn't mind. Of course we both said: 'By all means,' or 'Not at all,' and Long put away his cards. And we settled down to hear what his difficulty was.

'It began,' he said, 'more than a week ago, when I bicycled over to Froston, only about five or six miles, to see the church; I'm very much interested in architecture, and it's got one of those pretty porches with niches and shields. I took a photograph of it, and then an old man who was tidying up in the churchyard came and asked if I'd care to look into the church. I said yes, and he produced a key and let me in. There wasn't much inside, but I told him it was a nice little church, and he kept it very clean, 'But,' I said, 'the porch is the best part of it.' We were just outside the porch then, and he said, 'Ah, yes, that is a nice porch; and do you know, sir, what's the meanin' of that coat of arms there?'

'It was the one with the three crowns, and though I'm not

much of a herald, I was able to say yes, I thought it was the old arms of the kingdom of East Anglia.

"'That's right, sir,' he said, 'and do you know the meanin' of them three crowns that's on it?'

'I said I'd no doubt it was known, but I couldn't recollect to have heard it myself.

"'Well, then,' he said, 'for all you're a scholard, I can tell you something you don't know. Them's the three 'oly crowns what was buried in the ground near by the coast to keep the Germans from landing – ah, I can see you don't believe that. But I tell you, if it hadn't have been for one of them 'oly crowns bein' there still, them Germans would a landed here time and again, they would. Landed with their ships, and killed man, woman and child in their beds. Now then, that's the truth what I'm telling you, that is; and if you don't believe me, you ast the rector. There he comes: you ast him, I says.'

'I looked round, and there was the rector, a nice-looking old man, coming up the path; and before I could begin assuring my old man, who was getting quite excited, that I didn't disbelieve him, the rector struck in, and said:

"'What's all this about, John? Good day to you, sir. Have you been looking at our little church?'

'So then there was a little talk which allowed the old man to calm down, and then the rector asked him again what was the matter.

"'Oh,' he said, 'it warn't nothink, only I was telling this gentleman he'd ought to ast you about them 'oly crowns.'

"'Ah, yes, to be sure,' said the rector, 'that's a very curious matter, isn't it? But I don't know whether the gentleman is interested in our old stories, eh?'

"'Oh, he'll be interested fast enough,' says the old man, 'he'll put his confidence in what you tells him, sir; why, you known William Ager yoursell, father and son too.'

'Then I put in a word to say how much I should like to hear all about it, and before many minutes I was walking up the village street with the rector, who had one or two words to say to parishioners, and then to the rectory, where he took me into his study. He had made out, on the way, that I really was capable of taking an intelligent interest in a piece of folklore, and not quite the ordinary tripper. So he was very willing to talk, and it is rather surprising to me that the particular legend he told me has not made its way into print before. His account of it was this: 'There has always been a belief in these parts in the three holy crowns. The old people say they were buried in different places near the coast to keep off the Danes or the French or the Germans. And they say that one of the three was dug up a long time ago, and another has disappeared by the encroaching of the sea, and one's still left doing its work, keeping off invaders. Well, now, if you have read the ordinary guides and histories of this county, you will remember perhaps that in 1687 a crown, which was said to be the crown of Redwald, King of the East Angles, was dug up at Rendlesham, and alas! alas! melted down before it was even properly described or drawn. Well, Rendlesham isn't on the coast, but it isn't so very far inland, and it's on a very important line of access. And I believe that is the crown which the people mean when they say that one has been dug up. Then on the south you don't want me to tell you where there was a Saxon royal palace which is now under the sea, eh? Well, there was the second crown, I take it. And up beyond these two, they say, lies the third.'

"Do they say where it is?' of course I asked.

'He said, 'Yes, indeed, they do, but they don't tell,' and his manner did not encourage me to put the obvious question. Instead of that I waited a moment, and said: 'What did the old man mean when he said you knew William Ager, as if that had something to do with the crowns?'

"To be sure,' he said, 'now that's another curious story. These Agers – it's a very old name in these parts, but I can't find that they were ever people of quality or big owners – these Agers say, or said, that their branch of the family were the guardians of the last crown. A certain old Nathaniel Ager was the first one I knew – I was born and brought up quite near here – and he, I believe, camped out at the place during the whole of the war of 1870. William, his son, did the same, I know, during the South African War. And young William, his son, who has only died fairly recently, took lodgings at the cottage nearest the spot; and I've no doubt hastened his end, for he was a consumptive, by exposure and night watching. And he was the last of that branch. It was a dreadful grief to him to think that he was the last, but he could do nothing, the only relations at all near to him were in the colonies. I wrote letters for him to them imploring them to come over on business very important to the family, but there has been no answer. So the last of the holy crowns, if it's there, has no guardian now.'

'That was what the rector told me, and you can fancy how interesting I found it. The only thing I could think of when I left him was how to hit upon the spot where the crown was supposed to be. I wish I'd left it alone.

'But there was a sort of fate in it, for as I bicycled back past the churchyard wall my eye caught a fairly new gravestone, and on it was the name of William Ager. Of course I got off and read it. It said 'of this parish, died at Seaburgh, 19 – , aged 28.' There it was, you see. A little judicious questioning in the right place, and I should at least find the cottage nearest the spot. Only I didn't quite know what was the right place to begin my questioning at. Again there was fate: it took me to the curiosity-shop down that way – you know – and I turned over some old books, and, if you please, one was a prayer-book of 1740 odd, in a rather handsome binding – I'll just go and get it, it's in my room.'

He left us in a state of some surprise, but we had hardly time to exchange any remarks when he was back, panting, and handed us the book opened at the fly-leaf, on which was, in a straggly hand:

'Nathaniel Ager is my name and England is my nation,
Seaburgh is my dwelling-place and Christ is my Salvation,
When I am dead and in my Grave, and all my bones are rotton,
I hope the lord will think on me when I am quite forgotton.'

This poem was dated 1754, and there were many more entries of Agers, Nathaniel, Frederick, William, and so on, ending with William, 19—.

'You see,' he said, 'anybody would call it the greatest bit of luck. I did, but I don't now. Of course I asked the shopman about William Ager, and of course he happened to remember that he lodged in a cottage in the North Field and died there. This was just chalking the road for me. I knew which the cottage must be: there is only one sizable one about there. The next thing was to scrape some sort of acquaintance with the people, and I took a walk that way at once. A dog did the business for me: he made at me so fiercely that they had to run out and beat him off, and then naturally begged my pardon, and we got into talk. I had only to bring up Ager's name, and pretend I knew, or thought I knew something of him, and then the woman said how sad it was him dying so young, and she was sure it came of him spending the night out of doors in the cold weather. Then I had to say: 'Did he go out on the sea at night?' and she said: 'Oh, no, it was on the hillock yonder with the trees on it.' And there I was.

'I know something about digging in these barrows: I've opened many of them in the down country. But that was with owner's leave, and in broad daylight and with men to help. I had to prospect very carefully here before I put a spade in: I couldn't trench across the mound, and with those old firs growing there I knew there would be awkward tree loots. Still the soil was very light and sandy and easy, and there was a rabbit hole or so that might be developed into a sort of tunnel. The going out and coming back at odd hours to the hotel was going to be the awkward part. When I made up my mind about the way to excavate I told the people that I was called away for a night, and I spent it out there. I made my tunnel: I won't bore you with the details of how I supported it and filled it in when I'd done, but the main thing is that I got the crown.'

Naturally we both broke out into exclamations of surprise and interest. I for one had long known about the finding of the crown at Rendlesham and had often lamented its fate. No one has ever seen an Anglo-Saxon crown – at least no one had. But our man gazed at us with a rueful eye. 'Yes,' he said, 'and the worst of it is I don't know how to put it back.'

'Put it back?' we cried out. 'Why, my dear sir, you've made one of the most exciting finds ever heard of in this country. Of course it ought to go to the Jewel House at the Tower. What's your difficulty? If you're thinking about the owner of the land, and treasure-trove, and all that, we can certainly help you through. Nobody's going to make a fuss about technicalities in a case of this kind.'

Probably more was said, but all he did was to put his face in his hands, and mutter: 'I don't know how to put it back.'

At last Long said: 'You'll forgive me, I hope, if I seem impertinent, but are you quite sure you've got it?' I was wanting to ask much the same question myself, for of course the story did seem a lunatic's dream when one thought over it. But I hadn't quite dared to say what might hurt the poor young man's feelings. However, he took it quite calmly – really, with the calm of despair, you might say. He sat up and said: 'Oh, yes, there's no doubt of that: I have it here, in my room, locked up in my bag. You can come and look at it if you like: I won't offer to bring it here.'

We were not likely to let the chance slip. We went with him; his room was only a few doors off. The boots was just collecting shoes in the passage: or so we thought: afterwards we were not sure. Our visitor – his name was Parton – was in a worse state of shivers than before, and went hurriedly into the room, and beckoned us after him, turned on the light, and shut the door carefully. Then he unlocked his kit-bag, and produced a bundle of clean pocket-handkerchief in which something was wrapped, laid it on the bed, and undid it. I can now say I have seen an actual Anglo-Saxon crown. It was of silver – as the Rendlesham one is always said to have been – it was set with some gems, mostly antique intaglios and cameos, and was of rather plain, almost rough workmanship. In fact, it was like those you see on the coins and in the manuscripts. I found no reason to think it was later than the ninth century. I was intensely interested, of course, and I wanted to turn it over in my hands, but Paxton prevented me. 'Don't you touch it,' he said, 'I'll do that.' And with a sigh that was, I declare to you, dreadful to hear, he took it up and turned it about so that we could see every part of it. 'Seen enough?' he said at last, and we nodded. He wrapped it up and locked it in his bag, and stood looking at us dumbly. 'Come back to our room,' Long said, 'and tell us what the trouble is.' He thanked us, and said: 'Will you go first and see if – if the coast is clear?' That wasn't very intelligible, for our proceedings hadn't been, after all, very suspicious, and the hotel, as I said, was practically empty. However, we were beginning to have inklings of – we didn't know what, and anyhow nerves are infectious. So we did go, first peering out as we opened the door, and fancying (I found we both had the fancy) that a shadow, or more than a shadow – but it made no sound – passed from before us to one side as we came out into the passage. 'It's all right,' we whispered to Paxton – whispering seemed the proper tone – and we went, with him between us, back to our sitting-room. I was preparing, when we got there, to be ecstatic about the unique interest of what we had seen, but when I looked at Paxton I saw that would be terribly out of place, and I left it to him to begin.

'What is to be done?' was his opening. Long thought it right (as he explained to me afterwards) to be obtuse, and said: 'Why not find out who the owner of the land is, and inform—' Oh, no, no!' Paxton broke in impatiently, 'I beg your pardon: you've been very kind, but don't you see it's got to go back, and I daren't be there at night, and daytime's impossible. Perhaps, though, you don't see: well, then, the truth is that I've never been alone since I touched it.' I was beginning some fairly stupid comment, but Long caught my eye, and I stopped. Long said: 'I think I do see, perhaps: but wouldn't it be a relief – to tell us a little more clearly what the situation is?'

Then it all came out: Paxton looked over his shoulder and beckoned to us to come nearer to him, and began speaking in a low voice: we listened most intently, of course, and compared notes afterwards, and I wrote down our version, so I am confident I have what he told us almost word for word. He said:

'It began when I was first prospecting, and put me off again and again. There was always somebody – a man – standing by one of the firs. This was in daylight, you know. He was never in front of me. I always saw him with the tail of my eye on the left or the right, and he was never there when I looked straight for him. I would lie down for quite a long time and take careful observations, and make sure there was no one, and then when I got up and began prospecting again, there he was. And he began to give me hints, besides; for wherever I put that prayer-book – short of locking it up, which I did at last – when I came back to my loom it was always out on my table open at the flyleaf where the names are, and one of my razors across it to keep it open. I'm sure he just can't open my bag, or something more would have happened. You see, he's light and weak, but all the same I daren't face him. Well, then, when I was making the tunnel, of course it was worse, and if I hadn't been so keen I should have dropped the whole thing and run. It was like someone scraping at my back all the time: I thought for a long time it was only soil dropping on me, but as I got nearer the – the crown, it was unmistakable. And when I actually laid it bare and got my fingers into the ring of it and pulled it out, there came a sort of cry behind me – oh, I can't tell you how desolate it was! And horribly threatening too. It spoilt all my pleasure in my find – cut it off that moment. And if I hadn't been the wretched fool I am, I should have put the thing back and left it. But I didn't. The rest of the time was just awful. I had hours to get through before I could decently come back to the hotel. First I spent time filling up my tunnel and covering my tracks, and all the while he was there trying to thwart me. Sometimes, you know, you see him, and sometimes you don't, just as he pleases, I think: he's there, but he has some power over your eyes. Well, I wasn't off the spot very long before sunrise, and then I had to get to the junction for Seaburgh, and take a train back. And though it was daylight fairly soon, I don't know if that made it much better. There were always hedges, or gorse-bushes, or park fences along the road – some sort of cover, I mean – and I was never easy for a second. And then when I began to meet people going to work, they always looked behind me very strangely: it might have been that they were surprised at seeing anyone so early; but I didn't think it was only that, and I don't now: they didn't look exactly at me. And the porter at the train was like that too. And the guard held open the door after I'd got into the carriage – just as he would if there was somebody else coming, you know. Oh, you may be very sure it isn't my fancy,' he said with a dull sort of laugh. Then he went on: 'And even if I do get it put back, he won't forgive me: I can tell that. And I was so happy a fortnight ago.' He dropped into a chair, and I believe he began to cry.

We didn't know what to say, but we felt we must come to the rescue somehow, and so – it really seemed the only thing – we said if he was so set on putting the crown back in its place, we would help him. And I must say that after what we had heard it did seem the right thing. If these horrid consequences had come on this poor man, might there not really be something in the original idea of the crown having some curious power bound up with it, to guard the coast? At least, that was my feeling, and I think it was Long's too. Our offer was very welcome to Paxton, anyhow. When could we do it? It was nearing half-past ten. Could we contrive to make a late walk plausible to the hotel people that very night? We looked out of the window: there was a brilliant full moon – the Paschal moon. Long undertook to tackle the boots and propitiate him. He was to say that we should not be much over the hour, and if we did find it so pleasant that we stopped out a bit longer we would see that he didn't lose by sitting up. Well, we were pretty regular customers of the hotel, and did not give much trouble, and were considered by the servants to be not under the mark in the way of tips; and so the boots was propitiated, and let us out on to the sea-front, and remained, as we heard later, looking after us. Paxton had a large coat over his arm, under which was the wrapped-up crown.

So we were off on this strange errand before we had time to think how very much out of the way it was. I have told this part quite shortly on purpose, for it really does represent the haste with which we settled our plan and took action. 'The shortest way is up the hill and through the churchyard,' Paxton said, as we stood a moment before, the hotel looking up and down the front. There was nobody about – nobody at all. Seaburgh out of the season is an early, quiet place. 'We can't go along the dyke by the cottage, because of the dog,' Paxton also said, when I pointed to what I thought a shorter way along the front and across two fields. The reason he gave was good enough. We went up the road to the church, and turned in at the churchyard gate. I confess to having thought that there might be some lying there who might be conscious of our business: but if it was so, they were also conscious that one who was on their side, so to say, had us under surveillance, and we saw no sign of them. But under observation we felt we were, as I have never felt it at another time. Specially was it so when we passed out of the churchyard into a narrow path with close high hedges, through which we hurried as Christian did through that Valley; and so got out into open fields. Then along hedges, though I world sooner have been in the open, where I could see if anyone was visible behind me; over a gate or two, and then a swerve to the left, taking us up on to the ridge which ended in that mound.

As we neared it, Henry Long felt, and I felt too, that there were what I can only call dim presences waiting for us, as well as a far more actual one attending us. Of Paxton's agitation all this time I can give you no adequate picture: he breathed like a hunted beast, and we could not either of us look at his face. How he would manage when we got to the very place we had not troubled to think: he had seemed so sure that that would not be difficult. Nor was it. I never saw anything like the dash with which he flung himself at a particular spot in the side of the mound, and tore at it, so that in a very few minutes the greater part of his body was out of sight. We stood holding the coat and that bundle of handkerchief, and looking, very fearfully, I must admit, about us. There was nothing to be seen: a line of dark firs behind us made one skyline, more trees and the church tower half a mile off on the right, cottages and a windmill on the horizon on the left, calm sea dead in front, faint barking of a dog at a cottage on a gleaming dyke between us and it: full moon making that path we know across the sea: the eternal whisper of the Scotch firs just above us, and of the sea in front. Yet, in all this quiet, an acute, an acrid consciousness of a restrained hostility very near us, like a dog on a leash that might be let go at any moment.

Paxton pulled himself out of the hole, and stretched a hand back to us. 'Give it to me,' he whispered, 'unwrapped.' We pulled off the handkerchiefs, and he took the crown. The moonlight just fell on it as he snatched it. We had not ourselves touched that bit of metal, and I have thought since that it was just as well. In another moment Paxton was out of the hole again and busy shovelling back the soil with hands that were already bleeding He would have none of our help though It was much the longest part of the job to get the place to look undisturbed yet – I don't know how – he made a wonderful success of it. At last he was satisfied and we turned back

We were a couple of hundred yards from the hill when Long suddenly said to him: 'I say you've left your coat there. That won't do. See?' And I certainly did see it – the long dark overcoat lying where the tunnel had been. Paxton had not stopped, however: he only shook his head, and held up the coat on his arm. And when we joined him, he said, without any excitement, but as if nothing mattered any more: 'That wasn't my coat.' And, indeed, when we looked back again, that dark thing was not to be seen.

Well, we got out on to the road, and came rapidly back that way. It was well before twelve when we got in, trying to put a good face on it, and saying – Long and I – what a lovely night it was for a walk. The boots was on the look-out for us, and we made remarks like that for his edification as we entered the hotel. He gave another look up and down the sea-front before he locked the front door, and said: 'You didn't meet many people about, I s'pose, sir?' 'No, indeed, not a soul,' I said; at which I remember Paxton looked oddly at me. 'Only I thought I see someone turn up the station road after you gentlemen,' said the boots. 'Still, you was three together, and I don't suppose he meant mischief.' I didn't know what to say; Long merely said

'Good night,' and we went off upstairs, promising to turn put all lights, and to go to bed in a few minutes.

Back in our room, we did our very best to make Paxton take a cheerful view. 'There's the crown safe back,' we said; 'very likely you'd have done better not to touch it' (and he heavily assented to that), 'but no real harm has been done, and we shall never give this away to anyone who would be so mad as to go near it. Besides, don't you feel better yourself? I don't mind confessing,' I said, 'that on the way there I was very much inclined to take your view about – well, about being followed; but going back, it wasn't at all the same thing, was it?' No, it wouldn't do: 'You've nothing to trouble yourselves about,' he said, 'but I'm not forgiven. I've got to pay for that miserable sacrilege still. I know what you are going to say. The Church might help. Yes, but it's the body that has to suffer. It's true I'm not feeling that he's waiting outside for me just now. But—' Then he stopped. Then he turned to thanking us, and we put him off as soon as we could. And naturally we pressed him to use our sitting-room next day, and said we should be glad to go out with him. Or did he play golf, perhaps? Yes, he did, but he didn't think he should care about that tomorrow. Well, we recommended him to get up late and sit in our room in the morning while we were playing, and we would have a walk later in the day. He was very submissive and piano about it all: ready to do just what we thought best, but clearly quite certain in his own mind that what was coming could not be averted or palliated. You'll wonder why we didn't insist on accompanying him to his home and seeing him safe into the care of brothers or someone. The fact was he had nobody. He had had a flat in town, but lately he had made up his mind to settle for a time in Sweden, and he had dismantled his flat and shipped off his belongings, and was whiling away a fortnight or three weeks before he made a start. Anyhow, we didn't see what we could do better than sleep on it – or not sleep very much, as was my case – and see what we felt like tomorrow morning.

We felt very different, Long and I, on as beautiful an April morning as you could desire; and Paxton also looked very different when we saw him at breakfast. 'The first approach to a decent night I seem ever to have had,' was what he said. But he was going to do as we had settled: stay in probably all the morning, and come out with us later. We went to the links; we met some other men and played with them in the morning, and had lunch there rather early, so as not to be late back. All the same, the snares of death overtook him.

Whether it could have been prevented, I don't know. I think he would have been got at somehow, do what we might. Anyhow, this is what happened.

We went straight up to our room. Paxton was there, reading quite peaceably. 'Ready to come out shortly?' said Long, 'say in half an hour's time?' 'Certainly,' he said: and I said we would change first, and perhaps have baths, and call for him in half an hour. I had my bath first, and went and lay down on my bed, and slept for about ten minutes. We came out of our rooms at the same time, and went together to the sitting-room. Paxton wasn't there – only his book. Nor was he in his room, nor in the downstairs rooms. We shouted for him. A servant came out and said: 'Why, I thought you gentlemen was gone out already, and so did the other gentleman. He heard you a-calling from the path there, and run out in a hurry, and I looked out of the coffee-room window, but I didn't see you. 'Owever, he run off down the beach that way.'

Without a word we ran that way too – it was the opposite direction to that of last night's expedition. It wasn't quite four o'clock, and the day was fair, though not so fair as it had been, so that was really no reason, you'd say, for anxiety: with people about, surely a man couldn't come to much harm.

But something in our look as we ran out must have struck the servant, for she came out on the steps, and pointed, and said, 'Yes, that's the way he went.' We ran on as far as the top of the shingle bank, and there pulled up. There was a choice of ways: past the houses on the sea-front, or along the sand at the bottom of the beach, which, the tide being now out, was fairly broad. Or of course we might keep along the shingle between these two tracks and have some view of both of them; only that was heavy going. We chose the sand, for that was the loneliest, and someone might come to harm there without being seen from the public path.

Long said he saw Paxton some distance ahead, running and waving his stick, as if he wanted to signal to people who were on ahead of him. I couldn't be sure: one of these sea-mists was coming up very quickly from the south. There was someone, that's all I could say. And there were tracks on the sand as of someone running who wore shoes; and there were other tracks made before those – for the shoes sometimes trod in them and interfered with them – of someone not in shoes. Oh, of course, it's only my word you've got to take for all this: Long's dead, we'd no time or means to make sketches or take casts, and the next tide washed everything away. All we could do was to notice these marks as we hurried on. But there they were over and over again, and we had no doubt whatever that what we saw was the track of a bare foot, and one that showed more bones than flesh.

The notion of Paxton running after – after anything like this, and supposing it to be the friends he was looking for, was very dreadful to us. You can guess what we fancied: how the thing he was following might stop suddenly and turn round on him, and what sort of face it would show, half-seen at first in the mist – which all the while was getting thicker and thicker. And as I ran on wondering how the poor wretch could have been lured into mistaking that other thing for us, I remembered his saying, 'He has some power over your eyes.' And then I wondered what the end would be, for I had no hope now that the end could be averted, and – well, there is no need to tell all the dismal and horrid thoughts that flitted through my head as we ran on into the mist. It was uncanny, too, that the sun should still be bright in the sky and we could see nothing. We could only tell that we were now past the houses and had reached that gap there is between them and the old martello tower. When you are past the tower, you know, there is nothing but shingle for a long way – not a house, not a human creature; just that spit of land, or rather shingle, with the river on your right and the sea on your left.

But just before that, just by the martello tower, you remember there is the old battery, close to the sea. I believe there are only a few blocks of concrete left now: the rest has all been washed away, but at this time there was a lot more, though the place was a ruin. Well, when we got there, we clambered to the top as quick as we could to take breath and look over the shingle in front if by chance the mist would let us see anything. But a moment's rest we must have. We had run a mile at least. Nothing whatever was visible ahead of us, and we were just turning by common consent to get down and run hopelessly on, when we heard what I can only call a laugh: and if you can understand what I mean by a breathless, a lungless laugh, you have it: but I don't suppose you can. It came from below, and swerved away into the mist. That was enough. We bent over the wall. Paxton was there at the bottom.

You don't need to be told that he was dead. His tracks showed that he had run along the side of the battery, had turned sharp round the corner of it, and, small doubt of it, must have dashed straight into the open arms of someone who was waiting there. His mouth was full of sand and stones, and his teeth and jaws were broken to bits. I only glanced once at his face.

At the same moment, just as we were scrambling down from the battery to get to the body, we heard a shout, and saw a man running down the bank of the martello tower. He was the caretaker stationed there, and his keen old eyes had managed to descry through the mist that something was wrong. He had seen Paxton fall, and had seen us a moment after, running up – fortunate this, for otherwise we could hardly have escaped suspicion of being concerned in the dreadful business. Had he, we asked, caught sight of anybody attacking our friend? He could not be sure.

We sent him off for help, and stayed by the dead man till they came with the stretcher. It was then that we traced out how he had come, on the narrow fringe of sand under the battery wall. The rest was shingle, and it was hopelessly impossible to tell whither the other had gone.

What were we to say at the inquest? It was a duty, we felt,

not to give up, there and then, the secret of the crown, to be published in every paper. I don't know how much you would have told; but what we did agree upon was this: to say that we had only made acquaintance with Paxton the day before, and that he had told us he was under some apprehension of danger at the hands of a man called William Ager. Also that we had seen some other tracks besides Paxton's when we followed him along the beach. But of course by that time everything was gone from the sands.

No one had any knowledge, fortunately, of any William Ager living in the district. The evidence of the man at the martello tower freed us from all suspicion. All that could be done was to return a verdict of wilful murder by some person or persons unknown.

Paxton was so totally without connections that all the inquiries that were subsequently made ended in a No Thoroughfare. And I have never been at Seaburgh, or even near it, since.

STIVINGHOE BANK

R. H. Malden

The coast-line of Norfolk is one of those which have altered considerably in historic times. Along some stretches the sea has encroached. At low water traces of lost villages can still be seen, and in stormy weather pieces of wood from drowned forests are sometimes washed ashore. At Cromer a lighthouse which I remember has disappeared long since, though it was not very near the edge of the cliff when I knew it. A new one has been built at some distance inland.

Along other stretches the sea has receded and towns which were once thriving ports are separated from it by a wide expanse of marsh, where cattle graze and abundant mushrooms can be found in early autumn. These marshes are intersected by deep and muddy channels up which the tide creeps sluggishly. But even at high water nothing larger than an open boat can use them. The harbours whence the cloth was shipped in the great days of East Anglia, when Norwich was the third city in the kingdom and nearly wrested the second place from Bristol, are almost useless now. The towns which lived by them have dwindled to small villages. Here and there a fine old house may still be seen on the water-front. But for the most part the large and magnificent churches are all that remain of their former glories.

Melancholy as these villages are they have a beauty and dignity of their own. The wide horizon of marsh, beach and sea beyond gives a sense of spaciousness which can hardly be found elsewhere. Anyone who knows them will understand why a Norfolk nurserymaid when taken to Grasmere complained that she felt unable to breathe and that the mountains spoilt the view.

They have always been well known to sportsmen as the marshes teem with wild-fowl in winter.

Of late years artists have begun to discover them. But I must admit that I hope they will never become popular resorts.

It was at one of them, which I will call Stivinghoe, that the experience (it hardly deserves to be called an adventure) which is set down here, befell me some years ago. If, when you have heard the story, you think it rather pointless, that is not my fault. I do not think that I should have admired Mr. Chadband had I met him. But his insistence on what he called 'The Terewth' always seemed to me worthy of imitation. And I could not make the story more exciting without departing from the standard set by that eloquent divine.

Stivinghoe differs from its neighbours in the possession of a bank; that is to say a causeway some eight feet high running across the marsh land and projecting beyond it into the sea. I suppose it is natural, as it is not easy to see why anyone should have taken the trouble to construct it. There is a rough track along the top. At the shoreward end the sides are clothed with coarse grass where sea-pinks and yellow horned poppies grow. The last half-mile is sand and shingle. At high water the sea comes up to it on both sides. When the tide is out it is flanked by a wide expanse of wet sand. At the far end there is a little hillock on which are the remains of a ruined chapel. It is as lonely and desolate a spot as can well be imagined. I suppose the chapel had escaped demolition because it had never been worth anyone's while to pull the walls down and cart the material away. It was a cell of the great house of Walsingham and had been established as a place where prayer might be offered continually for fishermen along the coast and all who got their living from the sea.

After the dissolution of the monasteries a large part of the lands of Walsingham had gone to the Earl of W., whose descendant is still one of the magnates of Norfolk. I had reason to believe that some books from the library had made their way to his great house at Folkham. There was no adequate catalogue of them and as I had known Lord W.'s son at Cambridge I ventured to write and ask whether I might come and look at them. His reply was very cordial. He regretted that he could not ask me to stay as the family was away and the house shut up. He had written to the housekeeper, telling her to let me see anything I wanted, and added that while the only inn in the village was not to be recommended I should be sufficiently comfortable at the 'Fishmongers' Arms' at Stivinghoe.

The map showed me that the distance from Stivinghoe to Folkham House was only about three miles. A bicycle would solve the question of transport. I had never slept at the 'Fishmongers' Arms', but had had tea there more than once when exploring the neighbourhood, and my recollection of it confirmed Lord W.'s opinion.

Accordingly I wrote engaging a bedroom (if possible with a table at which I could write) for a week and established myself there one fine afternoon in the middle of September.

The greater part of the next three days was spent in the library at Folkham. The result was, however, rather disappointing. The manuscripts were not many. Neither contents nor workmanship were of outstanding interest. I thought I had got to the end of them when I came upon a bundle of papers tied up with tape and docketed, in a modern hand, Stivinghoe Chapel.

The housekeeper had just come into the room with some tea and I noticed that she seemed to be disconcerted when she saw the bundle in my hand.

'Are these private papers, do you suppose?' I said. 'They were on the same shelf as the other manuscripts. Is there any, reason why I shouldn't read them? I see that somebody had them out not very long ago.'

'Yes, Sir,' she said. 'That were his lordship's father, that were. The day before the great storm, not that that had anything to do with it, I do suppose. No, I don't see there'd be no harm – if so be as you're careful, Sir.'

Of course I told her that I would take great care of them, that I was accustomed to handling old books and papers and so forth. But I couldn't help thinking that that was not quite what she meant.

It was too late to do any more that day. So I said I would come back and go through them to-morrow morning.

I mounted my bicycle at the front door expecting to enjoy the ride home as it was a beautiful evening. But somehow I did not. For some reason I felt uncomfortable and could not get rid of the idea that there was someone following me. Though after all why shouldn't there be on a public highroad? And what harm could he do me in broad daylight if he were evilly disposed? All the same so strong was the feeling that I looked behind me more than once. But I had the road to myself. All the same I rode faster than usual and was glad when I found myself at the 'Fishmongers' Arms'.

After dinner I went into the bar-parlour as usual and got into conversation with its frequenters. The talk was of the usual description in such places. Interesting enough to anyone who, like myself, can find pleasure in listening to reminiscences of past harvests, speculations as to quality of the next one, the market prices of beasts and local affairs generally. But not worth attempting to set down here.

The company broke up early and I went early to bed. Contrary to my usual custom I did not sleep very well. I was troubled by a recurrent dream, the details of which eluded me, try as I would to recall them. The general sense was that I was going somewhere where I expected to meet, or at least feared that I might meet, somebody whom I did not want to see. Just as I was on the point of coming face to face with him I always woke up. This performance was repeated with monotonous regularity four or five times between midnight (which I heard on the church clock) and dawn. As soon as it was light I gave up trying to go to sleep and read until it was time to get up.

After breakfast I bicycled to Folkham House as usual and got out the bundle of papers.

They proved more interesting than I had expected. They belonged to the years 1531-2 and appeared to relate to the incumbent of the chapel at the end of the bank. John of

Costessey was his name.

The first document was brief. It was addressed to the Prior and Convent of Walsingham and was a request bearing about a dozen signatures, of which three seemed to be those of the rectors of Stivinghoe and two neighbouring villages, that John might be recalled to Walsingham and someone else despatched to take his place.

Presumably the Prior wrote, as he was bound to do, to ask the reason for this request, for the next letter was considerably longer. It appeared that John was suspected of having entered into a compact with the powers of evil. He was a man of violent and vindictive temper and it was noticeable that those who offended him were dogged by persistent and inexplicable misfortune. Next time they went to sea they met with no fish; or nets broke mysteriously as a catch was being brought on board. Unaccountable accidents, some fatal, occurred on board their boats. More than once a boat had been lost with all hands in a sudden and very violent storm, which had not been foreseen by the most weather-wise seamen along the coast.

More than once he had been seen from boats rounding the end of the bank close inshore to make the harbour, standing at the water's edge with an imp seated on his shoulder. The said imp had screamed and waved its arms (here followed an illegible word which I guessed to be meant for *devilishly).*

More than once at night-time the window of the Chapel had been seen to be brightly lighted, and bursts of song were heard proceeding from it. These melodies did not suggest the familiar offices of the Church and more than one voice seemed to be taking part.

Next came a letter from John himself, obviously in answer to a communication from the Prior. He protested that he could not be expected to reply in detail to such malicious and unfounded charges *(crimina tam perfida ac dolosa et omnino nugatoria)* and hinted that if his nocturnal vigils had been solaced by celestial company no fault could be found with him on that score *(quid in hoc improperii vel quae increpationis causa?).*

The Prior's answer to this may be inferred to have been a

summons to repair to Walsingham forthwith. John's next letter was to the effect that his austerities, which it was his delight to practise, had made him too feeble to undertake the journey on foot, while the hard-heartedness and irreligion of the countryside, of which the Prior had had ample proof *(litteris supradictis satis probatum),* made it unlikely that any attempt to borrow so much as an ass would be successful.

The Prior could hardly be expected to put up with this, nor did he. He must have told John that he proposed to visit him in person, for the last letter was as follows:

Quamquam in rebus humus vitae delectari non fas, attamen cum hic viderim oculis meis sanctissimum Priorem una cum duo bus fratribus dilectissimis libenter dicam Domine nunc dimittis servum tuum, etc.

(Although we are forbidden to take pleasure in the things of this life, yet when I have seen here with my eyes the most holy Prior together with two of my dearly beloved brethren I shall gladly say, 'Lord, now lettest thou Thy servant depart,' etc.)

'Well,' I said to myself, 'he may have been an impudent rascal if nothing worse. But he seems to have had a sense of humour and to have been pretty sure of his ground. I wonder how the story ended?'

Next moment I gave a violent start, for I heard what sounded like a laugh close behind me. I whipped round in my chair. But there was no one there. The library was a large room and I was some distance from the door. Although the carpet was thick I did not think anyone could have come in without my knowledge. However, I got up, and went all round the room and even looked behind the window curtains. Of course I found nobody, and sat down again feeling rather ashamed of myself for being so fanciful.

There was only one more paper to be examined. Unfortunately the top had been torn off and the first words remaining were *nusquan inveniri potuit* (could not be found anywhere).

Then followed an inventory of the contents of the Chapel and cell. The only unusual item was *Duae cerae nigrae* (two candles of black wax).

I concluded that the Prior had paid his visit, but that John's nerve had failed him at the last moment and he had disappeared. He could have made his way to Lynn without much difficulty and got on board a ship bound for the Low Countries.

No doubt the Prior was not sorry to be rid of him, and as the inventory was dated ***Festo S. Edithae MDXXXII*** (16 September 1532) the convent soon had other things to think about.

On my way home I speculated, not for the first time, upon the question whether there is or can be any foundation for any of the stories of compacts between human beings and evil spirits. In the abstract the possibility seems difficult to dispute. The belief is ancient and widely diffused. The real point seems to be whether the game could be worth the candle.

As I had finished all I meant to do at Folkham House I decided that I would spend to-morrow on a visit to the Chapel and perhaps sketch it. The day after I would return home.

When I imparted my plan to the landlord he naturally expressed a civil regret that my stay at Stivinghoe was coming to an end. He seemed doubtful whether the ruins (as I had learned the Chapel was called locally) were worth visiting, seeing as it were a dull trudge along the bank to get there. I thought from his manner that that was not his only reason for trying to discourage me. But he was summoned elsewhere before he had time to say more. While I was at dinner he looked in to see if I had everything I wanted. This was an unusual piece of condescension and I suspected an ulterior motive of some sort. I was not mistaken. After a moment or two he made an obvious effort.

'You'll excuse me, Sir. But the ruins is a queer place. Rare goings on there in those ancient times-by what I've heard.'

This was interesting as it suggested that some reminiscence of John of Costessey lingered on the scene of his activities. But before I could ask for details he went on rapidly, 'Not that I've any call to listen to the fishermen's talk – no more than what you 'ave.'

After this there was obviously no more to be got out of him. But I thought I would try a cast among the company in the parlour later on. After some miscellaneous conversation I mentioned that I thought of spending my last day in walking out along the bank and making a sketch of the ruins. For some reason the company seemed to find this proposal disturbing. No one made any comment but there was an awkward pause. Then two ancients near the fireplace held a short muttered conversation. The only words I could catch sounded like 'not lately, have he?'

Plainly they knew more than they meant to tell. Presently someone introduced some ordinary topic, and conversation flowed easily as before.

I went to bed about eleven and slept soundly.

Next morning I started soon after breakfast. I had ascertained that the tide would be low between 1 and 2 p.m. so that I should be able to find a position from which to make a sketch. I could hardly do this if I were confined to the bank itself. Also the day, though fine, was windy; windy enough, I thought, to make the top of the bank a wet place at high water.

I asked for some sandwiches to take with me and said that I should be back in time for dinner as usual, probably for tea. I thought the landlord looked at me rather reproachfully, but he said nothing when I had gone a few steps on my way I found that I had not filled my tobacco pouch that morning. I turned back to make the omission good and my eye was caught by a horseshoe nailed over the front door. Nothing remarkable in that, you may say, but I wondered that I had not noticed it before, as it now seemed to be unusually conspicuous.

The walk along the bank was pleasant enough. I could see over miles of marsh on either hand. Inland there were groups of red-roofed cottages to be seen, with occasional windmills and church towers. In front of me lay the sea. At the moment no fishing-boats were visible, but the smoke of one or two large ships could be seen on the horizon.

Altogether an exhilarating prospect. But somehow or other I did not feel at all exhilarated. On the contrary I had to admit that I was nervous and depressed.

Certainly I had had some odd little experiences since I had

touched the Stivinghoe papers, First there was the feeling that I was being followed on the way home. Then my uncomfortable and inconclusive dream. Then the laugh which I thought (no, *knew*) that I had heard in the library; and last of all the obvious conviction of the neighbourhood that the ruins were better left alone. What should I do if I saw a figure emerge from the Chapel and come along the bank to meet me? Should I enter into conversation or should I get down on to the sand and hope that he would pass me by? Or should I run for it? Or could I recall on the spur of the moment any form of exorcism which might prove effective? Fortunately I did not have to answer any of these questions.

The Chapel was a small building, roughly built of grey flint. It measured about twenty-two feet by ten and was lighted by a single lancet in the east wall. There was a door at the west end, I put its date at a little before 1350. Of course the roof was gone, but the walls looked fairly sound. The altar was still in place. But I noticed that the usual consecration crosses (one in the middle and one at each corner) had been deliberately obliterated. The chisel marks could be seen clearly. Such reforming zeal seemed to be almost excessive.

On the south (that is on the landward) side of the Chapel there were some small mounds which presumably indicated the site of the priest's dwelling. The superstructure had disappeared so completely that I wondered whether it had been of wood; also whether it could possibly be worth while to return with a spade.

I sat down on one of the mounds and ate my sandwiches. Then I thought it time to set about my sketch. I went down on to the sand and decided that the best position was a few yards to seaward. (In this part of Norfolk the coast runs east and west, so that the sea is to the north. The natives are fond of assuring visitors that there is nothing between them and the North Pole. No one who has been there in winter is likely to wish to dispute this statement.) The tide was still ebbing, so I should have plenty of time to do what I wanted.

I settled myself and my sketching materials, but somehow

I did not make very good progress. I had an uncomfortable feeling, as if there was somebody behind me, and caught myself wondering what I should do if a hand (probably a large and bony one) were suddenly laid upon my shoulder. I said aloud 'ridiculous' and as I did so a gull passed very close above my head and gave a derisive squawk, which seemed to indicate his complete concurrence.

The gulls were very many; which was not surprising. But they were so tame (or impudent, whichever you like to call it) that they were a positive nuisance. They flapped their wings almost in my face and one actually perched on my easel. I suppose they had never seen enough of men to be afraid of them. I had a sandwich or two left which I threw as far as I could towards the water's edge. This drew them off for a little, but they were soon as bad as ever. However, I got a sketch of some sort finished. I thought I would take one more look inside the Chapel before I started to walk home in case there were any detail of interest which I had missed. The floor was covered with coarse turf. Probably it had never been paved; if it had, the paving had been covered long since. But just in front of the altar I noticed a patch which somehow looked different from the rest. I had in my knife one of those curious implements said to be intended for taking stones out of horses' feet, and it seemed that at last I had a chance of using it. I scratched at the turf and very soon my hook grated upon a stone. A little scraping disclosed a small rectangular slab about twenty inches long by eight broad. A pentacle had been scratched upon it rather roughly. It was obviously the lid of something, if it were too small for any kind of coffin. A little more scraping of the earth round its edges and I got it up with less difficulty than I had expected. It was the lid of a coffin of sorts after all and in the coffin were some bones; clearly those of a small monkey. Its forepaws were crossed upon its breast and from some fragments of stuff which lay about I came to the conclusion that it had been buried in some sort of monastic habit.

This discovery explained the stories of the imp. Perhaps John had been really fond of his pet who must have been his only companion. Burial before the altar might perhaps be condoned. But the monastic habit looked like a profane jest. Or was it more than a jest? Taken in conjunction with the pentacle on the lid, the candles of black wax found by the Prior and the erasure of the consecration crosses (which I now began to think was John's handiwork and not the doing of any zealous follower of Dowsing) there was a definite suggestion of serious and sinister purpose. What unhallowed rites had been celebrated there, with what evil intent? And (I could not repress the, further question) in what company?

However, there seemed to be nothing for me to do but to leave things as I had found them. Which I did. The afternoon was wearing on, so I started for home. The tide had probably turned but was still very low. At the seaward end the line of the bank was curved, so I saw that I could shorten my walk considerably if I took to the sands and struck the bank again in about a mile. When I had gone a little way I turned to take a final look at the Chapel. It was a sunny day with big white clouds driving before the wind. As I looked the shadow of one passed across the Chapel, and by some odd trick of light made it seem as if a dark figure had emerged from the door and dropped down the far side of the bank. For a moment I was really startled.

I turned and went on with my walk. I have never considered myself a fanciful person, but it was borne in upon me very forcibly that the sooner I was sitting down to tea at the 'Fishmongers' Arms' the happier I should be.

Presently I reached the point at which I must take to the bank again. Just as I got to the edge of the sand I saw the print of a naked human foot, pointing towards the bank. It was very recent and could (apparently) only have been made by someone who had passed me quite close, having come across the sand as I had, and gone up the bank before me. This was frankly impossible. Had there been anyone else about I could not have failed to see him. The sand was too wet to hold impressions for long. Most of my own tracks had disappeared already. Yet there was the footprint, unmistakably. I stooped and looked at it (there was only one, which made it odder still) closely. It struck me as unusually bony, that is to say, the bones showed more plainly than I should have expected. I thought of the shadow which I had seen pass across the end of the Chapel. Had it, after all, emerged from the inside? If I went on, should I find someone waiting for me, and with what intent? However, there was nothing for it but to go on. I was within sight of the village now and there were people about who would see if any attack were made upon me, though what help they would be able to give was another matter. So on I went, and in a few minutes had reached my inn safely.

I turned on the doorstep to take a look over the marshes. Very lonely and solemn they were and very dark was the little Chapel. There was no one to be seen; I had not expected that there would be. By this time the wind had freshened and there was a hard brightness on the northeastern horizon which foretold a full gale before morning. There was an old barometer just inside the front door which had fallen so low that I wondered whether it were trustworthy, and hoped not. The landlord emerged and appeared ill at ease, and at the same time glad to see me – possibly by reason of the weather; possibly not. He murmured something to the effect of no harm done, as he returned to his occupations. I felt curiously tired, and when I had had tea, after a poor pretence of reading some book (I forget now what) dozed in an armchair by the fire.

I was roused by a clap of thunder and the storm broke with a roar like a train. The thunder was unusual, I thought, for the time of year, especially as the last few days had not been particularly hot. Also, the wind was off the sea, and I knew that there was a belief along the coast that when a thunderstorm comes up from the sea, that will be the beginning of the end of the world. The 'Fishmongers' Arms' was built to stand weather. But I doubt whether it ever had a worse buffeting than it got that night. There was no more thunder, but the rain came down in sheets and the wind tore at the house till I could almost imagine I felt it swaying to and fro. It was obvious that there would be no customers at the bar, so after dinner I invited the landlord to come to my sitting-room to smoke a cigar and drink a whisky and soda with me. I was really glad of his company, and he seemed to be of mine. We tried to talk of indifferent subjects, but could not do much save listen to the wind. We went to bed about eleven, though there was not much prospect of sleep. I wished that I had not remembered at that moment that Richard Kidder, Bishop of Bath and Wells, had been killed in his bed, together with his wife, by the fall of a chimney-stack through the roof of the palace during the terrible storm of 26-7 November, 1703.

Soon after midnight there was a screech (I can call it nothing else) like that of an animal in pain. I could hardly have believed that the wind could have made such a sound. This seemed to be its last effort, and the storm died away almost as quickly as it had arisen.

When I looked out next morning the Chapel was gone. The whole end of the bank had been washed away. The gale had coincided with a spring tide and I suspect that most of the marsh had been under water for some hours. Of course the tip of the bank had caught the full force of the sea.

I must confess that I felt relieved At first I was glad that I had made a sketch of the Chapel. But after a little reflection I burned it. Somehow I felt safer as I saw it turn to ashes.

THE BURE AT NIGHT

Gladys Mitchell

A curiously assorted party, impressed by real-life ghost stories heard on a bleak and windy All Hallows Eve, agree to go on a ghost hunt in Norfolk the following summer. Curious experiences will happen to them all – some of them deadly. Dee Crieff-Tweedle is the organizer of the ghost hunt. She and her husband ('Dum') soon recruit a party of enthusiasts, including a curiously muscular clergyman, a male medium calling himself Madame Arcati, and Eiladh Gavin, Laura's daughter and Dame Beatrice Bradly's (sleuth extraordinare) goddaughter. Among the sites to be investigated are: a ghostly mass in a Salhouse churchyard, a body thrown over a Roman Fort wall in Burgh Castle, and a benevolent ghost monk (with dutiful ghost dog) in a ghost boat in the waters of Ranworth Broad. In Eiladh's letters to Dame Beatrice, she reports that there's trouble from the start, due to ill will between hostess and just about everyone else in the party. Now read on...

'Earth, let not thy envious shade
Dare itself to interpose;
Cynthia's shining orb was made
Heaven to clear when day did close. . .'

Ben Jonson – 'Hymn to Diana'

As she had explained to her mother and Dame Beatrice just before the ghost-hunters set out, Eiladh liked to put herself abreast of a situation before she actually faced the facts of it. To this end she had immersed herself in what she termed 'spook-literature' and had been entertained by it to an extent unattained by Dame Beatrice, but (she believed at the time) she remained, like her godmother, unconvinced that ghosts really existed, or, at any rate, that they could be seen.

She had read Christina Hole's 'Haunted England', Harry Price's 'Poltergeist Over England' and his now rather controversial account of the hauntings at Borley Rectory; Dee Crieff-Tweedle had lent her 'Ghosts of the Broads' by Dr Charles Sampson (re-issued, after he had obtained copyright, by Mr Richard Sutton of Pulham Market) and from Dame Beatrice she had borrowed 'Haunted Britain', by Mr Anthony D. Hippisley Coxe and books on the folklore of Dame Beatrice's own Hampshire and the neighbouring county of Dorset. She had been deeply impressed by the works of Mr J. Wentworth Day, but remained a sceptic.

'Not that some of these accounts will be of much use in Norfolk,' she had announced when she returned her borrowings. Dame Beatrice disagreed.

'So far as my own researches go,' she said, 'which is not very far because I found the subject-matter both repetitive and boring, ghosts run to type. The ghostly hound, the grey lady, the headless coachman, the screaming woman, the empty gibbet on the moors which no horse can be persuaded to pass, the dog which follows a phantom all round the room with its eyes although no human being can see anything, the bells which ring of their own volition, the entity which flings unsuspecting visitors out of their beds, the phantom pack of hounds urged on by a ghostly horseman – everything, I believe, except the talking mongoose on the Isle of Man, has been duplicated over and over again. It is like these tiresome spirit-controls who are either little girls of below-average intelligence or Red Indians whose vocabulary seems limited to How and Wah, although, so far as my admittedly cursory study of their idiom goes, neither ejaculation means even Yes or No.'

The ghost-stories, however, must have made some impact upon Eiladh, for her dreams, that first night on the banks of the River Bure, were, so far as she could remember them afterwards, almost wholly concerned with what she had read.

The dreams themselves were strangely clear, although they

were without colour and the events she experienced in them took place in a shifting mist. As so often happens to dreamers whose chief means of communication when awake is the spoken word, whether to themselves, their possessions or to other people, her thoughts were coherent and logical.

'I'm seeing pale kings and princes, too,' she said to herself, as, at the entrance to Wroxham Broad, which, incidentally, she had never set eyes on, she dreamt she saw a tall figure standing, it seemed, upon the water. He raised an imperious hand, but said nothing. Eiladh, however, knew exactly who he was and what he was doing there. He was keeping the entrance to the Broad clear for Caesar's procession of boats.

As she realised this, the dream changed. She herself was walking on the water and was unable to stop herself approaching a vast bed of reeds. They were whistling; not with the gentle, furtive rustling she associated with reeds, but with a sort of hideous ribaldry. Then she saw that, caught up among them, was the heavy branch of a tree which must have floated down stream (she told herself) until the eddies had trapped it by the reed-bed.

She felt a sensation of panic. The branch, which was large and bifurcated had, first of all, two animal faces, one a dragon, the other a dog. They were menacing one another and, as she watched, they turned into the faces of the Crieff-Tweedles. Mrs Crieff-Tweedle was the dragon. Her husband the menacing dog.

She tried to swim towards them, but, suddenly, there was no water in the river and she was scrabbling towards them over stones and mud. Before she could reach them they had disappeared and she was back in college again facing a Finals paper of which she could not understand a single word.

'It's written in Japanese,' she thought, 'and I haven't attended a Japanese lecture since Christmas. I had better say the Lord's Prayer.' She woke up saying it. She had a recipe for banishing uneasy dreams which had never failed. This was to get out of bed, make sure that she was fully awake and then smoke a cigarette. She was anxious not to wake Liz, so she slipped out of the bedroom into the sitting-room, switched on the light and looked on the sideboard for the packer of cigarettes she had left there. It was gone.

'Oh, damn!' she said softly. 'Tom must have picked it up, thinking it was his.'

It was a tantalising thought, the more so because, although she was a very moderate smoker, having decided upon a cigarette she felt that at all costs she must have one. It occurred to her that the moonlight which she had blotted out in her own room must be flooding Tom's, and that young men with no troubles on their minds are heavy sleepers. This judgment she based upon knowledge of her brother Hamish, who habitually slept through the wildest thunderstorms and once had been known to mutter, 'Oh, get off my neck, you bitch,' when a tent he was sharing with another man and two girls fell in on him.

Secure in the thought that her furtive groping in Tom's jacket pocket would not disturb the sleeper, she switched off the sitting-room light, found the handle of his bedroom door, turned it and glided in.

She had been right about the moonlight. It filled the room and slanted in brilliance across the single bed. There was Tom's jacket draped across the back of a chair with his shin upon the seat and his trousers laid out neatly upon the floor so that their creases were respected.

Her error was in supposing that Tom, like Hamish, was a heavy sleeper. With her back to the bed she was fumbling in the pockets of the jacket when a pair of tough male aims pinioned her and Tom's voice said in her ear, 'What the hell? – Oh, Good Lord, it's you!'

'Let go,' said Eiladh. He let go, but swung her round to face him. 'So what?' he said. 'Why are you turning out my pockets? That's a wife's privilege, and we aren't married – yet.'

'Cigarettes. You pinched my cigarettes.'

'Did I? Sorry! Well, you'd better not stay in here. If Liz wakes up you'll need to do some explaining. Come on, let's smoke one together in the sitting-room. Here, shove this on. It's chilly.' He handed her the jacket she had been searching and himself donned the dressing-gown which lay across the foot of the bed.

They seated themselves upon the settee in the sitting-room and smoked in silence and in an intimacy rendered closer by the darkness. As Tom stubbed out his cigarette after Eiladh had extinguished hers, he put his arm round her and said, 'Taking a mean advantage of your burglarious intentions, I am going to kiss you.'

'All right,' she said, 'but hurry up about it because I want to go back to bed.'

'You're damn lucky that I don't carry you off to mine. Do you usually sneak into other people's rooms and search their jacket pockets?'

'Don't be a low hound. Let go of me.'

'For the second time of asking? There you are.'

'Thank you. I say, Tom, let's go for a row on the river.'

'At this time of night?'

'Father Melrose does.'

'Does what?'

'Goes for a moonlight row on the river.'

'The devil he does! Must have a guilty conscience,

'That's what I thought. I don't like him.'

'I don't like him. We must be twin souls. I suspected it from the first. Are you serious about going for a moonlight paddle on the water?'

'Yes, I'd like it above all things.'

'Well, you can't go boating in your jim-jams and my jacket and with nothing on your feet.'

'And I may wake Liz if I go back to my room dressed, so that's that. Goodnight and thank you for being a little gentleman.'

'Training, not inclination, I assure you. Look here, I've got plenty of spare gear in my room if you can just beetle in and get some shoes and socks from your's. I'll chick you out some trousers – you can turn the ends up – and a sweater. Put the lot on over your pyjamas and you'll be plenty warm enough. Which way do you want to go?'

'Downstream to Wroxham Broad. I want to break a rather beastly dream I had. It was to wake myself right up that I wanted a cigarette.'

'Nightmare?'

'No, just a bad dream.'

'Been reading too many ghost stories?'

'Yes, I expect so. Throw out the sweater and pants and I'll tap on your door when I'm dressed.'

'Unisex, here we come,' said Tom, and kissed the back of Eiladh's neck.

It was a dream-like expedition. The dinghy which went with the hiring of the bungalow was already in the tiny staithe by the side of the lawn and its short, heavy oars were lying in the bottom of the boat. Eiladh stepped delicately aboard, Tom cast off and a hefty shove away from the wooden planking at the end of the staithe sent them into the main flow of the river.

Tom settled to the oars and the boat, helped by the current, passed riverside bungalows and, on the opposite shore, a boat yard. All signs of habitation were left behind and there seemed nothing in the world but the great moon riding high in a clear sky, her reflection in the water, the black banks of the river fantastic with trees and reeds, and the boat itself travelling steadily along under Tom's long, lazy pull on the oars.

Eiladh dangled a hand in the water, but drew it out with a catch in her throat as her fingers touched a piece of floating, slimy weed.

'What's up?' asked Tom, whose ears had caught the slight gasp she gave.

'Nothing. A dead man's hand perhaps. No, it was only a bit of river-weed, but it was clammy and nasty. How far would you think is the entrance to the Broad?'

'I know roughly how far it is, and it's as far as I want to row because we're against the stream coming back.'

'Don't bother, then. It's only a silly fancy of mine to want to see the entrance to the Broad.,

'What was this dream you want to break?'

'I saw the ghost of the man Charles Sampson calls Flavius Mantus, the *Custos Rotulorum* appointed by Marcus Aurelius to control the Bure and its environs.,

'You have been reading too many ghost-stories!'

'Yes, but that dream wasn't frightening. It was what came next.'

'Tell me.'

'I hardly like to, because I've eaten their bread and salt.'

'The Crieff-Tweedles?'

'Yes.'

'I wonder he hasn't strangled that woman long ago. She treats him like a dog.'

'Oh, but, Tom, that's what he was in my dream! It began as a dead bough with two branches. One was like a dragon and it turned into Dee, and the other was like a dog and it turned into poor old Dum. In my dream I knew they were going to fight and one would kill the other. It was terrifying, so I said the Lord's Prayer and woke up just as I got to Lead us not into temptation. Please don't laugh.'

'I wasn't intending to. We'll certainly get to the entrance to the Broad and break that sort of dream. Let's hope it isn't a prophecy, that's all.'

'Please don't say that. One of my ancestresses is said to have had the Gift, and my mother comes out with some rather startling things at times. I hope I haven't inherited anything uncanny.'

'Not you. One only has to catch a glimpse of Crieff-Tweedle's face when the madam comes out with one of her biting comments to see what he has to put up with and what he thinks about it. He cringes. All the same, I don't think you are cut out for a ghost-hunter. Too much imagination by far.'

They lapsed into silence and the boat gradually drew nearer the entrance to Wroxham Broad. There was no sign of Flavius Mantus, the reed-beds which bordered the opening on to the Broad were unstirred by the slightest breeze, for the night was unusually calm, and, far from the infernal whistling which Eiladh had heard in her dream, they made no sound at all.

There was no dead branch, either; nothing to alarm or surprise.

'O.K., then?'asked Tom, resting on his oars.

'Yes. As James Elroy Flecker has said:

'She sank into the moonlight
And the sea was only sea.'

'Good enough.' With long, sweeping strokes he turned the boat, settled to his oars again and pulled strongly up-stream for the bungalow. When they had stepped ashore and tied up, he took both Eiladh's hands but, to her relief and disappointment, he did not kiss her.

'How old are you?' he asked.

'Twenty-two.'

'Hm! Know that thing of Yeats, called Politics?'

'Yes.'

'Ah!' He retained her left hand and side by side they walked across the dew-wet lawn. The moon had paled. The first light of dawn was in the east. Noiselessly Tom opened the door and noiselessly they tip-toed in. 'Good night', he whispered. 'No more bad dreams. '

'Goodnight,' she whispered back. 'Where shall I put your trousers and sweater?'

'Leave 'em on the settee and tap on my door. I'll give you a minute to nip into your room and then I'll come out and collect them.'

This time Liz was awake.

'Hullo,' she said, as Eiladh entered. 'Have you been for a swim?'

'No. I've been breaking up a bad dream and turning it into moonshine.'

'I hope Tom helped.'

Eiladh got into bed.

'How did you know I'd been out with Tom?', she asked.

'I didn't. I do now, though. Are your intentions honourable?'

'Don't rag me.'

'I'm not ragging. Are they?'

'Why do you want to know?'

'Because I'm fond of Tom and I wouldn't mind having you for a sister.'

'Good Lord! I've only known the two of you for a couple of days!'

'That has nothing to do with it. Besides, diagnosis is supposed to be my strong point.'

'I'd forgotten that you are a doctor.'

'I thought you had. You haven't answered my question.'

'It's one of those questions which will answer itself in time. Liz, do you think Dum hates Dee?'

'If he doesn't, he ought to. Why?'

'In my dream one of them was going to kill the other.'

'Which was which?'

'I don't know. I woke up before I found out. I'm glad I did. It was a horrible dream.'

'Where did you go with Tom?'

'As far as the entrance to Wroxham Broad.'

'And it broke up your dream?'

'Yes, and it's a dream I don't want repeated.'

THE HEADLESS HOUND

R. H. Mottram

'THERE!' cried Ginever, like the retired lawyer and admirable Uncle that he was. In obedience to his raised hand, his niece Marjorie stopped the car, with a squeak of the brakes. They were going due north, in a very narrow sandy lane which suddenly sloped sharply downhill. Overhead leaned one of those violent twisted dwarf oaks, only to be found on exposed coast-line. Either bank was knee-deep with wild scabious and campion, wild rose and orchis. In the V made by the tree and the bank were framed patches of cornfield, clumps of green, a huddle of red-roofed houses, and then, piercingly blue, cutting the horizon with its sweeping curve, the sea. Ginever drew along breath.

'Delicious.'

'Umps!'

'Do you know, I don't believe we shall find a better place for tea. Shall we stop here?'

'Let's.' Jean and Olive had the tea-basket out, and Marjorie backed the car a few yards into a convenient gateway, while their Uncle selected a spot on the top of the bank. Beneath the dwarf oak there were twenty square yards of sandy rough heath and gorse and wild flowers, before you came to the hedge of the cultivated field. But while the kettle was singing, Ginever had adjusted his glasses.

'Dear, dear, what a number of houses. That must have been because Clement Scott discovered this place in the 'nineties' But when I first remember, from this spot – this lane is the only road from civilisation – was just this horse-shoe of low hills-at one end the church – good gracious, it's repaired and roofed, it used to be a ruin – at the other end the Manor, Inaccessible, of course – in the gap of the horseshoe, that one little street of grey flint hovels – you can still trace them trending down there, to the cliff edge. But right in the middle of the horse-shoe – I can't find it!'

'What, Uncle?'

'Bullen's Mill! Ah, gone, of course; there, below us, half-way to the village is a mound, and a lot of poppies growing. That was the windmill, always 'Bullen's Mill.' That was where poor little Euphrosyne got her fright'

'Euphrosyne. That's the name of the old Miss Frost who used to keep the school in the Close, isn't it, Uncle?'

'Yes, my dear, but do not be so final. Some day perhaps you'll be old Miss, or old Mrs, and people will laugh when you tell them you tell them you used to have bobbed hair and silk stockings on view. Old Miss Frost was a little girl here, in pantalettes and ringlets. She was sent to stay at Bullen's Mill because she was so white and small, and her parents' good old servant Martha had married Bullen. There was no lodgings or hotels here then. Just a few score fishermen, some one in the Manor one never saw, some one in the parish living who didn't live here, and the place was run by old Bullen, the miller and farmer, and by a certain Blazey, who kept the Lobster inn at the top of the street there.'

'One minute, Uncle. If I put your cup there, you won't knock it over, will you? Scone? Or jam sandwich?'

'Scone, please.'

'Now, about Miss Frost'

'You must recollect that when I knew her she was an old woman. She had taught my mother. In those last years when she retired, I was her man of business, and came down here to see her at – it must be that Boarding House with the verandah. Then she told me of her childhood's fright – the terror that had overtaken her seventy years before.'

'Dates, dates, where are we getting to, Uncle?'

'It must have been the eighteen-twenties. Can you imagine what a schoolmissis looks like in her childhood?'

'Like anyone else.'

'I don't feel sure. Anyhow, Miss Frost's parents took the then unheard-of step of sending her out here for the month of September in her seventh year. It was no watering-place. There were no such things. Brighton was only just started, let alone this village of Beckhythe. It was not so much regarded as seaside as the country. Bullen never went near the sea. The great point was change of air and Martha Bullen's well-tried cookery, fresh milk and eggs, just beginning to be recognised as suitable for puling little girls. For Miss Frost admitted that she was undersized and peaky. Almost destined to scholasticism, I should say.'

'Rubbish, Uncle, look at our mistresses' golf, hockey, swimming the Channel, climbing the Alps!'

'A new species, my dear. Miss Frost was given the care of the daughters of gentlemen in order to make them into ladies, not into women. Of such was the Kingdom of Queen Victoria. Women did not come in for years after!'

'Lord!'

'Anyway, on some forgotten day in the eighteen-twenties, a thin, pale, rather frightened little girl must have seen this very view we are now looking at, from the seat of the carrier's cart. Somewhere down on that poppy-grown hump stood the great old black windmill waving its arms. I should think it impressed her as sinister. But in the little flint-bordered garden stood kind old Martha, the nurse of her babyhood reminiscent of a great wide, warm, safe lap, a coarse apron, custards and bedtime stories. Even across three-quarters of a century Miss Frost could recollect how, except for Martha, the country struck her as a wave strikes you between the shoulders when bathing. At first, it positively upset her. At the end of a week she was well again and a different girl. The thing that next beset her was an enormous curiosity. The little inhabitant of some great old house in Easthampton, where everything was known and fixed, began to grow, physically and mentally, in the new world of Beckhythe, confined between these low hills and the sea, watched over by the ruined church on one side and the inaccessible Manor-house on the other, with Bullen's Mill dead in the centre, and the village between it and the shore below those cliffs of gravel. There was no one for her to play with. Martha had been well trained. Little Miss Frossy couldn't associate with rough fisher children, of course. Martha had none of her own; Bullen by his first marriage had two grown up sons, but neither they nor Bullen himself had any time to spare from the mill and the farm. Martha was busy in her kitchen, and the little visitor played in the garden. It was when she ventured beyond its green paling and sunflowers that, as the song says, her troubles began.

'It seems that, even in childhood, she was susceptible to the charms of the picturesque.

'The first thing she wanted to see was the ruined church. No wonder that, starting so early, she became one of a race of school folk who trained the young in the romantic tradition. Anyhow, it seems she walked out of the garden one day, and had got as far as the coast road on her way, when she met Blazey. To the end of her life she never knew whether this was his surname or Christian – it was the only one ever used, she knew him because he was frequent visitor at the Mill, where he and Bullen would arrange such small supplies and services as the fisher people needed. Between them they owned all the horses and carts in the parish, and Blazey's Lobster Inn was also shop, post-office, posting-house – in a word, the carrier's cart called there once a week, and that was all the communication Beckhythe then needed to the outer world, ostensibly.

'Blazey impressed little Miss Frossy. After all those years she could describe him as if seen but yesterday. He had a very big head, perfectly hairless, bald and shaven, great pouchy eyes, flat nose with no bridge like a dog's and great ears that he could move. He habitually wore his mouth open, his tongue lolling out, his hands in the pockets of his knee-breeches. Only in the worst of weather did he produce an old three-cornered hat; usually he went bare-headed at a sort of trot. Such was the figure which little Miss Frossy must have found barring her way through the ruined church of Beckhythe, that golden, still, September afternoon.

"'And where might you be a-going, Miss?' he asked, breathing at her such a concentrated blast of rum and tobacco as seemed to the strictly brought-up child nothing less than the fire and brimstone of Sunday reading.

"'Going to look at the church, please!'

"'Shouldn't do that', breathed Blazey.

'Now Miss Frossy had been reared with a nice sense of social distinction. Blazey was repugnant, but she understood well enough that he was not entitled to give her an order. I suppose she did nothing, so he went on:

"'There's queer folk and rum doings in there!' and he turned his great bloodshot eyes towards the church.

"'What sort of folk?' asked little curiosity.

"'Folk that might carry you straight away!'

'This time a delicious horror thrilled the little girl: 'What are they like?'

"'Like — aint you never heard of Ole Shuck Dawg?'

"'No, never!'

"'Lor'— well, he's just like a great big Hound — with no 'ead on's shoulders!'

'I'm afraid it sounds foolish rather than awful as I say it. I can only tell you that after decades of life had rolled over that incident, Miss Frost could still remember how dreadful it seemed to little Miss Frossy, I suppose you girls don't believe in ghosts?'

'Believe, no. But we've been frightened as kids!'

'Then no doubt you found that it is always the intangible that frightens. The face that has no features, the body that is nobody - often mere sound or movement is most terrifying of all. The Headless Hound seemed to her the last refinement of evil. How could it she help it! Nowadays folklore experts have sorted out some mythological dog with no head, of Scandinavian origin, in whom older men and women downt here in the village probably still believe in. But little Miss Frossy was a child in an age when even grown-ups saw the Devil, erect on two legs, and Hell was only a few feet below the road you walked on. And the personality of Blazey helped darken her vision. He was, I suppose, what we should call deficient, with criminal tendencies – a lump of bone and muscle informed by a single streak of acquisitive cunning. He looked, I expect, like a hound. She turned and ran back to the farm. Of course, I can only give you a very imperfect story, as it was given me by an old lady, unused to story-telling, who remembered certain incidents happen to her as a little girl. I suspect that if she had been more receptive or older, she might have noticed a lot of nodding and whispering going on over her head or behind her back about then. The nights were drawing in. No longer was the darkness a semi-luminous affair of a few hours. The time was ripe for people who had any business to transact that could bear the light of day.

'You will see presently why I think so. Anyhow, the next thing Miss Frost remembered was a very beautiful evening when she had been put to bed early by Martha who was so busy; she had to cook a great meal for Bullen and the boys and possibly even for others. Why they wanted it at seven o'clock at night, and what was going to make them so busy, didn't interest little Frossy. But the last glow of sunset did, and she got up in her little bed, and leaned on the low window-sill, nearly on the floor level, as windows used to be in those old farmhouses.And when she looked at the view – very little different from that at which we are now looking – no doubt it was picturesque enough. Purple Hill and rosy sky, and wonderful opaline sea – and little starts coming out as the sunset dwindled. And then, just as if to please her, one bright little star came out, quite down in the sea, twinkled a moment and vanished. If she had been a boisterous modern girl she might have said 'Bully!'

'Go it, Uncle. What did the little nincompoop say?'

'Nothing, my dear, except perhaps a little murmured prayer of thanks for the Wonders of Creation. And the Wonders of Creation immediately justified her. For while she looked another star lit up on the half-tumbledown tower of the church, twinkled and vanished. This, I judge, was almost too picturesque for little Miss Frossy. The view from her window was wide, but not wide enough. There might be stars on the chimney of the Manor, invisible round the corner in the trees, on the top of the windmill, creaking somewhere above her head. So, curiosity overwhelming whatever recollection she retained of Blazey's warning, she slipped on some sufficient articles of clothing, popped out into the dark old passage – and evidently still retained some sense of naughtiness. For Miss Frost recollected that there were two stairs – one which descended into a sort of cupboard in the kitchen, and another that opened into the mill yard – relict no doubt of some ancient remodelling of the premises. She took the latter to avoid discovery, gropped her way down in the dark, found a latch, opened the door, and stepped out. The door swung to behind her – she wasn't tall enough to reach the sneck from outside – and there she was, confirmed in her star-gazing.

'The tower of the mill with its crucifix of sails must have stood above her like some great symbol. All around – can't you imagine it? – the autumn dusk, and that little girl from the town, going out into the unknown, no street pavement beneath her feet, no lamp to guide her. And then – clean across the years Miss Frost had never forgotten it – the sudden halt, the sense of impeding danger, the awfulness of the danger that was not there. Rooted to the spot, by the gate where the cart road entered the mill yard, she heard Fate approaching her. There was a pad-pad of soft heavy footsteps and some great animal brushed against her.

'Dimly outlined, in the darkness she only recalled one thing about it. There was no head. At this she fainted.'

'Little silly!'

'I'm not so sure. Fainting was the fashion then. There was something to be said for it. Nothing else provided the woman of these days with such relief from the various catastrophes that threatened. her. Anyhow, when little Miss Frossy came up, she was in the kitchen, lying in Martha's lap; Martha had drawn the big settle up to the great fire, which, more than the guttering candle, lit the old barn of a place. When she opened her eyes,

Martha left off rubbing her feet, and gave her a sip out of a glass of something that stung, burned the throat, and gave a pleasant warmth lower down. I very much suspect it was hot spirits. Three or four people at the table paid no regard to her. What with Martha and the great fire, and the hot stuff, a complete reaction took her, a delicious lassitude, so that presently when Martha carried her upstairs, she went soundly to sleep and did not wake until broad daylight, with Martha standing over her.

"How's your best feelin's this morning?'

"Quite well, thank you, Martha!'

"Will you have somethin' to take?' (East Anglian for 'Can you eat anything?').

"Yes, please. Oh, Martha, what was it I saw?'

"Never you mind. And don't you go trapassin' about at night. You might come to harm.'

'Something like this, it must have been. I know, Martha's sort was not extinct when I was a little boy. After this there came a gap in Miss Frost's memories, of a week or so, I judge, for it must have been about the Equinox when she remembered it being so wet.

'It is difficult to imagine on a day like this how the first October rains come in off the sea, over Reckhythe. Little Miss Frossy was playing about the kitchen when a couple of horsemen clattered into the yard, and one of them dismounted and tilted the water out of the brim of his shiny top-hat – the sort of hat you may have seen one of the pirates wearing in Peter Pan. That, and the semi-uniform he wore, had a peculiar effect on Martha, for little Miss Frossy, clutching from shyness her big floury hand that was always warm and strong, found it cold and lifeless, fiddling with Martha's apron.

"Good morning, Mrs Bullen; where's the miller?'

"Gone to market, sir.'

"Extraordinary thing,' remarked the gentleman; 'every one's gone to market. Not a man in the village!'

"Gone to sea, sir!' Martha was trembling.

"Gone to catch the fish as they fall out of the sky on a day like this, I warrant!'

'Martha said nothing, but Miss Frossy could feel her all a-tremble. The gentleman went on:

"And the landlord of the Lobster Inn. Has he gone to the sea, too?' No answer. 'Or to market, Mrs Bullen?'

"To market, I should think, sir.'

"What market?' The words came out of the gentleman's mouth with a pop, and terrified Miss Frossy as much as they appeared to terrify Martha.

"Lynn,sir, I think.'

"Funny that. What market do they hold at Lynn on a Sunday?'

"Perhaps he's gone to Easthampton, sir.'

"Don't think so. I've just come from there. Unless he's gone by sea, eh, Mrs Bullen?'

'Martha stood still, garping, as they say here.

"You don't mind if we wait a bit, and see if someone turns up, do you, Mrs Bullen?'

"Not at all, sir.'

"No. I thought you wouldn't!' And the gentleman called out through the window, to his companion: 'Lead 'em round into the yard, Jim.'

"Won't you take a seat, sir?' asked Martha politely, bringing forward Bullen's chair. It was one of the old fiddlebacks, with arms and a patchwork cushion. Miss Frost remembered that. Martha set it to the left of the hearth, and the gentleman therefore faced the window. When he was seated, he spoke to her:

"Now, what's this child doing here?' with great emphasis.

"This is Miss Frost, from Easthampton. The young lady from the house where I used to be in service. She's here for her health.'

"Good day to you, Miss Frost. My name is Vardigans. Mr. Exciseman Yardigans. I hope we may be better acquainted.'

'Frossy hoped not, but it didn't seem to matter. He went on: 'And do you wear any lace, Miss Frost?'

"Mercy no, what would the child do with lace!' put in Martha. Mr. Vardigans turned on her: 'What does anybody do with lace. Who does anything with it?' Martha fidgeted in silence.

"What do you do, if I may ask, Miss Frost?'

"She just plays about with me!'

'Mr. Vardigans turned sharply: 'You haven't such a thing as a glass of spirits, Mrs Bullen?'

"No, sir, but you can have a glass of ale, if you like.'

'Mr. Vardigans did not answer, and Miss Fossy was twitched away from wondering how Martha could tell such lies, by his next question.

"And do you sleep well o'nights, Miss Frost?'

'Miss Frost didn't answer, and Mr. Vardigans went on:

"Curious set of children round here. Can't answer questions. As I came up the road I took a look over the bank, and found a boy in a furze bush. 'What are you doing there?' I asked him; 'scaring birds,' says he. 'What, birds in October!' say's I. 'Come, Wiliam, where's Bullen's Mill?' says I. 'How do you know my name's William?' says he; 'I guessed it,' says I; 'Then guess the other,' says he!'

'The effect of some such tirade as this upon Miss Frossy, was precisely that of the snake's eye on the bird. She became fascinated and when Mr. Vardigans suddenly stopped and turned on her with:

"And do you ever see anything queer about here at nights?' there is no doubt she would have told him about the stars that went out, and the Ole Shuck Dawg. But just as the moment she was prevented. I have said that Martha had placed Mr. Vardigans facing the garden. Well, in the wall behind him was one of those meaningless little windows that you will find in old houses, looking from one room into another, lightening a cupboard, or allowing one to spy on one's visitors before one opened the door. Miss Frost had long forgotten the use of this one, she merely recalled a little square opening in the wall behind Mr. Vardigans. At the moment he asked that question what should appear in that window but a head. Nobody was visible, of course. It was Blazey's head, but the mouth and eyes, contrary to habit, were closed, and the ears pricked up, like a dog's, so that to little Miss Frossy it signified Blazey, and no head at all, and the Headless Hound. Can you understand what she felt?'

'Rather. Nightmares!'

'Just so. We must give Blazey credit for a certain knowledge of children. He wanted to stop the conversation. To do so he wanted to frighten Miss Frossy. He did it so effectually that she remembered it for seventy years. At the moment she screamed, and Martha seized her in a motherly embrace and began to rate Mr. Vardigans. It was a shame, that it was, frightening the poor little thing. Martha didn't know what things were coming to, when folk went about frightening children like that, and so on, at the same time lifting the sobbing little girl and bearing her away up the stair to her own room. Removal from the face at the window and the presence of Martha soon comforted her. And then she noticed that Martha, big strong Martha, who could carry her without feeling it, was sitting on the floor of the bedroom besides her, white and gasping. This was mysterious, and more mysterious still the bumping and creaking that went on below in the house, people trying doors, other people walking about upstairs. Finally there was the sound of horses clattering out of the yard, and Martha, peeping round the curtain, heaved a great sigh and wiped her face.

"Stop you here!' she said as she left the room.

'But that was more than little Miss Frossy could do. How many minutes – a lifetime to her, no doubt – she remained alone there, in the gathering dust, you may guess. She slipped down into the kitchen. More mysterious than ever, it was full of people. Evidently Mr. Bullen and the boys had come back quickly from Lynn or wherever they had been. But had they been at all? There were other men there too, that Frossy had never seen before, eating and drinking and discussing, so far as she could make out, Mr. Vardigans, the way he had gone, and the distance he would make. Nobody paid any attention to her, Martha was very busy over by the fire, and she just slipped out into the porch and, finding the rain abated, out into the yard.

'It was a wet lowering evening, a streak of violet in the

west, and growing early dark. After the excitement of the day it seemed to her a relief to go and say good-night to the cows, as they were being milked, as she had been used to do all the summer. But no sooner did she enter the stable, at the far end of which was the cowhouse, than she stopped, petrified. There was Blazey. She could not move under his eye. She could not ask him what he was doing with Billy, the stout cobby little trotter, of that forgotten breed of 'punches' that farmers about here used to fancy so much. Blazey didn't wait. He asked her:

"See what I'm a-doin'?'

'He was swathing Billy's feet in bits of old sacking tied with straw. She couldn't guess what for. He told her.

'I'm tyin 'im up where Ole Shuck Dawg bit 'im. Tew mind 'e don't bite yew!'

"She ran back to the house. The kitchen was emptying fast. Men spoke to each other in low tones and vanished. Bullen, usually kind and jocular, seemed suddenly to remember her, and whispered a word in his wife's ear, evidently about her, and soon Martha took her upstairs, undressed her in the dark, put her to bed and lay down beside her fully clothed. Now she may or may not have gone to sleep – who would trust the memory of a child so far? But it is certain that a little later she was awake – awake enough to know that the night was full of rumours, very dark, with an everlasting patter of raindrops off the mill sails and the bushes in the lane. And presently the darkness and silence – and something that wasn't there – grew so oppressive that she said aloud:

"Martha – are you awake?'

"Sh-sh-sh!' was all she got. So she lay still, and then, with a faint mutter, that might have been voices of the wind, a tiny stir outside that might or might not be the thing that wasn't there, the Terror of the Night began to move. And in spite of Martha and her own fear, it made her sit up, just as it made the hair shiver on her head. And so, squinting out through the low window, she saw it pass. Whether man or beast, muffle-footed and loaded, really moved along the cart lane – there, that cobbled piece that joins the road – or whether it was merely the shapes that darkness makes on the undersides of the eyelids; whether she heard thudding footfall and smothered breathing, or merely her own heart beating and the blood surging in her ears, the terror passed. She tried to count the shapes, but how can you count something that isn't, and clung to Martha, and one supposes, finally slept. All next day there was no Bullen, but the following day Bullen and the boys and Blazey were back, and she was dressed and her box packed and they put her on the carrier's cart and sent her home. And the very last thing of all was, that just as the cart topped the rise, she saw, sitting here, very much where we are sitting, Blazey. He said never a word. He just shut his mouth and eyes and erected his ears. That was the last she last she saw of him. She went home to Easthampton, and never mentioned a word of what she had seen.

'Well, Acts of Parliament were passed, manners and customs altered; the whole atmosphere of that incident borders on the ridiculous. But, as late as the 'nineties, when I came over here to see the old lady who had been little Miss Frossy, who since that time had had three-quarters of a century to learn all about superstitions and the use smugglers made of them – and the use they made of dogs and punches and church towers – in spite of the prosaic rationalistic knowledge that flourished in that decade – I remember that she still shivered when she told me parts of the story.

Which shows how impressionable children are, and what a deal of reason it takes to obliterate an image, once formed in their minds, like that of the Headless Hound.'

OH WHISTLE AND I'LL COME TO YOU, MY LAD

M. R. James

'I suppose you will be getting away pretty soon, now Full term is over, Professor,' said a person not in the story to the Professor of Ontography, soon after they had sat down next to each other at a feast in the hospitable hall of St James's College.

The Professor was young, neat, and precise in speech. 'Yes,' he said; 'my friends have been making me take up golf this term, and I mean to go to the East Coast – in point of fact to Burnstow – (I dare say you know it) for a week or ten days, to improve my game. I hope to get off tomorrow.'

'Oh, Parkins,' said his neighbour on the other side, 'if you are going to Burnstow, I wish you would look at the site of the Templars' preceptory, and let me know if you think it would be any good to have a dig there in the summer.'

It was, as you might suppose, a person of antiquarian pursuits who said this, but, since he merely appears in this prologue, there is no need to give his entitlements.

'Certainly,' said Parkins, the Professor: 'if you will describe to me whereabouts the site is, I will do my best to give you an idea of the lie of the land when I get back; or I could write to you about it, if you would tell me where you are likely to be.'

'Don't trouble to do that, thanks. It's only that I'm thinking of taking my family in that direction in the Long, and it occurred to me that, as very few of the English preceptories have ever been properly planned, I might have an opportunity of doing something useful on off days.'

The Professor rather sniffed at the idea that planning out a preceptory could be described as useful. His neighbour continued:

'The site – I doubt if there is anything showing above ground – must be down quite close to the beach now. The sea has encroached tremendously, as you know, all along that bit of coast. I should think, from the map, that it must be about three-quarters of a mile from the Globe Inn, at the north end of the town. Where are you going to stay?'

'Well, at the Globe Inn, as a matter of fact,' said Parkins; 'I have engaged a room there. I couldn't get in anywhere else; most of the lodging-houses are shut up in winter, it seems; and, as it is, they tell me that the only room of any size I can have is really a double-bedded one, and that they haven't a corner in which to store the other bed, and so on. But I must have a fairly large room, for I am taking some books down, and mean to do a bit of work; and though I don't quite fancy having an empty bed – not to speak of two – in what I may call for the time being my study, I suppose I can manage to rough it for the short time I shall be there.'

'Do you call having an extra bed in your room roughing it. Parkins?' said a bluff person opposite. 'Look here, I shall come down and occupy it for a bit; it'll be company for you.' The Professor quivered, but managed to laugh in a courteous manner.

'By all means, Rogers; there's nothing I should like better. But I'm afraid you would find it rather dull; you don't play golf, do you?' No, thank Heaven!' said rude Mr. Rogers. 'Well, you see, when I'm not writing I shall most likely be out on the links, and that, as I say, would be rather dull for you. I'm afraid.'

'Oh, I don't know! There's certain to be somebody I know in the place; but, of course, if you don't want me, speak the word. Parkins; I shan't be offended. Truth, as you always tell us, is never offensive.'

Parkins was, indeed, scrupulously polite and strictly truthful. It is to be feared that Mr Rogers sometimes practised upon his knowledge of these characteristics. In Parkins's breast there was a conflict now raging, which for a moment or two did not allow him to answer. That interval being over, he said:

'Well, if you want the exact truth, Rogers, I was considering whether the room I speak of would really be large enough to accommodate us both comfortably; and also whether (mind, I shouldn't have said this if you hadn't pressed me) you would not constitute something in the nature of a hindrance to my work.' Rogers laughed loudly.

'Well done. Parkins!' he said. 'It's all right. I promise not to interrupt your work; don't you disturb yourself about that. No, I won't come if you don't want me; but I thought I should do so nicely to keep the ghosts off.' Here he might have been seen to wink and to nudge his next neighbour. Parkins might also have been seen to become pink. 'I beg pardon. Parkins,' Rogers continued; 'I oughtn't to have said that. I forgot you didn't like levity on these topics.' 'Well,' Parkins said, 'as you have mentioned the matter, I freely own that I do not like careless talk about what you call ghosts. A man in my position,' he went on, raising his voice a little, 'cannot, I find, be too careful about appearing to sanction the current beliefs on such subjects. As you know, Rogers, or as you ought to know; for I think I have never concealed my views—'

'No, you certainly have not, old man,' put in Rogers *sotto voce*.

'—I hold that any semblance, any appearance of concession to the view that such things might exist is equivalent to a renunciation of all that I hold most sacred. But I'm afraid I have not succeeded in securing your attention.'

'Your undivided attention, was what Dr Blimber actually said,' Rogers interrupted, with every appearance of an earnest desire for accuracy. 'But I beg your pardon. Parkins; I'm stopping you.'

'No, not at all,' said Parkins. 'I don't remember Blimber; perhaps he was before my time. But I needn't go on. I'm sure you know what I mean.'

'Yes, yes,' said Rogers, rather hastily – 'just so. We'll go into it fully at Burnstow, or somewhere.'

In repeating the above dialogue I have tried to give the impression which it made on me, that Parkins was something of an old woman – rather hen-like, perhaps, in his little ways; totally destitute, alas! of the sense of humour, but at the same time dauntless and sincere in his convictions, and a man deserving of the greatest respect. Whether or not the reader has gathered so much, that was the character which Parkins had.

On the following day Parkins did, as he had hoped, succeed in getting away from his college, and in arriving at Burnstow. He was made welcome at the Globe Inn, was safely installed in the large double-bedded room of which we have heard, and was able before retiring to rest to arrange his materials for work in apple-pie order upon a commodious table which occupied the outer end of the room, and was surrounded on three sides by windows looking out seaward; that is to say, the central window looked straight out to sea, and those on the left and right commanded prospects along the shore to the north and south respectively. On the south you saw the village of Burnstow. On the north no houses were to be seen, but only the beach and the low cliff backing it. Immediately in front was a strip – not considerable – of rough grass, dotted with old anchors, capstans, and so forth; then a broad path; then the beach. Whatever may have been the original distance between the Globe Inn and the sea, not more than sixty yards now separated them.

The rest of the population of the inn was, of course, a golfing one, and included few elements that call for a special description. The most conspicuous figure was, perhaps, that of an *ancien militaire*, secretary of a London club, and possessed of a voice of incredible strength, and of views of a pronouncedly Protestant type. These were apt to find utterance after his attendance upon the ministrations of the Vicar, an estimable man with inclinations towards a picturesque ritual, which he gallantly kept down as far as he could out of deference to East Anglian tradition.

Professor Parkins, one of whose principal characteristics was pluck, spent the greater part of the day following his arrival at Burnstow in what he had called improving his game, in company with this Colonel Wilson: and during the afternoon – whether the process of improvement were to blame or not, I am not sure – the Colonel's demeanour assumed a colouring so lurid that even Parkins jibbed at the thought of walking home with him from the links. He determined, after a short and furtive look at that bristling moustache and those incarnadined features, that it would be wiser to allow the influences of tea and tobacco to do what they could with the Colonel before the dinner-hour should render a meeting inevitable. 'I might walk home tonight along the beach,' he reflected – 'yes, and take a look – there will be light enough for that – at the ruins of which Disney was talking. I don't exactly know where they are, by the way; but I expect I can hardly help stumbling on them.' This he accomplished, I may say, in the most literal sense, for in picking his way from the links to the shingle beach his foot caught, partly in a gorse-root and partly in a biggish stone, and over he went. When he got up and surveyed his surroundings, he found himself in a patch of somewhat broken ground covered with small depressions and mounds. These latter, when he came to examine them, proved to be simply masses of flints embedded in mortar and grown over with turf. He must, he quite rightly concluded, be on the site of the preceptory he had promised to look at. It seemed not unlikely to reward the spade of the explorer; enough of the foundations was probably left at no great depth to throw a good deal of light on the general plan. He remembered vaguely that the Templars, to whom this site had belonged, were in the habit of building round churches, and he thought a particular series of the humps or mounds near him did appear to be arranged in something of a circular form. Few people can resist the temptation to try a little amateur research in a department quite outside their own, if only for the satisfaction of showing how successful they would have been had they only taken it up seriously. Our Professor, however, if he felt something of this mean desire, was also truly anxious to oblige Mr Disney. So he paced with care the circular area he had noticed, and wrote down its rough dimensions in his pocket-book. Then he proceeded to examine an oblong eminence which lay east of the centre of the circle, and seemed to his thinking likely to be the base of a platform or altar. At one end of it, the northern, a patch of the turf was gone – removed by some boy or other creature *ferae naturae*. It might, he thought, be as well to probe the soil here for evidences of masonry, and he took out his knife and began scraping away the earth. And now followed another little discovery: a portion of soil fell inward as he scraped, and disclosed a small cavity. He lighted one match after another to help him to see of what nature the hole was, but the wind was too strong for them all. By tapping and scratching the sides with his knife, however, he was able to make out that it must be an artificial hole in masonry. It was rectangular, and the sides, top, and bottom, if not actually plastered, were smooth and regular. Of course it was empty. No! As he withdrew the knife he heard a metallic clink, and when he introduced his hand it met with a cylindrical object lying on the floor of the hole. Naturally enough, he picked it up, and when he brought it into the light, now fast fading, he could see that it, too, was of man's making – a metal tube about four inches long, and evidently of some considerable age.

By the time Parkins had made sure that there was nothing else in this odd receptacle, it was too late and too dark for him to think of undertaking any further search. What he had done had proved so unexpectedly interesting that he determined to sacrifice a little more of the daylight on the morrow to archaeology. The object which he now had safe in his pocket was bound to be of some slight value at least, he felt sure.

Bleak and solemn was the view on which he took a last look before starting homeward. A faint yellow light in the west showed the links, on which a few figures moving towards the club-house were still visible, the squat martello tower, the lights of Aldsey village, the pale ribbon of sands intersected at intervals by black wooden groynes, the dim and murmuring sea. The wind was bitter from the north, but was at his back when he set out for the Globe. He quickly rattled and clashed through the shingle and gained the sand, upon which, but for the groynes which had to be got over every few yards, the going was both good and quiet. One last look behind, to measure the distance he had made since leaving the ruined Templars' church, showed him a prospect of company on his walk, in the shape of a rather indistinct personage, who seemed to be making great efforts to catch up with him, but made little, if any, progress. I mean that there was an appearance of running about his movements, but that the distance between him and Parkins did not seem materially to lessen. So, at least, Parkins thought, and decided that he almost certainly did not know him, and that it would be absurd to wait until he came up. For all that, company, he began to think, would really be very welcome on that lonely shore, if only you could choose your companion. In his unenlightened days he had read of meetings in such places which even now would hardly bear thinking of. He went on thinking of them, however, until he reached home, and particularly of one which catches most people's fancy at some time of their childhood. 'Now I saw in my dream that Christian had gone but a very little way when he saw a foul fiend coming over the field to meet him.' What should I do now,' he thought, 'if I looked back and caught sight of a black figure sharply defined against the yellow sky, and saw that it had horns and wings? I wonder whether I should stand or run for it. Luckily, the gentleman behind is not of that kind, and he seems to be about as far off now as when I saw him first. Well, at this rate he won't get his dinner as soon as I shall; and, dear me! it's within a quarter of an hour of the time now. I must run!'

Parkins had, in fact, very little time for dressing. When he met the Colonel at dinner, peace – or as much of her as that gentleman could manage – reigned once more in the military bosom; nor was she put to flight in the hours of bridge that followed dinner, for Parkins was a more than respectable player. When, therefore, he retired towards twelve o'clock, he felt that he had spent his evening in quite a satisfactory way, and that, even for so long as a fortnight or three weeks, life at the Globe would be supportable under similar conditions – 'especially,' thought he, 'if I go on improving my game.'

As he went along the passages he met the boots of the Globe, who stopped and said: 'Beg your pardon, sir, but as I was a-brushing your coat just now there was somethink fell out of the pocket. I put it on your chest of drawers, sir, in your room, sir – a piece of a pipe or somethink of that, sir. Thank you, sir. You'll find it on your chest of drawers, sir – yes, sir. Good night, sir.'

The speech served to remind Parkins of his little discovery of that afternoon. It was with some considerable curiosity that he turned it over by the light of his candles. It was of bronze, he now saw, and was shaped very much after the manner of the modern dog-whistle; in fact it was – yes, certainly it was – actually no more nor less than a whistle. He put it to his lips, but it was quite full of a fine, caked-up sand or earth, which would not yield to knocking, but must be loosened with a knife. Tidy as ever in his habits. Parkins cleared out the earth on to a piece of paper, and took the latter to the window to empty it out. The night was clear and bright, as he saw when he had opened the casement, and he stopped for an instant to look at the sea and note a belated wanderer stationed on the shore in front of the inn. Then he shut the window, a little surprised at the late hours people kept at Burnstow, and took his whistle to the light again. Why, surely there were marks on it, and not merely marks, but letters! A very little rubbing rendered the deeply-cut inscription quite legible, but the Professor had to confess, after some earnest thought, that the meaning of it was as obscure to him as the writing on the wall to Belshazzar. There were legends both on the front and on the back of the whistle. The one read thus: FLA FUR BIS FLE The other: QUIS EST ISTE QUI VENIT 'I ought to be able to make it out,' he thought; 'but I suppose I am a little rusty in my Latin. When I come to think of it, I don't believe I even know the word for a whistle. The long one does seem simple enough. It ought to mean, 'Who is this who is coming?' Well, the best way to find out is evidently to whistle for him.'

He blew tentatively and stopped suddenly, startled and yet pleased at the note he had elicited. It had a quality of infinite distance in it, and, soft as it was, he somehow felt it must be audible for miles round. It was a sound, too, that seemed to have the power (which many scents possess) of forming pictures in the brain. He saw quite clearly for a moment a vision of a wide, dark expanse at night, with a fresh wind blowing and in the midst a lonely figure – how employed, he could not tell. Perhaps he would have seen more had not the picture been broken by the sudden surge of a gust of wind against his casement, so sudden that it made him look up, just in time to see the white glint of a sea-bird's wing somewhere outside the dark panes.

The sound of the whistle had so fascinated him that he could not help trying it once more, this time more boldly. The note was little, if at all, louder than before, and repetition broke the illusion – no picture followed, as he had half hoped it might. 'But what is this? Goodness! what force the wind can get up in a few minutes! What a tremendous gust! There! I knew that window-fastening was no use! Ah! I thought so – both candles out. It's enough to tear the room to pieces.'

The first thing was to get the window shut. While you might count twenty Parkins was struggling with the small casement, and felt almost as if he were pushing back a sturdy burglar, so strong was the pressure. It slackened all at once, and the window banged to and latched itself. Now to relight the candles and see what damage, if any, had been done. No, nothing seemed amiss; no glass even was broken in the casement. But the noise had evidently roused at least one member of the household: the Colonel was to be heard slumping in his stockinged feet on the floor above, and growling.

Quickly as it had risen, the wind did not fall at once. On it went, moaning and rushing past the house, at times rising to a cry so desolate that, as Parkins disinterestedly said, it might have made fanciful people feel quite uncomfortable; even the unimaginative, he thought after a quarter of an hour, might be happier without it.

Whether it was the wind, or the excitement of golf, or of the researches in the preceptory that kept Parkins awake, he was not sure. Awake he remained, in any case, long enough to fancy (as I am afraid I often do myself under such conditions) that he was the victim of all manner of fatal disorders: he would lie counting the beats of his heart, convinced that it was going to stop work every moment, and would entertain grave suspicions of his lungs, brain, liver, etc. – suspicions which he was sure would be dispelled by the return of daylight, but which until then refused to be put aside. He found a little vicarious comfort in the idea that someone else was in the same boat. A near neighbour (in the darkness it was not easy to tell his direction) was tossing and rustling in his bed, too.

The next stage was that Parkins shut his eyes and determined to give sleep every chance. Here again over-excitement asserted itself in another form – that of making pictures. *Experto crede*, pictures do come to the closed eyes of one trying to sleep, and are often so little to his taste that he must open his eyes and disperse them.

Parkins's experience on this occasion was a very distressing one. He found that the picture which presented itself to him was continuous. When he opened his eyes, of course, it went; but when he shut them once more it framed itself afresh, and acted itself out again, neither quicker nor slower than before. What he saw was this: A long stretch of shore – shingle edged by sand, and intersected at short intervals with black groynes running down to the water – a scene, in fact, so like that of his afternoon's walk that, in the absence of any landmark, it could not be distinguished therefrom. The light was obscure, conveying an impression of gathering storm, late winter evening, and slight cold rain. On this bleak stage at first no actor was visible. Then, in the distance, a bobbing black object appeared; a moment more, and it was a man running, jumping, clambering over the groynes, and every few seconds looking eagerly back. The nearer he came the more obvious it was that he was not only anxious, but even terribly frightened, though his face was not to be distinguished. He was, moreover, almost at the end of his strength. On he came; each successive obstacle seemed to cause him more difficulty than the last. 'Will he get over this next one?' thought Parkins; 'it seems a little higher than the others.' Yes; half-climbing, half throwing himself, he did get over, and fell all in a heap on the other side (the side nearest to the spectator). There, as if really unable to get up again, he remained crouching under the groyne, looking up in an attitude of painful anxiety.

So far no cause whatever for the fear of the runner had been shown; but now there began to be seen, far up the shore, a little flicker of something light-coloured moving to and fro with great swiftness and irregularity. Rapidly growing larger, it, too, declared itself as a figure in pale, fluttering draperies, ill-defined. There was something about its motion which made Parkins very unwilling to see it at close quarters. It would stop, raise arms, bow itself toward the sand, then run stooping across the beach to the water-edge and back again; and then, rising upright, once more continue its course forward at a speed that was startling and terrifying. The moment came when the pursuer was hovering about from left to right only a few yards beyond the groyne where the runner lay in hiding. After two or three ineffectual castings hither and thither it came to a stop, stood upright, with arms raised high, and then darted straight forward towards the groyne.

It was at this point that Parkins always failed in his resolution to keep his eyes shut. With many misgivings as to incipient failure of eyesight, over-worked brain, excessive smoking, and so on, he finally resigned himself to light his candle, get out a book, and pass the night waking, rather than be tormented by this persistent panorama, which he saw clearly enough could only be a morbid reflection of his walk and his thoughts on that very day.

The scraping of match on box and the glare of light must have startled some creatures of the night – rats or what not – which he heard scurry across the floor from the side of his bed with much rustling. Dear, dear! the match is out! Fool that it is! But the second one burnt better, and a candle and book were duly procured, over which Parkins pored till sleep of a wholesome kind came upon him, and that in no long space. For about the first time in his orderly and prudent life he forgot to blow out the candle, and when he was called next morning at eight there was still a flicker in the socket and a sad mess of guttered grease on the top of the little table.

After breakfast he was in his room, putting the finishing touches to his golfing costume – fortune had again allotted the Colonel to him for a partner – when one of the maids came in.

'Oh, if you please,' she said, 'would you like any extra blankets on your bed, sir?'

'Ah! thank you,' said Parkins. 'Yes, I think I should like one. It seems likely to turn rather colder.'

In a very short time the maid was back with the blanket.

'Which bed should I put it on, sir?' she asked. 'What? Why, that one – the one I slept in last night,' he said, pointing to it.

'Oh yes! I beg your pardon, sir, but you seemed to have tried both of 'em; leastways, we had to make 'em both up this morning.'

'Really? How very absurd!' said Parkins. 'I certainly never touched the other, except to lay some things on it. Did it actually seem to have been slept in?'

'Oh, yes, sir!' said the maid. 'Why, all the things was crumpled and throwed about all ways, if you'll excuse me, sir – quite as if anyone 'adn't passed but a very poor night, sir.'

'Dear me,' said Parkins. 'Well, I may have disordered it more than I thought when I unpacked my things. I'm very sorry to have given you the extra trouble. I'm sure. I expect a friend of mine soon, by the way – a gentleman from Cambridge – to come and occupy it for a night or two. That will be all right, I suppose, won't it?'

'Oh yes, to be sure, sir. Thank you, sir. It's no trouble. I'm sure,' said the maid, and departed to giggle with her colleagues.

Parkins set forth, with a stern determination to improve his game.

I am glad to be able to report that he succeeded so far in this enterprise that the Colonel, who had been rather repining at the prospect of a second day's play in his company, became quite chatty as the morning advanced; and his voice boomed out over the flats, as certain also of our own minor poets have said, 'like some great bourdon in a minster tower'.

'Extraordinary wind, that, we had last night,' he said. 'In my old home we should have said someone had been whistling for it.'

'Should you, indeed!' said Parkins, 'Is there a superstition of that kind still current in your part of the country?'

'I don't know about superstition,' said the Colonel. 'They believe in it all over Denmark and Norway, as well as on the Yorkshire coast; and my experience is, mind you, that there's generally something at the bottom of what these country-folk hold to, and have held to for generations. But it's your drive' (or whatever it might have been: the golfing reader will have to imagine appropriate digressions at the proper intervals).

When conversation was resumed. Parkins said, with a slight hesitancy:

'Apropos of what you were saying just now. Colonel, I think I ought to tell you that my own views on such subjects are very strong. I am, in fact, a convinced disbeliever in what is called the 'supernatural'.'

'What!' said the Colonel, 'do you mean to tell me you don't believe in second-sight, or ghosts, or anything of that kind?'

'In nothing whatever of that kind,' returned Parkins firmly.

'Well,' said the Colonel, 'but it appears to me at that rate, sir, that you must be little better than a Sadducee.'

Parkins was on the point of answering that, in his opinion, the Sadducees were the most sensible persons he had ever read of in the Old Testament; but, feeling some doubt as to whether much mention of them was to be found in that work, he preferred to laugh the accusation off.

'Perhaps I am,' he said; 'but – Here, give me my cleek, boy! – Excuse me one moment. Colonel.' A short interval. 'Now, as to whistling for the wind, let me give you my theory about it. The laws which govern winds are really not at all perfectly known – to fisher-folk and such, of course, not known at all. A man or woman of eccentric habits, perhaps, or a stranger, is seen repeatedly on the beach at some unusual hour, and is heard whistling. Soon afterwards a violent wind rises; a man who could read the sky perfectly or who possessed a barometer could have foretold that it would. The simple people of a fishing-village have no barometers, and only a few rough rules for prophesying weather. What more natural than that the eccentric personage I postulated should be regarded as having raised the wind, or that he or she should clutch eagerly at the reputation of being able to do so? Now, take last night's wind: as it happens, I myself was whistling. I blew a whistle twice, and the wind seemed to come absolutely in answer to my call. If anyone had seen me–'

The audience had been a little restive under this harangue, and Parkins had, I fear, fallen somewhat into the tone of a lecturer; but at the last sentence the Colonel stopped.

'Whistling, were you?' he said. 'And what sort of whistle did you use? Play this stroke first.' Interval.

'About that whistle you were asking. Colonel. It's rather a curious one. I have it in my – No; I see I've left in it my room. As a matter of fact, I found it yesterday.'

And then Parkins narrated the manner of his discovery of the whistle, upon hearing which the Colonel grunted, and opined that, in Parkins's place, he should himself be careful about using a thing that had belonged to a set of Papists, of whom, speaking generally, it might be affirmed that you never knew what they might not have been up to. From this topic he diverged to the enormities of the Vicar, who had given notice on the previous Sunday that Friday would be the Feast of St Thomas the Apostle, and that there would be service at eleven o'clock in the church. This and other similar proceedings constituted in the Colonel's view a strong presumption that the Vicar was a concealed Papist, if not a Jesuit; and Parkins, who could not very readily follow the Colonel in this region, did not disagree with him. In fact, they got on so well together in the morning that there was no talk on either side of their separating after lunch.

Both continued to play well during the afternoon, or, at least, well enough to make them forget everything else until the light began to fail them. Not until then did Parkins remember that he had meant to do some more investigating at the preceptory; but it was of no great importance, he reflected. One day was as good as another; he might as well go home with the Colonel.

As they turned the corner of the house, the Colonel was almost knocked down by a boy who rushed into him at the very top of his speed, and then, instead of running away, remained hanging on to him and panting. The first words of the warrior were naturally those of reproof and objurgation, but he very quickly discerned that the boy was almost speechless with fright. Inquiries were useless at first. When the boy got his breath he began to howl, and still clung to the Colonel's legs. He was at last detached, but continued to howl.

'What in the world is the matter with you? What have you been up to? What have you seen?' said the two men.

'Ow, I seen it wive at me out of the winder,' wailed the boy, 'and I don't like it.'

'What window?' said the irritated Colonel. 'Come, pull yourself together, my boy.' 'The front winder it was, at the 'otel,' said the boy. At this point Parkins was in favour of sending the boy home, but the Colonel refused; he wanted to get to the bottom of it, he said; it was most dangerous to give a boy such a fright as this one had had, and if it turned out that people had been playing jokes, they should suffer for it in some way. And by a series of questions he made out this story. The boy had been playing about on the grass in front of the Globe with some others; then they had gone home to their teas, and he was just going, when he happened to look up at the front winder and see it a-wiving at him. It seemed to be a figure of some sort, in white as far as he knew – couldn't see its face; but it wived at him, and it warn't a right thing – not to say not a right person. Was there a light in the room? No, he didn't think to look if there was a light. Which was the window? Was it the top one or the second one? The seckind one it was – the big winder what got two little uns at the sides.

'Very well, my boy,' said the Colonel, after a few more questions. 'You run away home now. I expect it was some person trying to give you a start. Another time, like a brave English boy, you just throw a stone – well, no, not that exactly, but you go and speak to the waiter, or to Mr Simpson, the landlord, and – yes – and say that I advised you to do so.'

The boy's face expressed some of the doubt he felt as to the likelihood of Mr Simpson's lending a favourable ear to his complaint, but the Colonel did not appear to perceive this, and went on:

'And here's a sixpence – no, I see it's a shilling – and you be off home, and don't think any more about it.'

The youth hurried off with agitated thanks, and the Colonel and Parkins went round to the front of the Globe and reconnoitred. There was only one window answering to the description they had been hearing.

'Well, that's curious,' said Parkins; 'it's evidently my window the lad was talking about. Will you come up for a moment. Colonel Wilson? We ought to be able to see if anyone has been taking liberties in my room.'

They were soon in the passage, and Parkins made as if to open the door. Then he stopped and felt in his pockets.

'This is more serious than I thought,' was his next remark. 'I remember now that before I started this morning I locked the door. It is locked now, and, what is more, here is the key.' And he held it up. 'Now,' he went on, 'if the servants are in the habit of going into one's room during the day when one is away, I can only say that – well, that I don't approve of it at all.' Conscious of a somewhat weak climax, he busied himself in opening the door (which was indeed locked) and in lighting candles. 'No,' he said, 'nothing seems disturbed.' Except your bed,' put in the Colonel. 'Excuse me, that isn't my bed,' said Parkins. 'I don't use that one. But it does look as if someone has been playing tricks with it.'

It certainly did: the clothes were bundled up and twisted together in a most tortuous confusion. Parkins pondered. 'That must be it,' he said at last: 'I disordered the clothes last night in unpacking, and they haven't made it since. Perhaps they came in to make it, and that boy saw them through the window; and then they were called away and locked the door after them. Yes, I think that must be it.'

'Well, ring and ask,' said the Colonel, and this appealed to Parkins as practical. The maid appeared, and, to make a long story short, deposed that she had made the bed in the morning when the gentleman was in the room, and hadn't been there since. No, she hadn't no other key. Mr Simpson he kep' the keys; he'd be able to tell the gentleman if anyone had been up.

This was a puzzle. Investigation showed that nothing of value had been taken, and Parkins remembered the disposition of the small objects on tables and so forth well enough to be pretty sure that no pranks had been played with them. Mr and Mrs Simpson furthermore agreed that neither of them had given the duplicate key of the room to any person whatever during the day. Nor could Parkins, fair-minded man as he was, detect anything in the demeanour of master, mistress, or maid that indicated guilt. He was much more inclined to think that the boy had been imposing on the Colonel.

The latter was unwontedly silent and pensive at dinner and throughout the evening. When he bade good night to Parkins, he murmured in a gruff undertone: 'You know where I am if you want me during the night.' 'Why, yes, thank you. Colonel Wilson, I think I do; but there isn't much prospect of my disturbing you, I hope. By the way,' he added, 'did I show you that old whistle I spoke of? I think not. Well, here it is.'

The Colonel turned it over gingerly in the light of the candle.

'Can you make anything of the inscription?' asked Parkins, as he took it back. 'No, not in this light. What do you mean to do with it?'

'Oh, well, when I get back to Cambridge I shall submit it to some of the archaeologists there, and see what they think of it; and very likely, if they consider it worth having, I may present it to one of the museums.'

'Mm!' said the Colonel. 'Well, you may be right. All I know is that, if it were mine, I should chuck it straight into the sea. It's no use talking, I'm well aware, but I expect that with you it's a case of live and learn. I hope so, I'm sure, and I wish you a good night.'

He turned away, leaving Parkins in act to speak at the bottom of the stair, and soon each was in his own bedroom.

By some unfortunate accident, there were neither blinds nor curtains to the windows of the Professor's room. The previous night he had thought little of this, but tonight there seemed every prospect of a bright moon rising to shine directly on his bed, and probably wake him later on. When he noticed this he was a good deal annoyed, but, with an ingenuity which I can only envy, he succeeded in rigging up, with the help of a railway-rug, some safety-pins, and a stick and umbrella, a screen which, if it only held together, would completely keep the moonlight off his bed. And shortly afterwards he was comfortably in that bed. When he had read a somewhat solid work long enough to produce a decided wish for sleep, he cast a drowsy glance round the room, blew out the candle, and fell back upon the pillow. He must have slept soundly for an hour or more, when a sudden clatter shook him up in a most unwelcome manner. In a moment he realized what had happened: his carefully-constructed screen had given way, and a very bright frosty moon was shining directly on his face. This was highly annoying. Could he possibly get up and reconstruct the screen? Or could he manage to sleep if he did not?

For some minutes he lay and pondered over the possibilities; then he turned over sharply, and with all his eyes open lay breathlessly listening. There had been a movement, he was sure, in the empty bed on the opposite side of the room. Tomorrow he would have it moved, for there must be rats or something playing about in it. It was quiet now. No! the commotion began again. There was a rustling and shaking: surely more than any rat could cause. I can figure to myself something of the Professor's bewilderment and horror, for I have in a dream thirty years back seen the same thing happen; but the reader will hardly, perhaps, imagine how dreadful it was to him to see a figure suddenly sit up in what he had known was an empty bed. He was out of his own bed in one bound, and made a dash towards the window, where lay his only weapon, the stick with which he had propped his screen. This was, as it turned out, the worst thing he could have done, because the personage in the empty bed, with a sudden smooth motion, slipped from the bed and took up a position, with outspread arms, between the two beds, and in front of the door. Parkins watched it in a horrid perplexity. Somehow, the idea of getting past it and escaping through the door was intolerable to him; he could not have borne – he didn't know why – to touch it; and as for its touching him, he would sooner dash himself through the window than have that happen. It stood for the moment in a band of dark shadow, and he had not seen what its face was like. Now it began to move, in a stooping posture, and all at once the spectator realized, with some horror and some relief, that it must be blind, for it seemed to feel about it with its muffled arms in a groping and random fashion. Turning half away from him, it became suddenly conscious of the bed he had just left, and darted towards it, and bent over and felt the pillows in a way which made Parkins shudder as he had never in his life thought it possible. In a very few moments it seemed to know that the bed was empty, and then, moving forward into the area of light and facing the window, it showed for the first time what manner of thing it was.

Parkins, who very much dislikes being questioned about it, did once describe something of it in my hearing, and I gathered that what he chiefly remembers about it is a horrible, an intensely horrible, face of crumbled linen. What expression he read upon it he could not or would not tell, but that the fear of it went nigh to maddening him is certain.

But he was not at leisure to watch it for long. With formidable quickness it moved into the middle of the room, and, as it groped and waved, one corner of its draperies swept across Parkins's face. He could not – though he knew how perilous a sound was – he could not keep back a cry of disgust, and this gave the searcher an instant clue. It leapt towards him upon the instant, and the next moment he was half-way through the window backwards, uttering cry upon cry at the utmost pitch of his voice, and the linen face was thrust close into his own. At this, almost the last possible second, deliverance came, as you will have guessed: the Colonel burst the door open, and was just in time to see the dreadful group at the window. When he reached the figures only one was left. Parkins sank forward into the room in a faint, and before him on the floor lay a tumbled heap of bedclothes.

Colonel Wilson asked no questions, but busied himself in keeping everyone else out of the room and in getting Parkins back to his bed; and himself, wrapped in a rug, occupied the other bed for the rest of the night. Early on the next day Rogers arrived, more welcome than he would have been a day before, and the three of them held a very long consultation in the Professor's room. At the end of it the Colonel left the hotel door carrying a small object between his finger and thumb, which he cast as far into the sea as a very brawny arm could send it. Later on the smoke of a burning ascended from the back premises of the Globe. Exactly what explanation was patched up for the staff and visitors at the hotel I must confess I do not recollect. The Professor was somehow cleared of the ready suspicion of delirium tremens, and the hotel of the reputation of a troubled house.

There is not much question as to what would have happened to Parkins if the Colonel had not intervened when he did. He would either have fallen out of the window or else lost his wits. But it is not so evident what more the creature that came in answer to the whistle could have done than frighten. There seemed to be absolutely nothing material about it save the bedclothes of which it had made itself a body. The Colonel, who remembered a not very dissimilar occurrence in India, was of opinion that if Parkins had closed with it it could really have done very little, and that its one power was that of frightening. The whole thing, he said, served to confirm his opinion of the Church of Rome.

There is really nothing more to tell, but, as you may imagine, the Professor's views on certain points are less clear cut than they used to be. His nerves, too, have suffered: he cannot even now see a surplice hanging on a door quite unmoved, and the spectacle of a scarecrow in a field late on a winter afternoon has cost him more than one sleepless night.

BLACK SHUCK: THE DEVIL'S DOG

Piers Warren

A low mist clung to the dew-soaked salt-marsh as the woman left her cottage garden through the small wooden gate. She set off along the narrow path, as she did every morning, on the way to work at the village store. To her left the marsh stretched out, with its covering of samphire and sea lavender, to the distant sea, a few small boats scattered along the banks of the creeks. To her right an occasional flint cottage punctuated the thick shrubs that lined the path.

This morning there was a strange yellowish tint to the mist and she noticed an unusual smell – sulphurous and unsettling. She glanced at her watch and quickened her pace, despite having plenty of time. The air was absolutely still and the marsh eerily silent. Normally it would be ringing with the whistles of oyster catchers, cries of curlew, and distant rhythmic twanging from the rigging of the many sailing dinghies lying along the bank of the main creek. But today the thick mist seemed to have swallowed all sounds. Way above her head a skein of pink-footed geese headed out from their roost on The Wash to graze on the fields inland. But why were they not calling to each other as they usually did? Her thoughts momentarily wandered to her husband, still sleeping in their warm bed at home. Having recently taken early retirement from Powergen, his task for the day was to start the re-wiring of their ancient cottage. She hoped there wouldn't be a mess when she got home but at least it was saving them a lot of money, and she was getting a nice new cooker into the bargain.

Suddenly something intangible made her stop dead. The acrid smell was stronger, burning her nostrils, and ahead of her, where the path dipped slightly, the mist seemed to be swirling slowly despite the stillness of the air. Something must have disturbed it. Despite knowing every twist and turn of the path she felt strangely disorientated. She glanced back but saw nothing but the outlines of shrubs in the whiteness. Above all she couldn't understand why she felt so instinctively scared when she had seen nothing frightening. She just needed to get to the shop, see her colleagues and have a cup of tea. It wasn't far now; it would be just the start of another ordinary day. So why the lump in her throat and the gathering tears?

Fearing her legs had locked solid she shifted her weight from one foot to the other and stared intently at the patch of swirling mist. Could there be something there: an animal perhaps? She took a step forward, but again stopped when she saw a large black shape appear fleetingly in the mist. Too big for a dog, surely? Maybe it was one of the young black cattle, escaped from the field next to the marsh. But then her chest tightened as the mist in the hollow evaporated rapidly to reveal the beast. It was a dog, but larger than any she had seen before. As big as a calf, with a massive heavy head, huge blazing red eyes and a thick shaggy coat. The dog stared at her in complete silence. As the woman watched with ever-widening eyes her focus was drawn to the hound's upper canines: long and yellowing, a string of saliva hanging from one of them.

She knew full well this was no ordinary dog but rather Black Shuck – the spectral hound that frequented the Norfolk coast – harbinger of death. As a child she had been told many tales of Shuck – the spectral hound; tales to stop her from straying too far from home on the marshes, or simply as spooky entertainment in the long winter evenings, but to have him standing before her was terrifying. She opened her mouth but could not summon any sound. Every part of her body burned to retreat – to put distance between herself and the shaggy beast that could be upon her in a couple of bounds – yet she didn't dare take her eyes from it. The stinging in her nostrils made her want to hold the tissue she was squeezing in her pocket to her face, but her hand would not move.

The dog's head moved slightly, but its saucer-sized shining eyes never left hers, they seemed to bore into her very soul like red-hot drills. The woman's body started to fail her, and, before she fainted, an overwhelming feeling of sadness blanketed her; emanating from the dog.

His work done, Shuck turned slowly and disappeared into the mist.

Almost as soon as he had gone, rays from the early sun lit the path and revived the woman who felt as if she were roused from a horrifying nightmare. She slowly stood and glanced jerkily around but knew in her heart that she would not see the hound again. There was no point in turning back now, in going home, so she heaved one wobbly leg forward, followed by the other, and was soon staggering on her way.

Her colleagues in the shop sat the shaking woman down with a cup of hot sweet tea, gathered round and heard her story. They consoled her that Black Shuck was often seen with no consequence. As the day wore on she gradually perked up, comforted by the lively atmosphere of the shop and chatting with the friendly locals. Her encounter on the path started to feel like a bad dream. But on return home that evening the woman opened her door to the smell of cooking meat. Still smoking slightly, with blackened, claw-like hands gripping the old socket he had been removing, her husband's body was deplete of any spark of life; his grey face twisted into a terrible, final grimace.

A STRANGE AND TERRIBLE WUNDER

Abraham Fleming

Sunday, being the fourth of August, in the year of our Lord 1577, to the amazing and singular astonishment of the present beholders, and absent hearers, at a certain town called Bungay, not past ten miles distant from the city of Norwich, there fell from heaven an exceeding great and terrible tempest, sudden and violent, between nine of the clock in the morning and ten of the day aforesaid.

The tempest began with rain, which fell with a wonderful force and with no less violence than abundance, which made the storm so much the more extreme and terrible.

The tempest was not simply of rain, but also of lightning and thunder, the flashing of the one whereof was so rare and vehement, and the roaring noise of the other so forcible and violent, that it made not only people perplexed in mind and at their wits end, but ministered such strange and unaccustomed cause of fear to be conceived, that dumb creatures with the horror of that which fortuned, were exceedingly disquieted, and senseless things void of all life and feeling, shook and trembled.

There were assembled at the same season, to hear divine service and common prayer, according to order, in the parish church of the said town of Bungay, the people thereabouts inhabiting, who were witnesses of the strangeness, the rareness, and suddenness of the storm, consisting of rain violently falling, fearful flashes of lightning, and terrible cracks of thunder, which came with such unwonted force and power, that to the perceiving of the people, at the time and in the place named, assembled, the Church did as it were quake and stagger, which struck into the hearts of those that were present, such a sore and sudden fear, that they were in a manner robbed of their right wits.

Immediately hereupon, there appeared in a most horrible similitude the likeness to the congregation then and there present, a dog as they might discern it, of a black colour; at the sight whereof, together with the fearful flashes of fire which then were seen, moved such admiration in the minds of the assembly, that they thought doomsday was already come.

This black dog, or the devil in such a likeness (God he knoweth all who worketh all) running all along down the body of the church with great swiftness, and incredible haste, among the people in visible form and shape, passed between two persons, as they were kneeling upon their knees, and occupied in prayer as it seemed, wrung the necks of them both at one instant clean backwards, in so much that even at a moment where they kneeled, they strangely died.

This is a wonderful example of God's wrath, no doubt to terrify us, that we might fear him for his justice, or pulling back our footsteps from the paths of sin, to love him for his mercy.

To our matter again. There was at the same time another wonder wrought; for the same black dog, still continuing and remaining in one and the same shape, passing by another man of the congregation in the church, gave him such a grip on the back, that therewith all he was presently drawn together and shrunk up, as it were a piece of leather scorched in the hot fire; or as the mouth of a purse or bag, drawn together with string. The man, albeit he was in so strange a taking, died not, but as it is thought is yet alive; which this is marvelous in the eyes of men, and offereth much matter of amazing the mind.

Moreover, and beside this, the Clark of the said Church being occupied in cleansing the gutter of the church, with a violent clap of thunder was smitten down, and beside his fall had no further harm; unto whom being all amazed this strange shape, whereof we have before spoken, appeared, howbeit he escaped without danger; which might peradventure seem to sound against the truth, and to be a thing incredible: but, let us leave thus or thus to judge, and cry out with the Prophet, O Domine, &c. – O Lord, how wonderful art thou in thy works.

At the time that these things in this order happened, the Rector, or Curate of the Church, being partaker of the people's perplexity, seeing what was seen, and done, comforted the people, and exhorted them to prayer, whose counsel, in such extreme distress they followed, and prayed to God as they were assembled together.

Now for the verifying of this report (which to some will see absurd, although the sensibleness of the thing itself confirmeth it to be the truth) as testimonies and witness of the force which rested in this strange shaped thing, there are remaining in the stones of the Church, and likewise in the Church door, which are marvelously rent and torn, the marks as it were of claws and talons. Beside that, all the wires, the wheels, and other things belonging to the clock, were wrung in sunder, and broken in pieces.

And (which I should have told you in the beginning of the report, if I had regarded the observing of order) at the time that this tempest lasted, and while these storms endured, the whole Church was so darkened, yea with such palpable darkness, that one person could not perceive another, neither yet might discern any light at all, though it were lesser than the least, but only when the great flashing of fire and lightning appeared.

These things are not lightly with silence to be over passed, but precisely and thoroughly to be considered.

Let us pray unto God, as it is the duty of Christians, to work all things to the best, to turn our flinty hearts into fleshy hearts, that we may feel the fire of God's mercy, and flee from the scourge of his justice.

THE EVERLASTING CLUB

'Ingulphus'

There is a chamber in Jesus College the existence of which is probably known to few who are now resident, and fewer still have penetrated into it or even seen its interior. It is on the right hand of the landing on the top floor of the precipitous staircase which for some forgotten story connected with it is traditionally called 'Cow Lane.' The padlock which secures its massive oaken door is very rarely unfastened, for the room is bare and unfurnished. Once it served as a place of deposit for superfluous kitchen ware, but even that ignominious use has passed from it, and it is now left to undisturbed solitude and darkness. For I should say that it is entirely cut off from the light of the outer day by the walling up, some time in the eighteenth century, of its single window, and such light as ever reaches it comes from the door, when rare occasion causes it to be opened.

Yet at no extraordinarily remote day this chamber has evidently ben tenanted, and, before it was given up to the darkness, was comfortably fitted, according to the standard of comfort which was known in college in the days of George II. There is still a roomy fireplace before which legs have been stretched and wine and gossip have circulated in the days of wigs and brocade. For the room is spacious and, when it was lighted by the window looking eastward over the fields and common, it must have been a cheerful place for the sociable don.

Let me state in brief, prosaic outline the circumstances which account for the gloom and solitude in which this room has remained now for nearly a century and a half.

In the second quarter of the eighteenth century the University possessed a great variety of clubs of a social kind. There were clubs in college parlours and clubs in private rooms, or in inns and coffee-houses: clubs flavoured with politics, clubs clerical, clubs purporting to be learned and literary. Whatever their professed particularity, the aim of each was convivial. Some of them, which included undergraduates as well as seniors, were dissipated enough, and in their limited provincial way aped the profligacy of such clubs as the Hell Fire Club of London notoriety.

Among these last was one which was at once more select and of more evil fame than any of its fellows. By a singular accident, presently to be explained, the Minute Book of this Club, including the years from 1738 to 1766, came into the hands of the Master of Jesus College, and though, so far as I am aware, it is no longer extant, I have before me a transcript of it which, though it is in a recent handwriting, presents in a bald shape such a singular array of facts that I must ask you to accept them as veracious. The original book is described as a stout duodecimo volume bound in red leather and fastened with red silken strings. The writing in it occupied some 40 pages, and ended with the date November 2, 1766.

The Club in question was called the Everlasting Club — a name sufficiently explained by its rules, set forth in the pocket-book. Its number was limited to seven, and it would seem that its members were all young men, between 22 and 30. One of them was a Fellow-Commoner of Trinity: three of them were Fellows of Colleges, among whom I should especially mention a Fellow of Jesus, named Charles Bellasis: another was a landed proprietor in the county, and the sixth was a young Cambridge physician. The Founder and President of the Club was the Honorable Alan Dermot, who, as the son of an Irish peer, had obtained a nobleman's degree in the University, and lived in idleness in the town. Very little is known of his life and character, but that little is highly in his disfavor. He was killed in a duel in Paris in the year 1743, under circumstances which I need not particularise, but which point to an exceptional degree of cruelty and wickedness in the slain man.

I will quote from the first page of the Minute Book some of the laws of the Club, which will explain its constitution:—

'1. This Society consisteth of seven Everlastings, who may be Corporeal or Incorporeal, as Destiny may determined.

2. The rules of the Society, as herein written, are immutable and Everlasting.

3. None shall hereafter be chosen into the Society and none shall cease to be members.

4. The Honorable Alan Dermot is the Everlasting President of the Society.

5. The Senior Corporeal Everlasting, not being President, shall be the Secretary of the Society, and in the Book of Minutes shall record its transactions, the date at which any Everlasting shall cease to be Corporeal, and all fines due to the Society. And when such Senior Everlasting shall cease to be Corporeal he shall, either in person or by some sure hand, deliver this Book of Minutes to him who shall be next Senior and at the time Corporeal, and he shall in like manner record the transactions therein and transmit it to the next Senior. The neglect of these provisions shall be visited by the President with fine or punishment according to his discretion.

6. On the Second day of November in every year, being the Feast of All Souls, at ten o'clock post meridiem, the Everlastings shall meet at supper in the place of residence of that Corporeal member of the Society to whom it shall fall in order of rotation to entertain them, and they shall all subscribe in this Book of Minutes their names and present place of abode.

7. It shall be the obligation of every Everlasting to be present at the yearly entertainment of the Society,

and none shall allege for excuse that he has not been invited thereto. If any Everlasting shall fail to attend the yearly meeting, or in his turn shall fail to provide entertainment for the Society, he shall be mulcted at the discretion of the President.

8. Nevertheless, if in any year, in the month of October and not less than seven days before the Feast of All Souls, the major part of the Society, that is to say, four at least, shall meet and record in writing in these Minutes that it is their desire that no entertainment be given in that year, then, notwithstanding the two rules rehearsed, there shall be no entertainment in that year, and no Everlasting shall be mulcted on the ground of his absence.'

The rest of the rules are either too profane or too puerile to be quoted here. They indicate the extraordinary levity with which the members entered on their preposterous obligations. In particular, to the omission of any regulation as to the transmission of the Minute Book after the last Everlasting ceased to be 'Corporeal,' we owe the accident that it fell into the hands of one who was not a member of the society, and the consequent preservation of its contents to the present day.

Low as was the standard of morals in all classes of the University in the first half of the eighteenth century, the flagrant defiance of public decorum by the members of the Everlasting Society brought upon it the stern censure of the authorities, and after a few years it was practically dissolved and its members banished from the University. Charles Bellasis, for instance, was obliged to leave the college, and, though he retained his fellowship, he remained absent from it for nearly twenty years. But the minutes of the society reveal a more terrible reason for its virtual extinction.

Between the years of 1738 and 1743 the minutes record many meetings of the Club, for it met on other occasions besides that of All Souls Day. Apart from a great deal of impious jocularity on the part of the writers, they are limited to the formal record of the attendance of the members, fines inflicted, and so forth, The meeting on November 2nd in the latter year is the first about which there is any departure from the stereotyped forms. The supper was given in the house of the physician. One member, Henry Davenport, the former Fellow-Commoner of Trinity, was absent from the entertainment, as he was then serving in Germany, in the Dettingen campaign. The minutes contain an entry, 'Mulctatus propter absentiam per Presidentem, Hen. Davenport.' An entry on the next page of the book runs, 'Henry Davenport by a cannon-shot became an Incorporeal Member, November 3, 1743.'

The minute give in their handwriting, under date November 2, the names and addresses of the six other members. First in the list, in a large bold hand, is the autograph of 'Alan Dermot, President, at the Court of His Royal Highness.' Now in October Dermot had certainly been in attendance on the Young Pretender at Paris, and doubtless the address which he gave was understood at the time by the other Everlastings to refer to the fact. But on October 28, five days before the meeting of the Club, he was killed, as I have already mentioned, in a duel. The news of his death cannot have reached Cambridge on November 2, for the Secretary's record of it is placed below that of Davenport, and with the date of November 10: 'this day was reported that the president was become an Incorporeal by the hands of a french chevalier.' And in a sudden ebullition, which is in glaring contrast with his previous profanities, he has dashed down, 'The Good God shield us from ill.'

The tidings of the President's death scattered the Everlastings like a thunderbolt. They left Cambridge and buried themselves in widely parted regions. But the Club did not cease to exist. The Secretary was still bound to his hateful records: the five survivors did not dare to neglect their fatal obligations. Horror of the presence of the President made the November gathering once and for ever impossible: but the horror, too, forbade them to neglect the meeting in October of every year to put in writing their objection to the celebration. For five years five names are appended to that entry in the minutes, and that is all the business of the Club. Then another member died, who was not the Secretary.

For eighteen more years four miserable men met once each year to deliver the same formal protest. During those years we gather from the signatures that Charles Bellasis returned to Cambridge, now, to appearance, chastened and decorous. He occupied the rooms which I have described on the staircase on the corner of the cloister.

Then in 1766 comes a new handwriting and an altered minute: 'Jan. 27, on this day Francis Witherington, Secretary, became an incorporeal member. The same day this Book was delivered to me, James Harvey.' Harvey lived only a month, and a similar entry on March 7 states that the book has descended, with the same mysterious celerity, to William Catherton. Then, on May 18, Charles Bellasis writes that on that day, being the day of Catherton's decease, the Minute Book has come to him as the last surviving Corporeal of the Club.

As it is my purpose to record fact only I shall not attempt to describe the feelings of the unhappy Secretary when he penned that fatal record. When Witherington died it must have come home to the three survivors that after twenty-three years' intermission the ghastly entertainment must be annually renewed, with the addition of fresh incorporeal guests, or that they must undergo the pitiless censure of the President. I think it likely that the terror of the alternative, coupled with the mysterious delivery of the Minute Book, was answerable for the speedy decease of the first two successors to the Secretaryship. Now that the alternative was offered to Bellasis alone, he was firmly resolved to bear the consequences, whatever they might be, of an infringement of the Club rules.

The graceless days of George II. had passed away from the University. They were succeeded by times of outward respectability, when religion and morals were no longer publicly challenged. With Bellasis, too, the petulance of youth had passed: he was discreet, perhaps exemplary. The scandal of his early conduct was unknown to most of the new generation, condoned by the few survivors who had witnessed it.

On the night of November 2nd, 1766, a terrible event revived in the older inhabitants of the College the memory of those evil days. From ten o'clock to midnight a hideous uproar went on in the chamber of Bellasis. Who were his companions none knew. Blasphemous outcries and ribald songs, such as had not been heard for twenty years past, aroused from sleep or study the occupants of the court; but among the voices was not that of Bellasis. At twelve a sudden silence fell upon the cloisters. But the Master lay awake all night, troubled at the relapse of a respected colleague and the horrible example of libertinism set to his pupils.

In the morning all remained quiet about Bellasis' chamber. When his door was opened, soon after daybreak, the early light creeping through the drawn curtains revealed a strange scene. About the table were drawn seven chairs, but some of them had been overthrown, and the furniture was in chaotic disorder, as after some wild orgy. In the chair at the foot of the table sat the lifeless figure of the Secretary, his head bent over his folded arms, as though he would shield his eyes from some horrible sight. Before him on the table lay pen, ink and the red Minute Book. On the last inscribed page, under the date of November 2nd, were written, for the first time since 1742, the autographs of the seven members of the Everlasting Club, but without address. In the same strong hand in which the President's name was written there was appended below the signatures the note 'Mulctus per Presidentem propter neglectum obsonii, Car. Bellasis.'

The Minute Book was secured by the Master of the College and I believe that he alone was acquainted with the nature of its contents. The scandal reflected on the College by the circumstances revealed in it caused him to keep the knowledge rigidly to himself. But some suspicion of the nature of the occurrences must have percolated to students and servants, for there was a long-abiding belief in the College that annually on the night of November 2 sounds of unholy revelry were heard to issue from the chamber of Charles Bellasis. I cannot learn that the occupants of the adjoining rooms have ever been disturbed by them. Indeed, it is plain from the minutes that owing to their improvident drafting no provision was made for the perpetuation of the All Souls entertainment after the last Everlasting ceased to Corporeal. Such superstitious belief must be treated with contemptuous incredulity. But whether for that cause of another the rooms were shut up, and have remained tenantless from that day to this.

LOT 629

Noel Boston

A spinet in mahogany and banded case on fluted legs 5ft 9ins wide. That line in the Sale Catalogue, together with the fact that the sale was to be held at Mowbray House, one of Norfolk's greatest residences, decided me, and I made up my mind to attend the sale. Lord Senlac's family had owned Mowbray for seven hundred years and I was most anxious for a view of the great mansion which his ancestors had raised about 1680 for, hitherto, I had only caught tantalizing glimpses of a splendid Palladian facade across the park as I drove along the main Blakeney road which skirts it. Mowbray is no great distance from my house and in less than an hour of leaving home I was driving through a park in which the prospects of lakes and woods, little towers, and, above all, the great house itself hinted at the work of Capability Brown or one of his pupils.

Nature had been made to conform with late eighteenth century ideas of what a nobleman's park should be, probably about a hundred years after the present house was built. The house itself is of mellow red brick with stone facings, and the front is dominated by a great pediment, in the centre of which is a massive escutcheon displaying Senlac arms in brilliant colours. Each side of the pediment stretches a wealth of column, balustrade, and urn.

There are few more poignant sights than a great country house empty with no prospect of ever being lived in again. That all too common fate was not to be the lot of Mowbray, for it had been bought by the Duke of Lambeth and was already, once again, inhabited. This I felt to be a pity, since it meant that the sale was to be held in the stables and not in the house itself. The actual scene of the sale turned our to be the coachhouse. I arrived and parked the car and made my way there.

There was the usual sale crowd, many of whom were known to me. Lord Senlac had kept the best of the furniture and nearly all the pictures, but the yard in front of the coach house was filled with hip baths, iron bedsteads, and that yellow-coloured furniture which seems to be found almost exclusively in the servant's quarters of great houses and in the cheaper seaside boarding houses. There were glass cases and stag's heads and bundles of garden implements tied together with string. These lots were quickly bought up by second-hand dealers as distinct from antique dealers, who pressed into the stables with catalogues and pencils to examine the more valuable lots. By the time we got inside the auctioneer was ensconced on top of a large table, round which I recognized several friends. There was no sign of Lord Senlac, which was understandable, but George Nuneaton, whom I know quite well and who is Lord Senlac's cousin, was there chatting to the agent, a pleasant young man of the name of Hillman. I edged round to them and enquired about the spinet.

'I've spent all my boyhood in this house,' said George, 'but I have never seen half the stuff that is here today. It must have been in attics and places for hundreds of years.'

'Well, I hope it is not just another of those square pianos, that's all,' I said. It is a very common habit of auctioneers, and dealers too, to describe the very pleasant little square pianos of the late eighteenth and early nineteenth centuries as spinets. Needless to say, the spinet is a plucked instrument and the piano a struck one. A spinet, moreover, is a very valuable 'find' and there seemed every chance that one might have lain neglected at such a place as Mowbray.

My wife wanted such things as chair covers, stair carpets, curtains, and such-like so that, for a time, I was kept busy. As the stair carpets that were being sold were all a hundred feet or so long and George's wife and the agent's wife seemed to have similar ideas, we determined to buy some of the long carpets, if they went for a reasonable price, and thencut them up. We left the bidding to the agent and I went off in search of the spinet. After a good deal of searching and moving of miscellaneous objects, I ran Lot 629 to earth in a loose box. It was as I feared: Lot 629 was a pleasant square piano by Broadwood. I had no particular desire for a square piano but, since I was there, it seemed a pity not to have a look at it. On opening the top, I found the movements and 'works' generally in a surprisingly good condition, and the sound board responded to my thump with a pleasantly resonant note.

I am lucky in having at home a large music room, and there was one stretch of wall that would take such a piano. If it had been a spinet or a harpsichord I should probably have been extravagant and bid far more than I could afford. However, the 'square' was a fine piece of furniture and perhaps, if it went very cheap—

The morning wore on and the auction progressed as such occasions do. The excitement of bidding, the disappointment of being outbid, the interest in the prices, and even more of what one's friends and acquaitances were willing to pay, was interspersed by intervals of strolling with various people about the yard. About 12.30, a mobile canteen arrived and, realizing that Lot 629 would probably come up about one o'clock, I bought and ate an excellent lunch of new rolls split with ham and pastries afterwards. I had just finished a cup of coffee when Joe Rix came out of the coach-house.

'What have they got to?' I asked.

'620,' he replied.

I took my place by the long table. Lot 628 was a pleasant 'spark-guard' and I was beginning to wonder what the piano would fetch when there was a break. Old Mr Harket, who had been selling, climbed down from his table rostrum, obviously to fortify himself with lunch, and a dapper, spruce young man with a small moustache, obviously a representative of the London firm of auctioneers who were combining with the local firm, took his place.

'Lot 629,' he began. 'A handsome piece of late eighteenth century furniture. A spinet by Broadwood.' He did not seem very interested in the Lot, which was too large to exhibit. Many people had gone to lunch and there were several hundred more Lots.

'Well, gentlemen, what shall I say for the spinet?' There was a pause. We are not too quick about this sort of business in Norfolk.

'Come now, I have got to get the sale through today; will someone start me at ten pounds?'

'Ten bob,' said a dirty-looking old woman. The young auctioneer did not even pretend not to hear.

'Ten shillings I'm bid,' he said at once. Again there was a pause. 'Ten shillings,' he repeated, looking round the room.

'One pound,' said a ferrery-looking man in tweeds.

'One pound; any advance on one pound? At one pound, at one pound.'

'Thirty shillings,' I said.

'Thirty shillings, at thirty shillings.' I could see some whispering at the far end of the room, but the auctioneer obviously thought enough time had been given, and before anyone else could bid he knocked it down to me. I stayed to buy a few more things and then, having struck a bargain with one of the many furniture removers who haunt such auctions to have my purchases brought home, I left the sale and drove home to tea.

Returning home a few mornings later to lunch I was agreeably surprised to find that my purchases had arrived and that my wife thoroughly approved of the piano. we live in a comfortable old Georgian house of two storeys. The upper one is built round a landing and all the bedroom doors open on to it. until recently a friend lived with us and occupied rooms at the extreme east end of the house. These were now empty and into one of them the piano had been put.

That evening I got down to a thorough and minute examination of the instrument. I was delighted with it. The condition of the action, of the sound board, and of the woodwork was surprisingly good. On the wooden cover directly over the wires and also on the side of one of the keys was scrawled a signature: 'A.Wright, Jnr.' Presumably this was the particular craftsman at Broadwood's who made the instrument. . . . I dated the piano about 1790. I carefully polished the woodwork, cleaned the inside and the action, and then settled down happily to work with my tuning key. The restoration of old musical instruments holds a fascination for me. To enable an instrument to give out the same tones as it did a hundred and fifty years ago gives me an indescribable satisfaction. It is an unusual hobby, perhaps, but one which I believe is of very real assistance to music. However, I must not embark on that theme...

It is enough to say that a few hours' work sufficed to bring back the tonal beauty of a very fine old instrument. I was enthusiastic about it. Mr Wright, pianoforte maker though he was, had obviously served his apprenticeship on harpsichords. The delicate, rather poignant, tone of the plucked instrument was unmistakably there but not, of course, that glorious clarity of the pluck which is the outstanding feature of the harpsichord or the spinet. The personality of the instrument seemed to come flowing back into it. One blemish and one only there was. The hammer of the A octave above middle A was missing.

The piano was, eventually, given a place in the large music room. It was admired by connoisseurs, played on by pianists who dropped in to see my collection, and used by me in the accompaniment of instruments of a similar date and for contemporary music. And so the old piano became, so to speak, part of the household.

Nearly a year went by when, one night in late October, I suddenly woke up. My illuminated clock pointed to 1.30. For a moment I could not think what had awakened me; and then quite suddenly and quite distinctly there fell upon my ears the sound of the piano. My wife and I sleep in a room over the music room. Yes, it was unmistakable. Someone was playing the piano. Not for a moment was there any doubt about which piano. Someone was playing the old Broadwood at 1.30 in the morning. My wife was sleeping soundly and I did not know whether to be angry with my son for playing 'The Death of Nelson' at 1.30 or to congratulate him on his rendering.

Trills and grace notes abounded. I glanced out of the window expecting to see the lights from the music room illuminating the lawn. But all was in darkness.

Ever since the war days I have always kept my old army greatcoat handy by my bed; we who live in the country never know what alarms and excursions wait for us in the shape of cows in the garden, etc. bursting pipes, importunate neighbours, and the like. It was, therefore, the work of a moment to slip the coat over my pyjamas and tip-toe downstairs. The playing continued; who on earth could be playing like that in the dark? As I approached the music room door I suddenly became most conscious that I did not want to go in. It was a feeling I could not quite put into words. There was something odd about that playing. It was brilliant, indeed of its kind I have never heard better, and yet it was imperfect, inaccurate. It was almost as if whoever was playing had got right back into the period. The musical historian sees many signs, many indications of how a particular period rendered its music.

Here, beyond doubt, was something very remarkable. This was playing as piano playing was carried out a hundred and fifty years ago. There was no mistaking the technique. All I ever knew about the playing of that period was being enacted in my own music room in the middle of the night. But it was not just all I ever knew; it was a great deal more as well and yet, so to speak, it all fitted in and followed from what I did know. I was fascinated as I had not been fascinated since a ninety-year-old and semi-retired lay clerk once sang in the Cathedral (because nobody had noticed that the soloist who should have sung it was not there) a solo of Green's, putting in all the trills he had learned eighty years before from Dr Buck, who had learned them from a contemporary of Green's. I was fascinated but also frightened. But there was something else: the spirit, the flavour of the music was perfect, and yet it was inaccurate in elementary notarion. This supreme master of the period seemed, unbelievably, not to be able to play the piano very well. Every now and then the harmonies were at fault and several times there was distinct fumbling for the actual melody. It was then that I realized something else, too. That missing A was sounding. I had hardly realized this quite unexplainable fact when there came a tremendous chord on that very note, and then silence.

That silence was more impelling than the most imperative summons. The hypnotism of the music was broken. Whatever was going on in the music room, it was clearly my business to find out what it was. The spell was broken, though fear still held me in its grip. I flung open the door and at the same instant switched on the light.

Nothing. . . the room was empty of all save the familiar furniture.

The 'square' was indeed open and a chair was before it, but then I had left it all like that last night. The bright light and the familiar things gave me fresh courage. With the stout stick I had snatched up as I came down the stairs I poked the curtains, at first gingerly, and then went over the room foot by foot. The sash windows were all fastened. The only other door had a large radiogram standing in front of it. There was nowhere where anyone could possibly hide and . . . the room was empty. Besides, it could not have been more than ten seconds between the end of the music and my switching on the light.

My wife called my name. 'Henry, what on earth are you doing? I really do think you might draw the line at playing the piano at this time of night and waking us all up.' She came on down and must have seen from my face that something was amiss.

'Why, Henry, what is it? What has been happening?'

'I think, my dear, we will come out of this room, but we will leave the lights on.' And so we went back to bed and I told her. It was no dream; I was glad my wife had heard that playing as well as I. There are the facts. An eighteenth century piano was playing an early nineteenth century tune in the middle of the night and there was no human player.

That should really be the end. In the few experiences that have come my way of what are commonly called 'ghosts' something like that, something inexplicable, happens and no explanation, no reason, is ever forthcoming, and as often as not there is no story. (There was the eighteenth century woman who used to walk through the A.T.S. sleeping quarters at Datton – but this is nor a treatise on 'ghosts' and, in this particular case, we did get more information.)

A month or so later I received a note from George Nuneaton:

My dear Henry (it ran), you will remember buying the old square piano at the Mowbray sale. I told you at the time I could not remember it although I spent all my boy-hood at Mowbray. At the time of the sale my cousin, knowing my interest in such things, gave me some boxes of papers, diaries and letters, etc., which had long been preserved in the library. I have recently been going through these and found the enclosed letter which I know will interest you. Since you now have the piano I think you should have the letter. Come over soon and look at the other papers. I should like your opinion on several.

Eagerly I unfolded a somewhat faded letter. It was dated Dec. 1, 1811.

My dearest Mama (it ran), I have the most dreadful news. Cousin Sukie is dead. Papa has done all that could be done which is little enough, for the poor dear child was dead when we found her. You will remember that she was to have been married to Tom Topmast, a lieutenant in the Navy, who was known to be serving on the frigate ship Druid. Cousin Sukie was forever reading and talking of the Navy and on Tuesday she was sitting at the pianoforte in the red drawing-room playing – the pity of it! Mr Braham's new song, 'The Death of Nelson', when her maid Polly came bursting into the room saying a groom had just ridden over from my Lord Portsmouth's with a letter from Papa but that he had said that there had been ahorrid battle at some place called Tarifa and that Tom Topmast had been shot through the head and was dead. Poor, poor Sukie had just reached the end of the tune. As soon as she heard what that silly stupid Polly said she seemed to put all her strength into one more chord on the piano-forte and then fell insensible from the chair. We all rushed for Papa but the poor sweet was dead before he could come. We shall miss her vastly with her gentle ways and pretty playing. Poor Sukie! When she learned that Tom was dead she struck the pianoforte so violently that one of the notes was quite broken. I could not bear to see the pianoforte any more and told Jacob to carry it up to one of the attics. I have written to cousin Maria to apprise her of the grievous news, and, dear Mama, to see what the mantuamakers have to say about a becoming mourning, for, of course...

The letter was signed 'Letitia'. Letitia was the second daughter of Robert, ninth earl of Senlac, and the letter was written to her mother who was spending a month with her old friend, Lady Bumfidget (whom you can read about in the New Bath Guide) at Bath. There remained but one thing to do. I turned to my shelves and, after a certain amount of searching, found what I was looking for, an old song book, dated 1810.This, I knew, contained a rather florid and elaborate version of 'The Death of Nelson'. Yes, here it was. The song over, the final flourish of the piano did end on high A.

BONE TO HIS BONE

E. G. Swain

William Whitehead, Fellow of Emmanuel College, in the University of Cambridge, became Vicar of Stoneground in the year 1731. The annals of his incumbency were doubtless short and simple: they have not survived. In his day were no newspapers to collect gossip, no Parish Magazines to record the simple events of parochial life. One event, however, of greater moment then than now, is recorded in two places. Vicar Whitehead failed in health after 23 years of work, and journeyed to Bath in what his monument calls 'the vain hope of being restored'. The duration of his visit is unknown; it is reasonable to suppose that he made his journey in the summer, it is certain that by the month of November his physician told him to lay aside all hope of recovery.

Then it was that the thoughts of the patient turned to the comfortable straggling vicarage he had left at Stoneground, in which he had hoped to end his days. He prayed that his successor might be as happy there as he had been himself. Setting his affairs in order, as became one who had but a short time to live, he executed a will, bequeathing to the Vicars of Stoneground, for ever, the close of ground he had recently purchased because it lay next the vicarage garden. And by a codicil, he added to the bequest his library of books. Within a few days, William Whitehead was gathered to his fathers.

A mural tablet in the north aisle of the church, records, in Latin, his services and his bequests, his two marriages, and his fruitless journey to Bath. The house he loved, but never again saw, was taken down 40 years later, and re-built by Vicar James Devie. The garden, with Vicar Whitehead's 'close of ground' and other adjacent lands, was opened out and planted, somewhat before 1850, by Vicar Robert Towerson. The aspect of everything has changed. But in a convenient chamber on the first floor of the present vicarage the library of Vicar Whitehead stands very much as he used it and loved it, and as he bequeathed it to his successors 'for ever'.

The books there are arranged as he arranged and ticketed them. Little slips of paper, sometimes bearing interesting fragments of writing, still mark his places. His marginal comments still give life to pages from which all other interest has faded, and he would have but a dull imagination who could sit in the chamber amidst these books without ever being carried back 180 years into the past, to the time when the newest of them left the printer's hands.

Of those into whose possession the books have come, some have doubtless loved them more, and some less; some, perhaps, have left them severely alone. But neither those who loved them, nor those who loved them not, have lost them, and they passed, some century and a half after William Whitehead's death, into the hands of Mr Batchel, who loved them as a father loves his children. He lived alone, and had few domestic cares to distract his mind. He was able, therefore, to enjoy to the full what Vicar Whitehead had enjoyed so long before him. During many a long summer evening would he sit poring over long-forgotten books; and since the chamber, otherwise called the library, faced the south, he could also spend sunny winter mornings there without discomfort. Writing at a small table, or reading as he stood at a tall desk, he would browse amongst the books like an ox in a pleasant pasture.

There were other times also, at which Mr Batchel would use the books. Not being a sound sleeper (for book-loving men seldom are), he elected to use as a bedroom one of the two chambers which opened at either side into the library. The arrangement enabled him to beguile many a sleepless hour amongst the books, and in view of these nocturnal visits he kept a candle standing in a sconce above the desk, and matches always ready to his hand.

There was one disadvantage in this close proximity of his bed to the library. Owing, apparently, to some defect in the fittings of the room, which, having no mechanical tastes, Mr Batchel had never investigated, there could be heard, in the stillness of the night, exactly such sounds as might arise from a person moving about amongst the books. Visitors using the other adjacent room would often remark at breakfast, that they had heard their host in the library at one or two o'clock in the morning, when, in fact, he had not left his bed. Invariably Mr Batchel allowed them to suppose that he had been where they thought him. He disliked idle controversy, and was unwilling to afford an opening for supernatural talk. Knowing well enough the sounds by which his guests had been deceived, he wanted no other explanation of them than his own, though it was of too vague a character to count as an explanation. He conjectured that the window-sashes, or the doors, or 'something', were defective, and was too phlegmatic and too unpractical to make any investigation. The matter gave him no concern.

Persons whose sleep is uncertain are apt to have their worst nights when they would like their best. The consciousness of a special need for rest seems to bring enough mental disturbance to forbid it. So on Christmas Eye, in the year 1907, Mr Batchel, who would have liked to sleep well, in view of the labours of Christmas Day, lay hopelessly wide awake. He exhausted all the known devices for courting sleep, and, at the end, found himself wider awake than ever. A brilliant moon shone into his room, for he hated window-blinds. There was a light wind blowing, and the sounds in the library were more than usually suggestive of a person moving about. He almost determined to have the sashes 'seen to', although he could seldom be induced to have anything 'seen to'. He disliked changes, even for the better, and would submit to great inconvenience rather than have things altered with which he had become familiar.

As he revolved these matters in his mind, he heard the clocks strike the hour of midnight, and having now lost all hope of falling asleep, he rose from his bed, got into a large dressing gown which hung in readiness for such occasions, and passed into the library, with the intention of reading himself sleepy, if he could.

The moon, by this time, had passed out of the south, and the library seemed all the darker by contrast with the moonlit chamber he had left. He could see nothing but two blue-grey rectangles formed by the windows against the sky, the furniture of the room being altogether invisible. Groping along to where the table stood, Mr Batchel felt over its surface for the matches which usually lay there; he found, however, that the table was cleared of everything. He raised his right hand, therefore, in order to feel his way to a shelf where the matches were sometimes mislaid, and at that moment, whilst his hand was in mid-air, the matchbox was gently put into it!

Such an incident could hardly fail to disturb even a phlegmatic person, and Mr Batchel cried 'Who's this?' somewhat nervously. There was no answer. He struck a match, looked hastily round the room, and found it empty, as usual. There was everything, that is to say, that he was accustomed to see, but no other person than himself.

It is not quite accurate, however, to say that everything was in its usual state. Upon the tall desk lay a quarto volume that he had certainly not placed there. It was his quite invariable practice to replace his books upon the shelves after using them, and what we may call his library habits were precise and methodical. A book out of place like this, was not only an offence against good order, but a sign that his privacy had been intruded upon. With some surprise, therefore, he lit the candle standing ready in the sconce, and proceeded to examine the book, not sorry, in the disturbed condition in which he was, to have an occupation found for him.

The book proved to be one with which he was unfamiliar, and this made it certain that some other hand than his had removed it from its place. Its title was 'The Compleat Gard'ner' of M. de la Quintinye, made English by John Evelyn Esquire. It was not a work in which Mr Batchell felt any great interest. It consisted of divers reflections on various parts of husbandry, doubtless entertaining enough, but too deliberate and discursive for practical purposes. He had certainly never used the book, and growing restless now in mind, said to himself that some boy, having freedom of the house, had taken it down from its place in the hope of finding pictures.

But even whilst he made this explanation he felt its weakness. To begin with, the desk was too high for a boy. The improbability that any boy would place a book there was equaled by the improbability that he would leave it there. To discover its uninviting character would be the work only of a moment, and no boy would have brought it so far from its shelf.

Mr Batchel had, however, come to read, and habit was too strong with him to be wholly set aside. Leaving 'The Compleat Gard'ner' on the desk, he turned round to the shelves to find some more congenial reading.

Hardly had he done this when he was startled by a sharp rap upon the desk behind him, followed by a rustling of paper. he turned quickly about and saw the quarto lying open. In obedience to the instinct of the moment, he at once sought a natural cause for what he saw. Only a wind, and that of the strongest, could have opened the book, and laid back its heavy cover; and though he accepted, for a brief moment, that explanation, he was too candid to retain it longer. The wind out of doors was very light. The window sash was closed and latched and, to decide the matter fully, the book had its back, and not its edges, turned towards the only quarter from which a wind could strike.

Mr Batchel approached the desk again and stood over the book. With increasing perturbation of mind (for he still thought of the matchbox) he looked upon the open page. Without much reason beyond that he felt constrained to do something, he read the words of the half-completed sentence at the turn of the page:

> *'...at dead of night he left the house and passed into the solitude of the garden.'*

But he read no more, nor did he give himself the trouble of discovering whose midnight wandering was being decribed, although the habit was singularly like one of his own. He was in no condition for reading, and turning his back upon the volume he slowly paced the length of the chamber, 'wondering at that which had come to pass'.

He reached the opposite end of the chamber and was in the act of turning, when again he heard the rustling of paper, and by the time he had faced round, saw the leaves of the book again was turning over. In a moment the volume lay at rest, open in another place, and there was no further movement as he approached it. To make sure that he had not been deceived, he read again the words as they entered the page. The author was following a not uncommon practice of the time, and throwing common speech into forms suggested by Holy Writ: 'So dig,' it said, 'that ye may obtain.'

This passage, which to Mr Batchel seemed reprehensible in its levity, excited at once his interest and his disapproval. He was prepared to read more, but this time was not allowed. Before his eye could pass beyond the passage already cited, the leaves of the book slowly turned again and presented by a termination of five words and a colophon.

The words were 'to the North, an Ilex'. These three passages, in which he saw no meaning and no connection, began to entangle themselves together in Mr Batchel's mind. He found himself repeating them in different orders, now beginning with one, and now with another. Any further attempt at reading he felt to be impossible, and he was in no mind for any more experiences of the unaccountable. Sleep was, of course, further from him than ever, if that were conceivable. What he did, therefore, was to blow out the candle, to return to his moonlit bedroom and put on more clothing, and then to pass downstairs with the object of going out of doors.

It was no unusual with Mr Batchel to walk about his garden at nighttime. This form of exercise had often, after a wakeful hour, sent him back to his bed refreshed and ready for sleep. The conventient access to the garden at such times lay through his study, whose French windows opened on to a short flight of steps, and upon these he now paused for a moment to admire the snow-like appearance of the lawns, bathed as they were in the moonlight. As he paused, he heard the city clocks strike the half-hour after midnight, and he could not forbear repeating aloud:

> *'...at dead of night he left the house and passed into the solitude of the garden.'*

It was solitary enough. At intervals the screech of an owl, and now and then the noise of a train, seemed to emphasise the solitude by drawing attention to it and then leaving it in possession of the night. Mr Batchel found himself wondering and conjecturing what Vicar Whitehead, who had acquired the close of land to secure quiet and privacy for a garden, would have thought of the railways to the west and north. He turned his face northwards, whence a whistle had just sounded, and saw a tree beautifully outlined against the sky. His breath caught at the sight. Not because the tree was unfamiliar. Mr Batchel knew all his trees. But what he had seen was 'to the North, an Ilex.'

Mr Batchel knew not what to make of it all. He had walked into the garden hundreds of times and as often seen the Ilex, but the words out of 'The Compleat Card'ner' seemed to be pursuing him in a way that made him almost afraid. His temperament, however, as has been said already, was phlegmatic. It was commonly said, and Mr Batchel approved the verdict, whilst he condemnded its exactness, that 'his nerves were made of fiddle-string', so he braced himself afresh and set upon his walk round the silent garden, which he was accustomed to begin in a northerly direction, and was now too proud to change. He usually passed the Ilex at the beginning of his perambulation, and so would pass it now.

He did not pass it. A small discovery, as he reached it, annoyed and disturbed him. His gardener, as careful and punctilious as himself, neer failed to house all his tools at the end of a day's work. yet there, under the Ilex, standing upright in moonlight brilliant enough to cast a shadow of it, was a spade.

Mr Natchel's second thought was one of relief. After his extraordinary experiences in the library (he hardly knew now whether they had been real or not) something quite commonplace would act sedatively,and he determined to carry the spade to the tool-house.

The soil was quite dry, and the surface even a little frozen, so Mr Batchel left the path, walked upto the spade, and would have drawn it towards him. But it was as if he had made the attempt upon the trunk of the Ilex itself. The spade would not be moved. Then, first with one hand, and then with both, he tried to raise it, and still it stood firm. Mr Batchel, of course, attributed this to the frost, slight as it was. Wondering at the spade's being there, and annoyed at its being frozen, he was about to leave it and continue his walk, when the remaining words of 'The Compleat Gard'ner' seemed rather to utter themselves, than to await his will:

'So dig, that ye may obtain.'

Mr Batchel's power of independent action now deserted him. He took the spade, which no longer resisted, and began to dig. 'Five spadefuls and no more,' he said aloud. 'This is all foolishness.'

Four spadefuls of earth he then raised and spread out before him in the moonlight. There was nothing unusual to be seen. Nor did Mr Batchel decide what he would look for, whether coins, jewels, documents in canisters, or weapons. In point of fact, he dug against what he deemed his better judgement, and expected nothing. He spread before him the fifth and last spadeful of earth, not quite without result, but with no result that was at all sensational. The earth contained a bone. Mr Batchel's knowledge of anatomy was sufficient to show him that it was a human bone. He identified it, even by moonlight, as the *radius*, a bone of the forearm, as he removed the earth from it, with his thumb.

Such a discovery might be thought worthy of more than the

very ordinary interest Mr Batchel showed. As a matter of fact, the presence of a human bone was easily to be accounted for. Recent excavations within the church had caused the upturning of numberless bones, which had been collected and reverently buried. But an earth-stained bone is also easily overlooked, and this *radius* had obviously found its way into the garden with some of the earth brought out of the church.

Mr Batchel was glad, rather than regretful, at this termination to his adventure. he was once more provided with something to do. The reinterment of such bones as this had been his constant care, and he decided at once to restore the bone to consecrated earth. The time seemed opportune. The eyes of the curious were closed in sleep, he himself was still alert and wakeful. The spade remained by his side and the bone in his hand. So he betook himself, there and then, to the churchyard. By the still generous light of the moon, he found a place where the earth yeielded to his spade, and within a few minutes the bone was laid decently to earth, some 18 inches deep.

The city clocks struck one as he finished. The whole world seemed asleep, and Mr Batchel slowly returned to the garden with his spade. As he hing it in its accustomed place he felt stealing over him the welcome desire to sleep. he walked quietly on to the house and ascended to his room. It was now dark: the moon had passed on and left the room in shadow. He lit a candle, and before undressing passed into the library. He had an irresistable curiosity to see the passages in John Evelyn's book which had so strangely adapted themselves to the events of the past hour.

In the library a last surprise awaited him. The desk upon which the book had lain was empty. 'The Compleat Gard'ner' stood in its place on the shelf. And then Mr Batchel knew that he had handled a bone of William Whitehead, and that in response to his own entreaty.

A COLLECTOR'S COMPANY

R. H. Malden

The story which follows was told to me rather more than thirty years ago. The narrator was elderly then. He died very soon after the end of the last war with Germany, so there can be no harm in repeating it now. His name, if you want to know, was Arthur Harberton. As he was a young man when it happened to him I suppose it must be dated not long after the year 1870. I made notes of it at the time, and reproduce it now as nearly as I can in his own words.

'Three years after my ordination I was offered a post as a college lecturer at Cambridge. That was the kind of work which I had always thought that I should like, at any rate for a few years, so I accepted the offer very gladly. I have never regretted that I did so; nor that I did not devote the rest of my life to academic work.

'I was not dean of the college, and as in those days the number of Fellows in Holy Order was much larger than it is now it was very seldom necessary for me to be in the Chapel on a Sunday. Accordingly I used to go about the diocese a good deal, visiting the country churches. I don't think that I was under any illusion as to my powers as a preacher, even then. But I thought, without, I hope, undue vanity, that it might be good for village congregations to hear a fresh voice occasionally, and even for the incumbent if he were present. That was not always the case, for I was always willing to take the whole duty of the day if I were asked, so that the incumbent might secure a short holiday.

'As a rule I enjoyed these expeditions thoroughly. They began with a short train journey, followed by a drive from the station, sometimes of as much as ten miles. Country lanes were country lanes then. They had not been blackened with tar macadam and motor-cars were, of course, unknown. An occasional traction engine, preceded by a man on foot carrying a red flag, was the only disagreeable object likely to be encountered. From a dog-cart, which was usually the vehicle which came to meet me, it was possible to see over the hedges and to get a very fair idea of the country as you went along at eight to ten miles an hour.

'My hosts were generally interesting. For the most part they were country-bred men who belonged naturally to their surroundings. Many of them had a wide variety of interests (and sometimes a store of real knowledge) on which they were ready to discourse to a stranger. When I had the house to myself, it was amusing to try to deduce what manner of man the owner might be from his books and pictures.

'Most of the churches and a good many of the houses presented features of architectural interest, which appealed to me strongly. Besides, I used to enjoy such conversations as I might have with rural churchwardens, sextons and other parish officials. I remember one churchwarden (a farmer, I think) who had heard that Huntingdon was a fine town. Personally he had never penetrated farther than St. Neots. When I told him that I lived at Cambridge I might as well have said Pekin, or Timbuctoo.

'In another place the village school-master was opposed to elementary education in the abstract: not merely to the particular form of it which he was required to administer. He thought it unsettled children and took them off the land. There was, no doubt, something to be said on behalf of his views; but I couldn't help wondering whether he were *quite* the right man in the right place. Well – no doubt the countryside is more sophisticated now, and I won't bore you with speculations as to whether the gains outweigh the losses or not.

'So, as you see, I had good reason to look forward to these excursions. In fact, I only once got to a place which I should not care to visit again, and that is the one which I am going to tell you about now. All the same, I don't entirely regret that I did go there. Anyhow, it was a unique experience.

'Towards the end of one October term I got a letter from the bishop's chaplain, asking me if I could preach twice on the following Sunday at a village about twenty-five miles from Cambridge – I don't think I will tell you in what direction. The incumbent, it appeared, was not very well, and having no curate was doubtful of his ability to get through the day single-handed. As it would be the second Sunday in Advent it would not be difficult for me to preach at short notice. The collect and epistle for the day provided me with a subject ready-made: a subject, moreover, which I have always found particularly congenial.

'I discovered that there was a convenient train to the nearest station on the Saturday afternoon and from it on the Monday morning, so I telegraphed Yes, and wrote to my prospective host to say when I might be expected.

'It was a little after three when I got out at a wayside station. I was met by a groom with a dog-cart who brought a note from his master apologizing for not having come in person. As I had understood that he wasn't well I hadn't expected him. I will call him Melrose.

'As we drove away from the station I said to the groom, 'I hope Mr. Melrose has nothing serious the matter with him?' 'No,' he replied, 'but he *du* come over all queer – like at times – so he du. When he have one of his turns – well, it's not for me to be explaining of it, if you take my meaning, Sir.'

'I was not at all sure that I did, but thought it would be ill-bred on my part to ask for details. Also I was inclined to suspect that they might be copious rather than enlightening. However, as my companion seemed inclined to talk I did not feel bound to try to suppress him.

'I gathered that Mr. Melrose was wealthy and a bachelor. He had 'travelled furren,' which was regarded locally as a hazardous proceeding, on the ground that all foreigners are well known to be black, and that they blackamoors might be up to anything. He was much took up with reading: also in my companion's opinion a dubious proceeding. For if there was good in some books there was bad in others, and how'd you know which till arterwards, and then it was done.

'The general impression left on my mind was that while Mr. Melrose might be loved by his parishioners he was certainly feared. I thought that I might look forward to an unusually interesting week-end. As it turned out this expectation was not unduly sanguine, as I think you will agree when you have heard the rest of my story.

'After a drive of about seven miles we arrived. The light was failing, but I could see that the house was an old one. It was rather larger than the average, and I judged that there was probably a considerable garden behind it. I looked forward to examining both more closely between services on Sunday.

'Mr. Melrose made me very welcome. He was a tall man who stooped a little. I set him down as about seventy; probably over rather than under. He had abundant white hair and very prominent white eyebrows. His eyes were dark and his nose aquiline. The general effect was scholarly and striking. He would have been noticeable in any company, and once seen would always be remembered. My first impression was that he was very handsome.'

Here Mr. Harberton paused for a minute or two and then said rather abruptly, 'Did you ever see Thompson (W. H. Thompson, 1866-86.), the Master of Trinity?'

'No,' I said. 'He was some years before my time. But I know the portrait; by Richmond, I think.' 'No, of course you didn't,' he went on. 'Stupid of me. But one forgets how time passes. I don't think the portrait really does him justice. However, if you know it you'll understand what I am going to say.

'I knew him very well by sight and he was one of the most distinguished-looking men I have ever seen. He was handsome if you like, and you couldn't doubt his ability or force of character. You had only to look at him to see that he was a great man. Yet somehow I never could think his face a pleasing one. It always seemed to me to contain great possibilities of evil. I could believe him to be capable of absolutely diabolical conduct.'

'Well,' I said, 'I believe that when Richmond painted Lightfoot he declared that he had never had a sitter whose jaw was so obviously and unmistakably that of a murderer. And I have been told by people who knew the Bishop well that they could believe that he had a naturally violent temper, and that his complete mastery of it was part of his greatness. The same may have been true of Thompson.'

'Yes,' said Mr. Harberton, 'it may. Anyhow, this was the effect which Mr. Melrose produced on me. However, I tried to dismiss it from my mind as foolishness.

'After tea, which we had in a square hall by a log fire, Mr. Melrose asked me to excuse him until dinner-time as he had some letters to write and the post went out at six-thirty. He had a small study on the first floor opening out of his bedroom to which he proposed to betake himself. The library, which was on the ground floor and opened out of the hall, was at my disposal and there were writing materials there if I wanted them.

'The library was a large room, completely lined with bookcases. A cursory inspection of these showed that my host was a man of wide and miscellaneous reading. He seemed to be particularly interested in the later Neoplatonists and to be well supplied with Orphic literature. On a glass-topped table by the window was a collection of Gnostic gems. An Egyptian mummy-case stood upright in a corner. On a table by the fire was a book which he had presumably been reading when I arrived. I picked it up and found that it was Philostratus' *Life* of Apollonius of Tyana. It had been interleaved and was copiously annotated. I should have liked to read some of the notes, but thought that would be impertinent.

'Evidently I was in the house of a scholar whose interests were out of the common run, and the possessor of means which enabled him to indulge them freely.'

'At dinner he proved very good company. He had travelled widely and had visited places which were then very much off the beaten track, such as Sicily and Transylvania. He had spent some considerable time in the latter country and had made a careful study of its grim folklore.

'The dinner was good, and my host exerted himself to be pleasant. Interesting he undoubtedly was, but I was not at all sure how much I liked him. I had a vague feeling that in some way he was playing a part. But I could find no rational ground for my suspicion. And, after all, why should he think it worth while to try to impress anyone so much younger than himself?

'It struck me as curious that a man of his calibre should be content to bury himself in so obscure a place. Of course the country was much more prosperous then than it is now and rural life offered more interests than I fear it does to-day. But this particular neighbourhood was not specially attractive in any way. Most of the land had belonged to the see of Ely and was now administered by the Ecclesiastical Commissioners. I believe that they are always considered to be good landlords, but naturally there are seldom any country-houses other than farms on their estates. I could hardly see my host at ease in the society of farmers, nor could I imagine that they would be able to make much of him. (I had discovered that he did not shoot or hunt, and in those days a man who did neither was very much out of it in the country.)

'When he told me that he had been rector of the parish for more than thirty years I could not help expressing surprise – rather clumsily, I fear, and perhaps not too politely, but I was very young then – and saying something about the solitariness of the life which he led.

'Yes,' he said; 'I don't wonder that it strikes you like that. The road from the station is rather desolate. But I have plenty of occupation and interests here; and do you know I find some of my neighbours more companionable than you would expect.'

'The last sentence struck me as rather odd, not only in itself but in the way he said it. I felt that there was more behind the remark than I was meant to understand, and did not like the feeling. I liked the laugh which followed it even less. However, there was obviously no more to be said about that. Perhaps he thought I had been rather impertinent, and perhaps he was right.

'After dinner we went into the library for coffee, and somehow our talk drifted to witchcraft, necromancy and kindred topics. I had always taken an interest in such matters, if not a very serious one, and have often wondered what foundation, if any, there is or was for the belief that the powers to which witches lay claim have any real existence.

'At this distance of time I do not mind admitting that as an undergraduate I had once made an essay in Invultuadon. The object was the Vice-Chancellor of the day, whom I did not know by sight. He had annoyed me by refusing to allow a play which I had written to be acted publicly by the A.D.C., on the ground that it was disrespectful to authority. I adopted the only method of retaliation which seemed to be open. I made a waxen image and placed it on my mantelpiece. After some incantations which I thought appropriate (*Flectere si nequeo superos Acheronta movebo* [Aeneid, vii. 12.] is the only line which I remember now) I inserted a pin into one leg. The very next day I heard that the Vice-Chancellor had slipped going downstairs in his lodge and had sprained one of his ankles. I felt that my cause had been vindicated and took no further steps. But, as you will understand, I had not been serious in the matter. I never pretended to think that the accident had been more than a coincidence for which I need not reproach myself. The story leaked out somehow, and one comment on it which came to my ears was 'Whole religions have been founded upon less evidence.' I will not name the author, but I still think he ought to have known better.

'Mr. Melrose's discourse seemed to me to be a very different story. I could not help thinking that he knew more than he ought about a great deal which was very undesirable. And he spoke with an air of inside knowledge which I found disquieting. His tone was that of a lecturer on a subject which he had really made his own, and he gave the impression of having verified at least some of his knowledge by experiment. I felt that there was something malign about him, as well as creepy.

'Finally, I came to the conclusion that he was like an evil caricature of Dr. Hans Emmanuel Bryerley, the Sweden-borgian teacher in *Uncle Silas*. (By Joseph Sheridan Le Fanu.) Altogether I was extremely glad when he suggested a move bedwards, and was at pains to lock the door of my room. Perhaps that would not avail much if it came to the point. But the illusion of security which it produced was comforting.

'I do not know how long I had been asleep when I awoke with the impression which one sometimes has of having been disturbed by a loud and sudden noise. Probably the church clock, I thought, though I had not noticed its strike earlier in the evening. I was just disposing myself for a renewed period of slumber when it struck me that although my fire had burned low the room was curiously light; not with firelight either. I had drawn back the window curtains before going to bed, as I usually did, and the light was coming from the window.

"Moonlight,' you will say. 'But I knew that it was not. In the first place, the moon was several days short of full, and in the second, the light was not coming from a particular point. It was evenly diffused, like daylight on a cloudy day; and no moon could have produced so much light from behind clouds. It seemed to me to have a bluish tinge which was unnatural and unpleasant. I went to the window and looked out. It commanded a view of a good-sized lawn flanked by dark shrubberies of some sort – rhododendrons, I found out subsequently.

'This lawn sloped slightly upwards away from the house, and at the farther end was a low wall with a gateway in it leading to the churchyard. This and the church itself were as plainly visible as if it had been midday instead of just after midnight in December. But everything to right and left was in darkness. I felt as if I were looking down an illuminated tunnel, and it seemed obvious that something would appear at the upper end. I took my courage in both hands and waited. I did not have to wait long. Through the gate in the churchyard wall came my host. He seemed to be wearing a cassock with a long black cloak over it. On his head was a high-pointed cap, something like a mitre, and he carried a short rod in his right hand. He came straight down the lawn towards the house. I wondered whether I was as visible to him as he was to me; and hoped not. Anyhow I felt bound to see the performance through. He was followed by a number of figures: I think about twelve, but I could not be sure.

'Although there seemed to be plenty of light they were somehow curiously indistinct. They may have dodged behind each other from time to time in some odd fashion. Anyhow I found that it was no use to try to count them. They were dressed in long black cloaks with hoods, which prevented their faces from being seen. On the whole I felt glad of that. They moved rather stiffly, like marionettes. Of course their feet made no sound upon the grass. But I was conscious of a faint creaking, the source of which was not easy to determine. It might have been produced by the breeze in the shrubbery; but I did not think that it was.

'The procession advanced until it had reached the middle of the lawn. Then the leader stopped and the others formed a circle round him. Still I could not be sure how many they were. Every time I tried to count them I became confused and arrived at a different result.

'Then they began to dance while he beat time or conducted, however you like to put it, with his wand. They moved more quickly than I should have expected, though they still suggested marionettes. The faint creaking which I had heard before was more audible. There could be no doubt now that it came from the dancing figures.

'Do you remember a story told by one of the minor characters in Stevenson's *Catriona?* About Tod Lapraik, the warlock weaver of Leith. He used to fall into a dream in his house and once while he was in that state he, or something in his likeness, was seen dancing alone on the Bass Rock 'in the black glory of his heart.' Those words rose in my mind now. The performance which I was watching seemed to be inspired by an unholy – well, *joie de vivre* I suppose I must call it, though I don't know how far the dancers could be considered to be alive. The whole effect was abominably, indescribably evil. Yet, curiously enough, I did not feel afraid. I have never considered myself a particularly courageous person, and have not had many opportunities of discovering whether I am or not. But anyhow I was not conscious of any fear then. Partly perhaps I was too deeply interested in what I was watching to think of anything else. Also, youth and a good digestion will carry their possessor securely through many of the changes and chances of this mortal life.

'The dance grew faster, and the ring of dancers contracted. As it did so the mysterious light contracted too. I could no longer see the church, or the greater part of the lawn. Only the tall stationary figure with his black-shrouded companions whirling – it had come to that now – whirling round him. The group was illuminated as a particular figure sometimes is upon the stage (spotlight, I think they call it), but as before the light did not seem to be coming from any particular direction. Perhaps this was why I could see no shadow upon the grass.

'In another minute the dancers seemed to have closed in and then (as was perhaps to be expected) the light went out. I could neither see nor hear anything. The garden seemed to be as dark and deserted as you might expect between midnight and 1 a.m. on a moonless night in December. As I turned away from the window I heard the discordant cry of a night-jar (at least that was what I thought it sounded like) very loud and apparently very close to my window. Immediately afterwards I heard a low chuckle. It was not a pleasant one. I felt pretty sure that whatever the joke might be I should prefer not to meet the author of it. I made certain that my door was locked, made up my fire to last until daylight, got into bed and rather to my surprise fell asleep almost immediately.

'It was getting light when I woke. I got out of bed and unlocked my door. As I waited to be called I naturally thought of my experience of a few hours earlier. The more I considered it the less confident did I become that I had not dreamed the whole thing. I have always been an active and vivid dreamer, but have never had a vision of my head upon my bed worth taking seriously; even by the most nasty-minded psycho-analyst who ever came out of Vienna or anywhere else.

'At eight o'clock the butler brought me tea and hot water. On the tray was a note from Mr. Melrose saying that he regretted that he was unable to leave his room. The clerk would show me where everything was in the church. Would I make myself at home in the house and ask for anything I wanted, etc. etc.'

"Is your master seriously ill?' I asked the man. 'Ought a doctor to be sent for, or can you look after him?'

"No, Sir, not serious. But he don't come down as a rule, after one of his nights, not for a day or two.'

'For a moment I thought he was going to say more, but he turned away and began laying out my clothes. So I said something to the effect that old people often slept badly and that no doubt a wakeful night was very exhausting.

'To this he merely replied, 'Yes, Sir,' and left the room.

'While I was drinking my tea I thought I would look at the lessons for the day, as I should probably have to read them myself. There was a Bible beside my bed and I opened it at Isaiah (the first lesson was Chapter 5, as you probably remember), and it so happened that the first words which caught my eye were from Chapter 8, verse 19:

> *Seek unto them that have familiar spirits and unto the wizards that peep and that mutter.*

'No doubt a coincidence. But as I dressed I became more and more inclined to think that I had not been dreaming.

'The day passed uneventfully. Evensong was at three, as was not unusual in the country then during the winter months; I must confess that I was glad of this as I did not relish the prospect of coming down the lawn from the church in the dark. Of course it was getting dark by the time service was over, and as I went through the gate leading from the churchyard I had an uncomfortable feeling that my movements were being watched by some person or persons whom I could not see –and not with any amiable solicitude for my welfare.

'However, nothing untoward happened then or during the evening. I went to bed early and slept soundly all night.

Next morning the butler brought another note from my host, expressing his regret that he would be unable to see me before I left, the disappointment which he felt at having had so little of my society, and a hope that I had been made comfortable.

'I replied to the first two heads of this communication as politely as was consistent with the truth. As regards the third I could reassure him honestly. I left the house soon after breakfast. The butler had not seemed disposed to be communicative, nor was the groom who drove me to the station. Three days later I went down for the Christmas vacation.'

'Mr. Harberton was silent for a minute or two, so I asked – I must admit with a feeling of disappointment – 'Is that all?'

'Not quite,' he replied. 'But for the conclusion of the story you had better read this.'

He handed me a cutting from a newspaper, probably a local weekly, which he took from a large old-fashioned pocket-book. I had seen the book before, as it was his practice to carry it with him. The cutting was from the bottom of a column, so no date was visible. I judged it to be about thirty years old. It ran as follows:

RECTOR'S STRANGE DEATH

'A painful sensation was produced at [the name of the place was carefully erased] on Christmas morning.

'As soon as it was light the sexton (Mr. Jonas Day) had gone to the church to make up the fire in the stove. As he approached the south door he was horrified to observe the body of the rector lying face downwards on a flight of four steps leading from the churchyard to the rectory garden. He went at once to the house and summoned the butler (Mr. Thomas Blogg) and the groom (Mr. Henry Meekin). They carried the rev. gentleman to his room, but it was all too evident that the vital spark had ceased to pulsate. Dr. Horridge was sent for and arrived a little before ten o'clock. He reported that the neck of the deceased was broken and that death must have intervened some hours before.

'It may be presumed that the unfortunate gentleman had gone to the church at a late hour to satisfy himself that everything was in order for the morrow. The steps were slippery with frost and he did not appear to have taken a lantern.

'The Rev. [name erased] had held the rectory for thirty-two years and the sad occurrence cast a deep aroma of gloom over the festivities naturally incidental to the day.

'The inquest was held at the Fox and Grapes on the 30th ult., Dr. Horridge presiding as Coroner. Mr. Blogg deposed that his master not infrequently went to the church late at night. When asked by one of the Jury if he knew for what purpose, he replied that he had never demeaned himself to curiosity in his master's business. He was warmly commended by the Coroner for his reply.

'Mr. Day deposed that when he approached the body he saw some curious marks on the back of the coat. When pressed to describe them he said 'Like muddy claws.' Neither Mr. Blogg nor Mr. Meekin had noticed these. The coat was sent for, but it had been brushed. The Coroner thought that they might easily have been made by an owl or some other bird of the night perching upon the body after life was extinct, and by his direction the Jury returned a verdict of *Death by Misadventure*.

'The funereal obsequies were celebrated on the and instant.'

'May I take a copy of this?' I asked.

'Yes, if you like,' said Mr. Harberton. And I did.

A TALE OF AN EMPTY HOUSE

E. F. Benson

It had been a disastrous afternoon: rain had streamed incessantly from a low grey sky, and the road was of the vilest description. There were sections consisting of sharp flints, newly laid down and not yet rolled into amenity, and the stretches in between were worn into deep ruts and bouncing holes, so that it was impossible anywhere to travel at even a moderate speed. Twice we had punctured, and now, as the stormy dusk began to fall, something went wrong with the engine, and after crawling on for a hundred yards or so we stopped. My driver, after a short investigation, told me that there was a half-hour's tinkering to be done, and after that we might, with luck, trundle along in a leisurely manner, and hope eventually to arrive at Crowthorpe which was the proposed destination.

We had come, when this stoppage occurred, to a crossroad. Through the driving rain I could see on the right a great church, and in front a huddle of houses. A consultation of the map seemed to indicate that this was the village of Riddington. The guide-book added the information that Riddington possessed an hotel, and the sign-post at the corner endorsed them both. To the right along the main road, into which we had just struck, was Crowthorpe, fifteen miles away and straight in front of us, half a mile distant, was the hotel.

The decision was not difficult. There was no reason why I should get to Crowthorpe to-night instead of to-morrow, for the friend whom I was to meet there would not arrive until next afternoon and it was surely better to limp half a mile with a spasmodic engine than to attempt fifteen on this inclement evening.

'We'll spend the night here,' I said to my chauffeur. 'The road dips down hill, and it's only half a mile to the hotel. I daresay we shall get there without using the engine at all. Let's try, anyhow.'

We hooted and crossed the main road, and began to slide very slowly down a narrow street. It was impossible to see much, but on either side there were little houses with lights gleaming through blinds, or with blinds still undrawn, revealing cosy interiors. Then the incline grew steeper, and close in front of us I saw masts against a sheet of water that appeared to stretch unbroken into the rain-shrouded gloom of the gathering night.

Riddington then must be on the open sea, though how it came about that boats should be tied up to an open quay-wall was a puzzle, but perhaps there was some jetty, invisible in the darkness, which protected them. I heard the chauffeur switch on his engine, as we made a sharp turn to the left, and we passed below a long row of lighted windows, shining out on to a rather narrow road, on the right edge of which the water lapped. Again he turned sharply to the left, described a half-circle on crunching gravel, and drew up at the door of the hotel. There was a room for me, there was a garage, there was a room for him, and dinner had not long begun.

Among the little excitements and surprises of travel there is none more delightful than that of waking in a new place at which one has arrived after nightfall on the previous evening. The mind has received a few hints and dusky impressions, and probably during sleep it has juggled with these, constructing them into some sort of coherent whole and next morning its anticipations are put to the proof. Usually the eye has seen more than it has consciously registered, and the brain has fitted together as in the manner of a jig-saw puzzle a very fair presentment of its immediate surroundings. When I woke next morning a brilliantly sunny sky looked in at my windows; there was no sound of wind or of breaking waves, and before getting up and verifying my impressions of the night before I lay and washed-in my imagined picture. In front of my windows there would be a narrow roadway bordered by a quay-wall: there would be a breakwater, forming a harbour for the boats that lay at anchor there, and away, away to the horizon would stretch an expanse of still and glittering sea. I ran over these points in my mind; they seemed an inevitable inference from the glimpses of the night before and then, assured of my correctness, I got out of bed and went to the window.

I have never experienced so complete a surprise. There was no harbour, there was no breakwater, and there was no sea. A very narrow channel, three-quarters choked with sand-banks on which now rested the boats whose masts I had seen the previous evening, ran parallel to the road, and then turned at right angles and went off into the distance. Otherwise no water of any sort was visible; right and left and in front stretched a limitless expanse of shining grasses with tufts of shrubby growth, and great patches of purple sea-lavender. Beyond were tawny sand-banks, and further yet a line of shingle and scrub and sand-dunes. But the sea which I had expected to fill the whole circle of the visible world till it met the sky on the horizon, had totally disappeared.

After the first surprise at this colossal conjuring trick was over, I dressed quickly, in order to ascertain from local authorities how it was done. Unless some hallucination had poisoned my perceptive faculties, there must be an explanation of this total disappearance, alternately, of sea and land, and the key, when supplied, was simple enough. That line of shingle and scrub and sand dunes on the horizon was a peninsula running for four or five miles parallel with the land, forming the true beach, and it enclosed this vast basin of sand-banks and mud-banks and level lavender-covered marsh, which was submerged at high tide, and made an estuary. At low tide it was altogether empty but for the stream that struggled out through various channels to the mouth of it two miles away to the left, and there was easy passage across it for a man who carried his shoes and stockings, to the far sand dunes and beaches which terminated at Riddington Point, while at high tide you could sail out from the quay just in front of the hotel and be landed there.

The tide would be out of the estuary for five or six hours yet; I could spend the morning on the beach, or, taking my lunch, walk out to the Point, and be back before the returning waters rendered the channel impassable. There was good bathing on the beach, and there was a colony of terns who nested there.

Already, as I ate my breakfast at a table in the window overlooking the marsh, the spell and attraction of it had begun to work. It was so immense and so empty; it had the allure of the desert about it, with none of the desert's intolerable monotony, for companies of chiding gulls hovered over it, and I could hear the pipe of redshank and the babble of curlews. I was due to meet Jack Granger in Crowthorpe that evening, but if I went I knew that I should persuade him to come back to Riddington, and from my knowledge of him, I was aware that he would feel the spell of the place not less potent than I. So, having ascertained that there was a room for him here, I wrote him a note saying that I had found the most amazing place in the world, and told my chauffeur to take the car into Crowthorpe to meet the train that afternoon and bring him here. And with a perfectly clear conscience, I set off with a towel and a packet of lunch in my pocket to explore vaguely and goallessly that beckoning immensity of lavender-covered, bird-haunted expanse.

My way, as pointed out to me, led first along a sea-bank which defended the drained pastureland on the right of it from the high tides, and at the corner of that I struck into the basin of the estuary. A contour line of jetsam, withered grass, strands of seaweed, and the bleached shells of little crabs showed where the last tide had reached its height, and inside it the marsh growth was still wet. Then came a stretch of mud and pebbles, and presently I was wading through the stream that flowed down to the sea. Beyond that were banks of ribbed sand swept by the incoming tides, and soon I regained the wide green marshes on the further side, beyond which was the bar of shingle that fringed the sea.

I paused as I re-shod myself. There was not a sign of any living human being within sight, but never have I found myself in so exhilarating a solitude. Right and left were spread the lawns of sea-lavender, starred with pink tufts of thrift and thickets of suæda bushes. Here and there were pools left in depressions of the ground by the retreated tide, and here were patches of smooth black mud, out of which grew, like little spikes of milky-green asparagus, a crop of glass-wort, and all these happy vegetables flourished in sunshine or rain or the salt of the flooding tides with impartial amphibiousness. Overhead was the immense arc of the sky, across which flew now a flight of duck, hurrying with necks outstretched, and now a lonely black-backed gull, flapping his ponderous way seawards. Curlews were bubbling, and redshank and ringed plover fluting, and now as I trudged up the shingle bank, at the bottom of which the marsh came to an end, the sea, blue and waveless, lay stretched and sleeping, bordered by a strip of sand, on which far off a mirage hovered. But from end to end of it, as far as eye could see, there was no sign of human presence.

I bathed and basked on the hot beach, walked along for half a mile, and then struck back across the shingle into the marsh. And then with a pang of disappointment I saw the first evidence of the intrusion of man into this paradise of solitude, for on a stony spit of ground that ran like some great rib into the amphibious meadows, there stood a small square house built of brick, with a tall flagstaff set up in front of it. It had not caught my eye before, and it seemed an unwarrantable invasion of the emptiness. But perhaps it was not so gross an infringement of it as it appeared, for it wore an indefinable look of desertion, as if man had attempted to domesticate himself here and had failed. As I approached it this impression increased, for the chimney was smokeless, and the closed windows were dim with the film of salt air and the threshold of the closed door was patched with lichen and strewn with débris of withered grasses. I walked twice round it, decided that it was certainly uninhabited, and finally, leaning against the sun-baked wall, ate my lunch.

The glitter and heat of the day were at their height. Warmed and exercised, and invigorated by my bathe, I felt strung to the supreme pitch of physical well-being, and my mind, quite vacant except for these felicitous impressions, followed the example of my body, and basked in an unclouded content. And, I suppose by a sense of the Lucretian luxury of contrast, it began to picture to itself, in order to accentuate these blissful conditions, what this sunlit solitude would be like when some November night began to close in underneath a low, grey sky and a driving storm of sleet. Its solitariness would be turned into an abominable desolation: if from some unconjecturable cause one was forced to spend the night here, how the mind would long for any companionship, how sinister would become the calling of the birds, how weird the whistle of the wind round the cavern of this abandoned habitation. Or would it be just the other way about, and would one only be longing to be assured that the seeming solitude was real, and that no invisible but encroaching presence, soon to be made manifest, was creeping nearer under cover of the dusk, and be shuddering to think that the wail of the wind was not only the wind, but the cry of some discarnate being, and that it was not the curlews who made that melancholy piping? By degrees the edge of thought grew blunt, and melted into inconsequent imaginings, and I fell asleep.

I woke with a start from the trouble of a dream that faded with waking, but felt sure that some noise close at hand had aroused me. And then it came again: it was the footfall of someone moving about inside the deserted house, against the wall of which my back was propped. Up and down it went, then paused and began again; it was like that of a man who waited with impatience for some expected arrival. I noticed also that the footfall had an irregular beat, as if the walker went with a limp. Then in a minute or two the sound ceased altogether.

An odd uneasiness came over me, for I had been so certain that the house was uninhabited. Then turning my head I noticed that in the wall just above me was a window, and the notion, wholly irrational and unfounded, entered my mind that the man inside who tramped was watching me from it. When once that idea got hold of me, it became impossible to sit there in peace any more, and I got up and shovelled into my knapsack my towel and the remains of my meal. I walked a little further down the spit of land which ran out into the marsh, and turning looked at the house again, and again to my eyes it seemed absolutely deserted. But after all, it was no concern of mine and I proceeded on my walk, determining to inquire casually on my return to the hotel who it was that lived in so hermetical a place, and for the present dismissed the matter from my mind.

It was some three hours later that I found myself opposite the house again, after a long wandering walk. I saw that, by making an only slightly longer detour, I could pass close to the house again, and I knew that the sound of those footsteps within it had raised in me a curiosity that I wanted to satisfy. And then, even as I paused, I saw that a man was standing by the door: how he came there I had no idea, for the moment before he had not been there, and he must have come out of the house. He was looking down the path that led through the marsh, shielding his eyes against the sun, and presently he took a step or two forward and he dragged his left leg as he walked, limping heavily. It was his step then which I had heard within, and any mystery about the matter was of my own making. I therefore took the shorter path, and got back to the hotel to find that Jack Granger had just arrived.

We went out again in the gleam of the sunset, and watched the tide sweeping in and pouring up the dykes, until again the great conjuring trick was accomplished, and the stretch of marsh with its fields of sea-lavender was a sheet of shining water. Far away across it stood the house by which I had lunched, and just as we turned Jack pointed to it.

'That's a queer place for a house,' he said. 'I suppose no one lives there.'

'Yes, a lame man,' said I, 'I saw him to-day. I'm going to ask the hotel porter who he is.'

The result of this inquiry was unexpected.

'No; the house has been uninhabited several years,' he said. 'It used to be a watch-house from which the coastguards signalled if there was a ship in distress, and the lifeboat went out from here. But now the lifeboat and the coastguards are at the end of the Point.'

'Then who is the lame man I saw walking about there, and heard inside the house?' I asked.

He looked at me, I thought, queerly.

'I don't know who that could be,' he said. 'There's no lame man about here to my knowledge.'

The effect on Jack of the marshes and their gorgeous emptiness, of the sun and the sea, was precisely what I had anticipated. He vowed that any day spent anywhere than on these beaches and fields of sea-lavender was a day wasted, and proposed that the tour, of which the main object had originally been the golf links of Norfolk, should for the present be cancelled. In particular, it was the birds of this long solitary headland that enchanted him.

'After all, we can play golf anywhere,' he said. 'There's an oyster-catcher scolding, do you hear?—and how silly to whack a little white ball—ringed plover, but what's that calling as well?—when you can spend the day like this! Oh! don't let us go and bathe yet: I want to wander along that edge of the marsh—ha! there's a company of turnstones, they make a noise like the drawing of a cork—there they are, those little chaps with chestnut-coloured patches! Let's go along the near edge of the marsh, and come out by the house where your lame man lives.'

We took, therefore, the path with the longer detour, which I had abandoned last night. I had said nothing to him of what the hotel porter had told me that the house was unlived in, and all he knew was that I had seen a lame man, apparently in occupation there. My reason for not doing so (to make the confession at once) was that I already half believed that the steps I had heard inside, and the lame man I had seen watching outside, did not imply in the porter's sense of the word that the house was occupied, and I wanted to see whether Jack as well as myself would be conscious of any such tokens of a presence there. And then the oddest thing happened.

All the way up to the house his attention was alert on the birds, and in especial on a piping note which was unfamiliar to him. In vain he tried to catch sight of the bird that uttered it, and in vain I tried to hear it. 'It doesn't sound like any bird I know,' he said, 'in fact it doesn't sound like a bird at all, but like some human being whistling. There it is again! Is it possible you don't hear it?'

We were now quite close to the house.

'There must be someone there who is whistling,' he said, 'it must be your lame man.... Lord! yes, it comes from inside the house. So that's explained, and I hoped it was some new bird. But why can't you hear it?'

'Some people can't hear a bat's squeak,' said I.

Jack, satisfied with the explanation, took no more interest in the matter, and we struck across the shingle, bathed and lunched, and tramped on to the tumble of sand dunes in which the Point ended. For a couple of hours we strolled and lazed there in the liquid and sunny air, and reluctantly returned in order to cross the ford before the tide came in. As we retraced our way, I saw coming up from the west a huge continent of cloud: and just as we reached the spit of land on which the house stood, a jagged sword of lightning flickered down to the low-lying hills across the estuary, and a few big raindrops plopped on the shingle.

'We're in for a drenching,' he said. 'Ha! Let's ask for shelter at your lame man's house. Better run for it!' Already the big drops were falling thickly, and we scuttled across the hundred yards that lay between us and the house, and came to the door just as the sluices of heaven were pulled wide. He rapped on it, but there came no answer; he tried the handle of it, but the door did not yield, and then, by a sudden inspiration, he felt along the top of the lintel and found a key. It fitted into the wards and next moment we stood within.

We found ourselves in a slip of a passage, at the end of which went up the staircase to the floor above. On each side of it was a room, one a kitchen, the other a living-room, but in neither was there any stick of furniture. Discoloured paper was peeling off the walls, the windows were thick with spidery weavings, the air heavy with unventilated damp.

'Your lame man dispenses with the necessities as well as the luxuries of life,' said Jack. 'A Spartan fellow.'

We were standing in the kitchen: outside the hiss of the rain had grown to a roar, and the bleared window was suddenly lit up with a flare of lightning. A crack of thunder answered it, and in the silence that followed there came from just outside, audible now to me, the sound of a piping whistle. Immediately afterwards I heard the door by which we had just entered violently banged, and I remembered that I had left it open.

His eyes met mine.

'But there's no breath of wind,' I said. 'What made it bang like that?'

'And that was no bird that whistled,' said he.

There was the shuffle in the passage outside of a limping step: I could hear the drag of a man's lame foot along the boards.

'He has come in,' said Jack.

Yes, he had come in, and who had come in? At that moment not fright, but fear, which is a very different matter, closed in on me. Fright, as I understand it, is an emotion, startling, but not unnerving; you may under the finger of fright spring aside, you may scream, you may shout, you have the command of your muscles. But as that limping step moved down the passage I felt fear, the hand of the nightmare that, as it clutches, paralyses and inhibits not action only, but thought. I waited frozen and speechless for what should happen next.

Exactly opposite the open door of the kitchen in which we stood the step stopped. And then, soundlessly and invisibly, the presence that had made itself manifest to the outward ear, entered. Suddenly I heard Jack's breath rattle in his throat.

'O my God!' he cried in a voice hoarse and strangled, and he threw his left arm across his face as if defending himself, and his right arm shooting out, seemed to hit at something which I could not see, and his fingers crooked themselves as if clutching at that which had evaded his blow. His body was bent back as if resisting some invisible pressure, then lunged forward again, and I heard the noise of a resisting joint, and saw on his throat the shadow (or so it seemed) of a clutching hand. At that some power of movement came back to me, and I remember hurling myself at the empty space between him and me, and felt under my grip the shape of a shoulder and heard on the boards of the floor the slip and scoop of a foot. Something invisible, now a shoulder, now an arm, struggled in my grasp, and I heard a panting respiration that was not Jack's, nor mine, and now and then in my face I felt a hot breath that stank of corruption and decay. And all the time this physical contention was symbolical only: what he and I wrestled with was not a thing of flesh and blood, but some awful spiritual presence. And then....

There was nothing. The ghostly invasion ceased as suddenly as it had begun, and there was Jack's face gleaming with sweat close to mine, as we stood with dropped arms opposite each other in an empty room, with the rain beating on the roof and the gutters chuckling. No word passed between us, but next moment we were out in the pelting rain, running for the ford. The deluge was sweet to my soul, it seemed to wash away that horror of great darkness and that odour of corruption in which we had been plunged.

Now I have no certain explanation to give of the experience which has here been shortly recounted, and the reader may or may not connect with it a story that I heard a week or two later on my return to London.

A friend of mine and I had been dining at my house one evening, and we had discussed a murder trial then going on of which the papers were full.

'It isn't only the atrocity that attracts,' he said, 'I think it is the place where the murder occurs that is the cause of the interest in it. A murder at Brighton or Margate or Ramsgate, any place which the public associates with pleasure trips, attracts them because they know the place and can visualise the scene. But when there is a murder at some small unknown spot, which they have never heard of, there is no appeal to their imagination. Last spring, for instance, there was the murder at that small village on the coast of Norfolk. I've forgotten the name of the place, though I was in Norwich at the time of the trial and was present in court. It was one of the most awful stories I ever heard, as ghastly and sensational as this last affair, but it didn't attract the smallest attention. Odd that I can't remember the name of the place when all the rest is so vivid to me!'

'Tell me about it,' I said; 'I never heard of it.'

'Well, there was this little village, and just outside it was a farm, owned by a man called John Beardsley. He lived there with his only daughter, an unmarried woman of about thirty, a good-looking, sensible creature apparently, the last in the world you would have thought to do anything unexpected. There worked at the farm as a day labourer a young fellow called Alfred Maldon, who, in the trial of which I am speaking, was the prisoner. He had one of the most dreadful faces I ever saw, a cat-like receding forehead, a broad, short nose, and a great red sensual mouth, always on the grin. He seemed positively to enjoy being the central figure round whom all the interest of those ghoulish women who thronged the court was concentrated, and when he shambled into the witness-box—'

'Shambled?' I asked.

'Yes, he was lame, his left foot dragged along the floor as he walked. As he shambled into the witness-box he nodded and smiled to the judge, and clapped his counsel on the shoulder, and leered at the gallery.... He worked on the farm, as I was saying, doing jobs that were within his capacity, among which was certain housework, carrying coals and what-not, for John Beardsley, though very well-off, kept no servant, and this daughter Alice—that was her name—ran the house. And what must she do but fall in love, it was no less than that, with this monstrous and misshapen fellow. One afternoon her father came home unexpectedly and caught them together in the parlour, kissing and cuddling. He turned the man out of the house, neck and crop, gave him his week's wages, and dismissed him, threatening him with a fine thrashing if he ever caught him hanging about the place. He forbade his daughter ever to speak to him again, and in order to keep watch over her, got in a woman from the village who would be there all day while he was out on the farm.

'Young Maldon, deprived of his job, tried to get work in the village, but none would employ him, for he was a black-tempered fellow ready to pick a quarrel with anyone, and an unpleasant opponent, for, with all his lameness, he was of immense muscular strength. For some weeks he idled about in the village getting a chance job occasionally and no doubt, as you will see, Alice Beardsley managed to meet him. The village—its name still escapes me—lay on the edge of a big tidal estuary, full at high water, but on the ebb of a broad stretch of marsh and sand and mud-banks, beyond which ran a long belt of shingle that formed the seaward side of the estuary. On it stood a disused coastguard house, a couple of miles away from the village, and in as lonely a place as you would find anywhere in England. At low tide there was a shallow ford across to it, and in the sand-banks round about it some beds of cockle. Maldon, unable to get regular work, took to cockle-digging, and during the summer when the tide was low, Alice (it was no new thing with her) used to go over the ford to the beach beyond and bathe. She would go across the sand-banks where the cockle-diggers, Maldon among them, were at work, and if he whistled as she passed that was the signal between them that he would slip away presently and join her at the disused coastguard house, and there throughout the summer they used to meet.

'As the weeks went on her father saw the change that was coming in her, and suspecting the cause, often left his work and, hidden behind some sea-bank, used to watch her. One day he saw her cross the ford, and soon after she had passed he saw Maldon, recognisable from a long way off by his dragging leg, follow her. He went up the path to the coastguard house, and entered. At that John Beardsley crossed the ford, and hiding in the bushes near the house, saw Alice coming back from her bathe. The house was off the direct path to the ford, but she went round that way, and the door was opened to her, and closed behind her. He found them together, and mad with rage attacked the man. They fought and Maldon got him down and then and there in front of his daughter strangled him.

'The girl went off her head, and is in the asylum at Norwich now. She sits all day by the window whistling. The man was hanged.'

'Was Riddington the name of the village?' I asked.

'Yes. Riddington, of course,' he said. 'I can't think how I forgot it.'

THE SEVENTEENTH HOLE AT DUNCASTER

R. H. Wakefield

Mr. Baxter sauntered out of his office in the Dormy House at Duncaster Golf Club, just as the sun was setting one perfect evening late in September 192-, his meagre labours finished for the day. He gazed idly around him over one of the finest stretches of golfing country in the world. Duncaster is a remote hamlet on the Norfolk coast and, being twelve miles from a railway station, would have remained delicately secluded if some roaming enthusiast in the late 90's had not felt his heart seize by so fair, so promising, so Royal and Ancient a prospect, and rallied his golfing acquaintance to found the Duncaster Golf Club, with a small and select membership, and small and select it had remained. Almost deserted for most of the year, it was thickly sprinkled in August, and there was always a pleasant gathering of old friends at the Spring and Autumn meetings. Mr. Baxter, the popular and efficient secretary, was a portly little person, kindly, considerate, but not very happy. He let his eye roam placidly just over the superb sand dune country bordering the North Sea, where gleaming alley-ways of perfect turf burrowed their way through the golden ramparts above them, sweet isolated pathways ending in the World's Finest Greens – so the members considered – where little red flags gleamed, waving gently in a dying evening breeze; then his eyes wandered inland and became for a moment sharply intent as they reached the 17th green, the new 17th placed on a plateau in the big wood, the long shadows cast by the sleepy sun peeping through the trees, playing across it.

Mr. Baxter was in a slightly depressed and introspective mood. Golf secretaries, he decided, were born and not made, and born under no felicitous star.

There was he, a student and a philosopher by taste and temperament, condemned to oversee for a slender, remuneration the tiny activities of a blasted Golf Club. He had drifted into this blind alley as he had always drifted; it was all due, he supposed, to the fact that one of his glands functioned inadequately.

Yes, golf secretaries were only explicable on some such derogatory hypothesis. This 17th green, for example, because it was the only alteration made since the opening of the links, what a 'Yes and No,' what a discordant clamour of debate, what a fuss about almost nothing! Of course it was an improvement; by hacking a fairway through the wood and making the green on that ideal little plateau a bad 270-yarder had been changed into a very fine two-shotter – the best, though not the most pleasing hole, for the dunes made the real charm of the course. And yet – the student and philosopher rebelled.

He strolled across to the Pro.'s shop, whose tenant was standing in the doorway smoking a pipe, and gazing reflectively in front of him.

'Evening, Dakers,' said Mr. Baxter, 'I thought I saw someone on the seventeenth a little while ago. Is anyone still out?'

The Pro. took his pipe out of his mouth. His face did not command a wide range of expression, but for a moment a look of a certain sharpness and subtlety flitted across it.

'No, sir, everyone's in. Mr. and Mrs Stannard finished a quarter of an hour ago; they were the last.'

'That's funny,' said Mr. Baxter, 'I could have sworn I saw someone.'

The Pro. paused a moment, as if carefully choosing his reply. 'I think, sir, it's the shadows. I've fancied the same thing.'

'Well, what do you think of it?' asked the secretary.

'I'm sure it's a very fine hole, sir, but it's too good for me. I've played it seven times now, and done five fives and two sixes. It's funny, too, because it's just my length – a drive and push iron with the ground as hard as this, yet I haven't found the green with my second shot once. The ball seems to leave the club all right, and then – well, it's something I've never known happen before.'

'I hope it's going to be a success, for it's been enough bother and expense,' said Mr. Baxter.

The Pro. did not answer for a moment. He put his pipe back in his mouth and looked away over to the subject of discussion. At length he asked, 'Did they ever discover what the contractor's men died of, sir?'

'Not for certain,' replied the secretary, 'blood-poisoning of some kind – a very unfortunate affair'

'The other chaps thought it had something to do with those skulls and bones they dug up. They got talking to the villagers, who put the wind up them a bit, I'm thinking.'

'How was that?' asked Mr. Baxter.

'It's some sort of talk about the wood, it seems,' replied Dakers.

Mr. Baxter was interested. 'I should like to hear more about this,' he said, 'but I have no time now. I'll see you tomorrow.'

The next day, the Saturday before the opening of the Autumn meeting, Mr. Baxter played an afternoon round with Colonel Senlis. It was for both of them their first introduction to the new 17th. The Colonel had taken up the game after he retired, and he served it with an even more fanatical devotion than he had served his King. He was a jolly old maniac with a handicap of 16 and a style of his own.

Mr. Baxter might have been a very fine player; he had balance, rhythm, and a beautiful pair of hands, but his heart had never been in it, and he was content to be a perfectly reliable 2.

No incident of any moment occurred during the first sixteen holes. The Colonel collected much fine sand in various portions of his attire; Mr. Baxter played sound but listless golf. When they reached the seventeenth tee the wind, which had been wandering vaguely and gustily round the compass, suddenly settled down to blow half a gale from due east, and the seventeenth became a tiger indeed. Mr. Baxter, after a couple of nice blows dead into the wind, lay some twenty yards short of the wood, which was beginning to shout wildly in the gale. The Colonel was in the rough on the right, an alliterative position he usually occupied. He played his fourth – one of the few properly struck golf shots of his existence – dead on the pin. The secretary took his number three iron, and knew from the moment the ball left the club that he didn't want it back. It was ruled on the flag.

As the Colonel came up, a look of swelling pride on his rubicund visage, he remarked, 'Did you see mine, Baxter? Never say again I can't play a spoon shot! You hit yours, too, didn't you?'

'Yes' answered the secretary, smiling. 'I'm inside you by a yard or two, I fancy.'

'I don't,' said the Colonel. 'You'll be playing the odd stroke gone, all right.' They walked together along the avenue of lurching Scotch firs and larches, and climbed the bank of the plateau.

'My God!' cried the Colonel. 'We're neither of us on! Where the Hades are they?'

An exasperating search followed, which ended when the Colonel found his Dunlop No. 1 dozing behind a tree, and Mr. Baxter detected his No. 2 in a rabbit hole. The Colonel made robust use of an expletive much favoured by the gallant men he had once had the honour of commanding. Mr. Baxter quietly picked up his errant globe and walked off to the last tee.

'Damn it, Baxter!' cried the Colonel, 'that hole meant to fight me. I felt it all the time.'

The secretary had played many holes with the Colonel on many different courses, but had never noticed any of them displaying any Locarno spirit towards or desire to fraternize with him, but all the same he had voiced his own thoughts. It had been a ludicrous incident, but its humour did not appeal to him particularly. Both those shots should have been by the pin. Just what the Pro. had said. It was very curious. 'I'm going to hate that hole,' he thought.

'There's a damned funny mark on my ball,' grumbled the Colonel. 'I suppose it hit a tree, though I could swear it didn't. Looks more like a burn. Why, there's the same thing on yours!'

Mr. Baxter examined them. They were funny symmetrical

little marks, and they were remarkably like burns. 'The wind must have caught them and blown them into the trees,' he said, unconvincingly. 'It's rather a gloomy spot in there, and it's hard to follow the flight exactly.'

After tea the secretary went round to see Dakers.

'Well,' he said, 'I've tried the new hole.'

'I saw you out, sir,' said the Pro., smiling. 'Did you get your four?'

'I almost deserved it,' said Mr. Baxter. 'My third was played like a golfer, and lined on the pin. I found it in a rabbit hole underneath the left bank.'

'That's what I told you, sir. It's that sort of hole. I shall be interested to see how the members like it next week. In this wind it's certainly some hole.'

'You mentioned last night something about talk in the village,' insinuated Mr. Baxter. 'What kind of talk?'

'Well, sir, there's been quite a clack, still is, for that matter; they're a funny, old-fashioned lot, with funny ideas. Do you know, sir, they won't go into that wood after dusk!'

'Why on earth not?'

'They don't seem to think it's healthy somehow; they call it 'Blood Wood,' some old superstition or other. I think some of them were a bit ashamed of feeling that way till the contractor's men died; but that started them off again.'

'It's a pretty vague sort of yarn,' said the secretary musingly. 'Do they go into detail at all?'

'No, sir, it's a village tradition of very old standing, I should say. They are scared of the wood. Old Jim the Cobbler's father was found dead, apparently murdered, in it, and there are other tales of the old times like that.'

Sunday was a busy day for Mr. Baxter. The Dormy House filled up steadily, and by the evening the highly satisfactory total of forty-four, mostly hale and slightly too hearty, elderly gentlemen had assembled.

The Autumn meeting opened in a full easterly gale, and it was a battered and weary collection of competitors who arrived back at the club house. Mr. Baxter, greeting them as they came in, found them on one subject unanimously eloquent. They one and all cherished loathing mingled with respect for the new seventeenth. The secretary examined their cards with curiosity. Only one five was recorded, the average was eight. When young Cyril Ward, the only scratch player in the club, came in, the secretary asked him how he had fared. 'My ancient friend,' he replied, 'I accomplished seventeen holes in seventy-two strokes; good going in this wind; my total is eighty. I give you one guess as to the other hole.'

'Oh, the seventeenth, I suppose.'

'You've said it. Baxter, there's something funny about it. I hit two perfect shots and then took six more to hole out.'

'I'm sure of it,' said the secretary, 'but I'm getting most remarkably sick of hearing about it.'

After the second round of the thirty-six holes stroke competition Mr. Baxter found himself the centre of one of the fiercest indignation meetings in the history of the golf game. Everyone had something to say.

Eventually he was forced to promise that, if at the end of the week they were still of the same opinion, he would have the old seventeenth restored. 'But,' said he, 'all this chopping and changing will cost us a lot of money.'

'More likely save us a bit,' grumbled a protestant.

'I lost three new balls there today. Have you noticed what a stench there was coming from the back of the green?'

Cyril Ward went for a stroll with Mr. Baxter when the debate was over. 'I wish the old boys weren't so impatient,' he said. 'That hole has beaten me badly twice, but I'd like to have many more shots at it. I shall protest strongly if they decide to change back. Look at it now, the green's like a pool of blood!'

('A sinister but apt description,' thought Mr. Baxter.)

The sun was setting in a wild and tortured sky, and its fiery dying rays certainly painted the seventeenth a sanguine hue.

'It's funny you should say that' he remarked. 'It's called 'Blood Wood' by the locals.'

'From what I heard of the expletives used by our worthy fellow foozlers, they certainly agree with them,' laughed Ward.

That night Mr. Baxter had a short but disturbing dream. He seemed to hear a deep bell tolling sullenly, and then suddenly a voice cried, 'Sacred to the memory of Cyril Ward, who screamed once in Blood Wood,' and then came a discordant chorus of vile and bestial laughter, and he awoke feeling depressed and ill at ease.

'This absurd business is getting on my nerves,' he thought, 'I'm even dreaming about it,' and he suddenly felt he wanted to leave Duncaster, and the sooner the better. It was too lonely and idle a life, he decided.

The next day the gale continued, bringing torrents of rain with it, and there was no competition. The course was a melancholy and deserted waste. Mr. Baxter, as he worked in his office, could hear the great breakers booming beyond the Dunes. About six the rain dwindled into a light drizzle, and Cyril Ward came in to see him, a couple of clubs under his arm. 'There's just enough light to let me defeat that blasted hole,' he said; 'the swine fascinates me!'

Mr. Baxter found himself rather vehemently trying to persuade him otherwise. 'I shouldn't; it's still raining, and it will be almost dark in the wood.'

'Oh, rot,' said Ward, and presently the secretary saw him tee up and drive off. He watched him until he had almost reached the wood, and then someone called him to settle a point of bridge law. The windows of the smoking-room were open, and the gale suddenly increased in fury.

Mr. Baxter had just given his decision when there came a long scream of agony shaking down the wind.

He rushed to the door, the other occupants of the room hustling after him.

That terrible cry had come from the wood, and they began running towards it. Suddenly, just visible in the gloom, a figure came staggering out from the wood, threw up its arms, and fell. Mr. Baxter dashed towards it as he had not run for twenty years, the others after him.

Cyril Ward was lying on his back, his eyes wide, staring, and horrible – obviously dead.

Amongst those who came up was the local doctor, who knelt down and made a short examination'

'Must be heart. I believe he had a weakness there, poor Cyril!' Mr. Baxter helped to carry the-body tack to the Dormy House; his burden was Cyril's left leg, a disgusting dangling thing. The memory of his dream came back to him, and his nerves shook.

He tried to find reassurance by telling himself that such premonitions were common enough, however inexplicable.

It was decided at an informal meeting that the links should be closed the next day out of respect for the dead, but that the foursomes should be held on the Thursday. 'A very typically British compromise,' thought Mr. Baxter.

'Will an inquest be necessary?' he asked the doctor.

'I think not; it's clearly a case of heart.'

'Did you notice his eyes?' asked the secretary.

The doctor gave him a quick glance. 'I did, he replied, 'but these attacks are often very painful. But did you notice that appalling stink coming from the wood?'

'Yes,' said the secretary, shortly.

'Well, I should find out the cause, it can't be healthy.'

'I will tomorrow,' said Mr. Baxter.

The next day he spent in his office, and never before had a sense of the futility of his occupation so swept over him. This shifting of pieces of India-rubber from one spot to another! Oh, that a man should have to spend his few and gloriously potential days fussing about such banality! Perhaps he was only pitying himself. He went back to his card-marking.

He felt utterly weary when he went to bed, and fell immediately asleep. Boom! Boom! Boom!, there came that terrible tolling. He must wake! He must not hear what was to come. 'Sacred to the memory of Sybil Grant, who screamed twice in Blood Wood,' and once again came that foul and wicked laughter.

He awoke sweating and unnerved. He got up and mixed himself the strongest whisky and soda of his temperate existence.

'Sybil Grant! Sybil Grant! '

Thank God, he knew no one of that name! He tried to read, till light came.

He went down to the club house after breakfast, and met the doctor. 'Hullo,' said the latter, 'you're not looking very fit! What's the matter?'

'Oh, just a rotten night,' said the secretary. 'By the way, I sent the green-keeper to find out about that smell, but he couldn't discover any cause for it; and, as a matter of fact, says he couldn't smell anything.'

'Well, he's a lucky man,' said the doctor. 'It was the most loathsome reek I've encountered, and I've met a few!'

After the foursomes had started, everyone desperately light-hearted and pathetically determined to allow no echo of the horror of a few hours before to disturb the atmosphere of laboured cheerfulness, Mr. Baxter felt he must be alone. He wandered off to the long No Man's Land between the dunes and the sea, a famous haunt of sea birds; the sand showed everywhere the delicate tracings of their soft little feet.

As he reached the darker strata just surrendered by the angry, fading tide, his eye was caught by a patch of scarlet moving down to the sea some distance to his left. 'A girl going to bathe,' he thought casually. 'She must have warm blood in her to face such a sea on such a day. I hope she knows what she's about. It's none too safe a spot.' Presently he saw a man run down to join her, and felt reassured and yet depressed. 'To be a dingy old bachelor like myself is the one unanswerable indictment. Ten King's Councillors could not make it seem excusable.'

Then his mind turned to the question of the new post he was determined to secure. He would go up to London as soon as the meeting was over and get an exchange if possible.

His work kept him busy all the afternoon, and he did not emerge from his office till dusk was falling.

'Best figure in England,' he heard the Colonel declaring, as he entered the smoking-room. 'I believe she's engaged to Bob Renton.'

'Who's that?' asked the secretary.

'The Grant girl,' said the Colonel, 'Sybil Grant.'

The secretary felt a tug of horror at his heart.

'Is she coming down here?' he asked sharply.

'She is here,' replied the Colonel. 'If you'd been here ten minutes ago you'd have seen her.'

'Well, where is she now?' asked the secretary, seizing his arm.

'Where is this girl?' he cried, his voice rising.

'Hullo, young feller, what's all the excitement? I imagine she's about at the seventeenth green; she's staying with the Bartletts at the Old Cottage, and is walking back that way.'

At that moment a bell seemed to toll once shatteringly in the secretary's ears. He put his hands to his head, and without a word started running frantically down the seventeenth fairway. Suddenly there sprang down the wind a terrible cry of terror, followed by a desperate and prolonged scream. Mr. Baxter stopped dead and shuddered. He heard shouts behind him and the patter of others running.

He tottered on. Somebody – several people – passed him; as he reeled into the wood he could see the firefly gleam of electric torches, and as he neared them he could see they were focussed on some object on the ground. It was white, and someone was kneeling over it. When he saw what it was he was suddenly and violently sick. It was flung down the bank, it was naked, its head was lolling hideously. It was sprawling, one knee flung high, its face – but someone covered that face with his coat and told Mr. Baxter to go for the doctor. And that terrible Death stench kept him company.

The inquest was fixed for the following Monday, and Mr. Baxter was told that his testimony would be required.

The little village swarmed with police and reporters. There hadn't been a mystery of such possibilities for many moons, and the whole country was stirred.

Murder so foul cried out for vengeance. But there was no arrest, 'And there never will be' thought Mr. Baxter as he took his stand in the improvised witness-box in the village school. The Coroner, a corpulent, hirsute and pompous person, soon put to him the question he had anticipated. 'I understand that you started to run towards the scene of the tragedy before these screams were heard: is that so?'

'Yes,' replied the secretary.

'Why was that?'

And then Mr. Baxter uncontrollably laughed'

'I may be mistaken,' said the Coroner, 'but this hardly seems a laughing matter…'

'I must beg your pardon,' said Mr Baxter. 'I laughed against my will. I laughed because I suddenly realized how absurd you would consider my explanation to be.'

'That is quite possible,' said the Coroner, 'but I must ask you to let me hear it.'

'I had a premonition, a dream.'

'Of what character?'

'Well, I dreamed that Miss Grant would be killed.'

'Did you warn her?'

'I had never heard of her except in this dream. I did not know she was here till I was so informed a moment before these screams were heard.'

'A curious story,' replied the representative of Law and Order, who clearly regarded Mr. Baxter as a person of limited intelligence and dubious veracity.

'Murder by some person or persons unknown' was the verdict, and unknown he, she or they remained.

The nine days ran their course, police and reporters departed, and Mr. Baxter went off to London, where he secured a job at a new course in Surrey.

He was to have no successor at Duncaster. Resignations poured in, and it was decided at a final meeting of the committee that the links should be abandoned.

On arriving in London, it occurred to Mr. Baxter to call upon a friend of his, a Mr. Markes. He very much wanted an expert confidant, and Mr. Markes, besides being very wealthy, was by some trick of temperament fascinated by all types of psychic phenomena, and had amassed the finest library on such matters in the world.

'Jim,' asked the secretary, 'is there any mention of Duncaster in your records?'

'When I read about your troubles there,' replied Mr. Markes, 'I thought they sounded rather in the tradition, and so I looked up the history of Duncaster and was unexpectedly fortunate; for it is mentioned in a work, which, for the most part, is deservedly forgotten. The Memoirs of Simon Tylor, a peculiarly dull dog. I have them here,' he continued, walking over to a shelf and taking down a bulky volume.

'In the year 1839 Simon took a walking tour through Norfolk and arrived at Duncaster on September 10th. He liked the look of it, and decided to spend a couple of days there at the inn, "The Sleeping Sentinel".'

'It is there still,' said Mr. Baxter.

'All this,' went on Mr. Markes, 'is described at vast and damnable length, but his adventure, which occurred on the second evening of his stay, is much more crisply done. I will read it to you:

"I spent a pleasing and invigorating morning wandering over the wild expanse of moor and 'dunes' as they call the great sand mounds; and afterwards dined, rested and had some talk with my good host of the inn. Late in the afternoon I decided to make further exploration of the neighbourhood, and, noticing a fine wood of tall trees some distance away across the moor, I remarked to my host that I proposed to visit it. Greatly to my surprise he strongly opposed my doing so, but when I asked him for what reason, he returned me evasive replies – 'No one wanders there after nightfall,' he said. 'It has a bad repute.'

"On account of robbers?' I asked. And though he replied with a short laugh that that was so, I did not believe it was the thought in his mind. To satisfy him, I declared I would but walk towards it, a promise I had better have kept.

"So I wandered out as the light was fading, and drew near to the wood. Then I put it to myself that such village gossip was in most cases but idle tradition inscribed in the long and sparsely furnished memories of country folk. And this decision prevailing, I entered the wood, following a rough pathway. And then I had reason to doubt my hosts word, for instead of it being shunned by the local folk it seemed that the wood did house quite a company. The light being low and the trees growing close, I failed clearly to distinguish my companions, but only, as it were, out of the corner of my eye, I glimpsed them many times. 'Lovers', thought I. After I had traversed some two hundred paces I noted some little way in front of me a low mound with a single fine tree at its back. I was just fancying that I would go so far and then return when a movement in the gloom caught my eye, and at the same instant I perceived a very vile and curious stench. Something seemed to be reclining on the mound, a beast of some sort, and slowly gaining its feet. And then I knew the beginning of fear. This thing seemed to rise and rise till it towered above the tree, and then it couched its head as for a spring. I have no wish to see its like again. Seized with a great loathing and horror, I ran back along the path, and as I ran it seemed that many were running beside me and closing in upon me. I felt the Thing was close beside me, but I dared not turn to look. Just as my breath was leaving me I found myself at the edge of the wood, and then something seemed to touch me, and I screamed and swooned.

"When I regained my senses I found I was prone on the ground and my host and some others were standing round me conversing in low tones. They helped me back to the inn, no one saying a word. I left early the next morning, that stench still lingering in my nostrils and the host seeming to avoid talk with me. All this is the truth as I have set it down."

'And that's what happened to Simon,' said Markes.

'A curious story,' said Mr. Baxter.

'Far more curious than uncommon. I could find you a dozen almost identical experiences. Almost certainly the work of our friends the Druids, whoever they were! A mound and an oak – such places are death-traps. Not all the time; the peril is periodic, why, we don't know. But our friend Simon was very lucky to be able to leave 'early next morning,' though he didn't escape altogether. The rest of his book reads like a coda to this adventure. Bad dreams, depression and always that smell in his nose. He died within a year or two. And now tell me exactly what happened at Duncaster, for I gather it is still a disturbed area.'

So Mr. Baxter told him the curious events connected with the new seventeenth.

THE FACE

E. F. Benson

Hester Ward, sitting by the open window on this hot afternoon in June, began seriously to argue with herself about the cloud of foreboding and depression which had encompassed her all day and, very sensibly, she enumerated to herself the manifold causes for happiness in the fortunate circumstances of her life. She was young, she was extremely good-looking, she was well-off, she enjoyed excellent health, and above all, she had an adorable husband and two small adorable children. There was no break, indeed, anywhere in the circle of prosperity which surrounded her, and had the wishing-cap been handed to her that moment by some beneficent fairy, she would have hesitated to put it on her head, for there was positively nothing that she can think of which would have been worthy such solemnity. Moreover, she could not accuse herself of a want of appreciation of her blessings; she appreciated enormously, she enjoyed enormously, and she thoroughly wanted all those who so munificently contributed to her happiness to share in it.

She made a very deliberately review of these things, for she was really anxious, more anxious, indeed, than she admitted to herself, to find anything tangible which could possibly warrant this ominous feeling of approaching disaster. Then, there was the weather to consider; for the last week London has been stiflingly hot, but if that was the cause, why had she not felt it before? Perhaps the effect of these broiling, airless days had been cumulative. That was an idea, but frankly, it did not seem a very good one, for as a matter of fact she loved the heat. Dick, who hated it, said that it was odd he should have fallen in love with a salamander.

She shifted her position, sitting up straight in this low window seat, for she was intending to make a call on her courage. She had known from the moment she awoke this morning what was that lay so heavy on her, and now, having done her best to shift the reason of her depression on to anything else, and having completely failed, she meant to look the thing in the face. She was ashamed of doing so, for the cause of this leaden mood of fear which held her in its grip was so trivial, so fantastic, so excessively silly.

'Yes, there was never anything so silly,' she said to herself. 'I must look at it straight, and convince myself how silly it is.' She paused a moment, clenching her hands.

'Now for it,' she said.

She had had a dream the previous night, which, years ago, used to be familiar to her, for again and again when she was a child she had dreamed it. In itself the dream was nothing, but in those childish days whenever she had this dream which had visited her last night, it was followed on the next night by another, which contained the source and the core of horror and she would awaken screaming and struggling in the grip of over-whelming nightmare. For some ten years now she had not experienced it, and would have said that, though she remembered it, it had become dim and distant to her. But last night she had had that warning dream which used to herald the visitation of the nightmare, and now the whole storehouse of memory, crammed as it was with bright things and beautiful, contained nothing so vivid.

The warning dream, the curtain that was drawn up on the succeeding night, and disclosed the vision she dreaded, was simple and harmless enough in itself. She seemed to be walking on a high sandy cliff covered with short down-grass; twenty yards to the left came the edge of this cliff, which sloped steeply down to the sea that lay at its foot. The past she followed led through fields bounced by low hedges, and mounted gradually upwards. She vent through some half-dozen of these, climbing over the wooden stiles that gave communication; sheep grazed there, but she never saw another human being, and always it was dusk, as if evening was falling, and she had to hurry on, because someone (she knew not whom) was waiting for her, and had been waiting not a few minutes only, but for many years. Presently, as she mounted this slope, she saw in front of her a copse of stunted trees, growing crookedly under the continual pressure of the wind that blew from the sea, and when she saw those she knew her journey was nearly done, and that the nameless one, who had been waiting for her so long, was somewhat close at hand. The path she followed was cut through the wood, and the slanting boughs of the trees on the seaward side almost roofed it in; it was like walking through a tunnel. Soon the trees in front began to grow thin, and she saw through them the gray tower of a lonely church. It stood in a graveyard, apparently long disused , and the body of the church, which lay between the tower and the edge of the cliff, was in ruins, roofless, and with gaping windows around which ivy grew thickly.

At this point this prefatory dream always stopped. It was a troubled, uneasy dream for there was over it the sense of dusk and of the man who had been waiting for her so long, but it was not the order of the nightmare. Many times in childhood she had experienced it, and perhaps it was the subconscious knowledge of the night that so surely followed it which gave it its disquiet.

And now last night it had come again, identical in every particular but one. For last night it seems to her that in the course of these ten years which had intervened since last it had visited her the glimpse of the church and the churchyard had changed. The edge of the cliff had come nearer to the tower, so that it now was within a yard or two of it, and the ruined body of the church, but for one broken arch that remained, had vanished. The sea had encroached, and for ten years had been busily eating at the cliff.

Hester knew well that it was this dream and this alone which had darkened her day for her, by reason of the nightmares that used to follow it, and like a sensible woman, having looked it once in the face, she refused to admit into her mind any conscious calling-up of the sequel. If she let herself contemplate that, as likely or not the very thinking about it would be sufficient to ensure its return, and of one thing she was very certain, namely, that she didn't at all want it to do so. It was not like the confused jumble and jangle of ordinary nightmare, it was very simple, and she felt it concerned the nameless one waiting for her.

But she must not think of it; her whole will and intention was set on not thinking of it, and to aid her resolution there was a rattle of Dick's latchkey in the front door, and his voice calling her.

She went out into the little square front hall; there he was, strong and large, and wonderfully undreamlike.

'This heat's a scandal, it's an outrage, it is an abomination of desolation', he cried, vigorously mopping. 'What have we done that Providence should place us in this frying pan? Let us thward him, Hester! Let us drive out of this inferno and have our dinner at – I'll whisper it so that he can't overhear– at Hampton Court!'

She laughed: this plan suited her excellently. They would return late, after the distraction of a fresh scene; and dining out at night was both delicious and stupefying.

'The very thing', she cried, and I'm sure Providence didn't hear. Let's start now!'

'Rather. Any letters for me?'

He walked to the table where there were a few rather uninteresting-looking envelopes with half-penny stamps.

'Ah, receipted bill', he said. 'Just a reminder of one's folly in paying it. Circular...unasked advice to invest in German marks... Circular begging letter, beginning 'Dear Sir or Madame.' Such impertinence to ask one to subscribe to something without ascertaining one's sex.. private view, portraits at the Walton Gallery. Can't go, business meetings all day. You might like to have a look in it, Hester. Someone told me there were some fine Vandycks. That's all: let's be off.'

Hester spent a thoroughly reassuring evening, and though she thought of telling Dick about the dream that had so deeply imprinted itself on her consciousness all day, in being such a goose, she refrained in doing so, since nothing that he could say would be so tonic to these fantastic fears as his general robustness. Besides, she would have to account for its disturbing effect, tell him that it was once familiar to her, and recount the sequel of the nightmares that followed. She would neither think of them, nor mention them: it was wiser by far just to soak herself in his extraordinary sanity, and wrap herself in his affection…

They dined out-of-doors at a riverside restaurant and strolled about afterwards, and it was very nearly midnight when, soothed with coolness and fresh air, and the vigour of his strong companionship, she let herself into the house, while he took the car back to the garage. And now she marvelled at the mood which had beset her all day, so distant and unreal had it become. She felt as if she had dreamed of shipwreck, and had awoke to find herself in some secure and sheltered garden where no tempest raged nor waves beat. But was there, ever so remotely, ever so dimly, the noise of far-off breakers somewhere?

He slept in the dressing-room which communicated with her bedroom, the door of which was left open for the sake of air and coolness, and she fell asleep almost as soon as her light was out, and while his was still burning. And immediately she began to dream.

She was standing on the sea-shore; the tide was out, for level sands strewn with stranded jetsam glimmered in a dusk that was deepening into night. Though she had never seen the place it was awfully familiar to her. At the head of the beach there was a steep cliff of sand, and perched on the edge of it was a grey church tower. The sea must have encroached and undermined the body of the church, for tumbled blocks of masonry lay close to her at the bottom of the cliff, and there were gravestones there, while others still in place were silhouetted whitely against the sky. To the right of the church tower there was a wood of stunted trees, combed sideways by the prevalent sea-wind, and she knew that along the top of the cliff a few yards inland there lay a path through fields, with wooden stiles to climb, which led through a tunnel of trees and so out into the churchyard. All this she saw in a glance, and waited, looking at the sand-cliff crowned by the church tower, for the terror that was going to reveal itself. Already she knew what it was, and, as so many times before, she tried to run away. But the catalepsy of nightmare was already on her; frantically she strove to move, but her utmost endeavour could not raise a foot from the sand. Frantically she tried to look away from the sand-cliffs close in front of her, where in a moment now the horror would be manifested. . . .

It came. There formed a pale oval light, the size of a man's face, dimly luminous in front of her and a few inches above the level of her eyes. It outlined itself, short reddish hair grew low on the forehead, below were two grey eyes, set very close together, which steadily and fixedly regarded her. On each side the ears stood noticeably away from the head, and the lines of the jaw met in a short pointed chin. The nose was straight and rather long, below it came a hairless lip, and last of all the mouth took shape and colour, and there lay the crowning terror. One side of it, soft-curved and beautiful, trembled into a smile, the other side, thick and gathered together as by some physical deformity, sneered and lusted.

The whole face, dim at first, gradually focused itself into clear outline: it was pale and rather lean, the face of a young man. And then the lower lip dropped a little, showing the glint of teeth, and there was the sound of speech. 'I shall soon come for you now,' it said, and on the words it drew a little nearer to her, and the smile broadened. At that the full hot blast of nightmare poured in upon her. Again she tried to run, again she tried to scream, and now she could feel the breath of that terrible mouth upon her. Then with a crash and a rending like the tearing asunder of soul and body she broke the spell, and heard her own voice yelling, and felt with her fingers for the switch of her light. And then she saw that the room was not dark, for Dick's door was open, and the next moment, not yet undressed, he was with her.

'My darling, what is it?' he said. 'What's the matter?'

She clung desperately to him, still distraught with terror.

'Ah, he has been here again,' she cried. 'He says he will soon come to me. Keep him away,

Dick.'

For one moment her fear infected him, and he found himself glancing round the room.

'But what do you mean?' he said. 'No one has been here.'

She raised her head from his shoulder.

'No, is was just a dream,' she said. 'But it was the old dream, and I was terrified. Why, you've not undressed yet. What time is it?'

'You haven't been in bed ten minutes, dear,' he said.

'You had hardly put out your light when I heard you screaming.'

She shuddered.

'Ah, it's awful.' she said. 'And he will come again. . . .

He sat down by her.

'Now tell me all about it,' he said.

She shook her head.

'No, it will never do to talk about it,' she said, 'it will only, make it more real. I suppose the children are all right, are they?'

'Of course they are. I looked in on my way upstairs.'

'That's good. But I'm better now, Dick. A dream hasn't anything real about it, has it? It doesn't mean anything?'

He was quite reassuring on this point, and soon she quieted down. Before he went to bed he looked in again on her, and she was asleep.

Hester had a stern interview with herself when Dick had gone down to his office next morning. She told herself that what she was afraid of was nothing more than her own fear. How many times had that ill-omened face come to her in dreams, and what significance had it ever proved to possess? Absolutely none at all, except to make her afraid. She was afraid where no fear was: she was guarded, sheltered, prosperous, and what if a nightmare of childhood returned? It had no more meaning now than it had then, and all those visitations of her childhood had passed away without trace. . . . And then, despite herself, she began thinking over that vision again. It was grimly identical with all its previous occurrences, except . . . And then, with a sudden shrinking of the heart, she remembered that in earlier years those terrible lips had said: 'I shall come for you when you are older,' and last night they had said: 'I shall soon come for you now.' She remembered, too, that in the warning dream the sea had encroached, and it had now demolished the body of the church. There was an awful consistency about these two changes in the otherwise identical visions. The years had brought their change to them, for in the one the encroaching sea had brought down the body of the church, in the other the time was now near…

It was no use to scold or reprimand herself, for to bring her mind to the contemplation of the vision meant merely that the grip of terror closed on her again; it was far wiser to occupy herself, and starve her fear out by refusing to bring it the sustenance of thought. So she went about her household duties, she took the children out for their airing in the park, and then, determined to leave no moment unoccupied, set off with the card of invitation to see the pictures in the private view at the Walton Gallery. After that her day was full enough, she was lunching out, and going on to a matinee, and by the time she got home

Dick would have returned, and they would drive down to his little house at Rye for the week-end. All Saturday and Sunday she would be playing golf, and she felt that fresh air and physical fatigue would exorcise the dread of these dreaming fantasies.

The gallery was crowded when she got there; there were friends among the sightseers, and the inspection of the pictures was diversified by cheerful conversation. There were two or three fine Raeburns, a couple of Sir Joshuas, but the gems, so she gathered, were three Vandycks that hung in a small room by themselves. Presently she strolled in there, looking at her catalogue. The first of them, she saw, was a portrait of Sir Roger

Wybum. Still chatting to her friend she raised her eye and saw it...

Her heart hammered in her throat, and then seemed to stand still altogether. A qualm, as of some mental sickness of the soul overcame her, for there in front of her was he who would soon come for her. There was the reddish hair, the projecting ears, the greedy eyes set close together, and the mouth smiling on one side, and on the other gathered up into the sneering menace that she knew so well. It might have been her own nightmare rather than a living model which had sat to the painter for that face.

'Ah, what a portrait, and what a brute!' said her companion. 'Look, Hester, isn't that marvellous?'

She recovered herself with an effort To give way to this ever-mastering dread would have been to allow nightmare to invade her waking life, and there, for sure, madness lay. She forced herself to look at it again, but there were the steady and eager eyes regarding her; she could almost fancy the mouth began to move. All round her the crowd bustled and chattered, but to her own sense she was alone there with Roger Wyburn.

And yet, so she reasoned with herself, this picture of him—for it was he and no other —should have reassured her. Roger Wyburn, to have been painted by Vandyck, must have been dead near on two hundred years; how could he be a menace to her? Had she seen that portrait by some chance as a child; had it made some dreadful impression on her, since overscored by other memories, but still alive in the mysterious subconsciousness, which flows eternally, like some dark underground river, beneath the surface of human life? Psychologists taught that these early impressions fester or poison the mind like some hidden abscess. That might account for this dread of one, nameless no longer, who waited for her.

That night down at Rye there came again to her the prefatory dream, followed by the nightmare, and clinging to her husband as the terror began to subside, she told him what she had resolved to keep to herself. Just to tell it brought a measure of comfort, for it was so outrageously fantastic, and his robust common sense upheld her. But when on their return to London there was a recurrence of these visions, he made short work of her demur and took her straight to her doctor.

'Tell him all, darling,' he said. 'Unless you promise to do that, I will. I can't have you worried like this. It's all nonsense, you know, and doctors are wonderful people for curing nonsense.'

She turned to him.

'Dick, you're frightened,' she said quietly.

He laughed.

'I'm nothing of the kind,' he said, 'but I don't like being awakened by your screaming. Not my idea of a peaceful night. Here we are.'

The medical report was decisive and peremptory. There was nothing whatever to be alarmed about; in brain and body she was perfectly healthy, but she was run down. These disturbing dreams were, as likely as not, an effect, a symptom of her condition, rather than the cause of it, and Dr. Baring unhesitatingly recommended a complete change to some bracing place. The wise thing would be to send her out of this stuffy furnace to some quiet place to where she had never been. Complete change; quite so. For the same reason her husband had better not go with her; he must pack her off to, let us say, the East coast. Sea-air and coolness and complete idleness. No long walks; no long bathings; a dip, and a deck-chair on the sands. A lazy, soporific life. How about Rushton? He had no doubt that Rushton would set her up again. After a week or so, perhaps, her husband might go down and see her. Plenty of sleep – never mind the nightmares – plenty of fresh air.

Hester, rather to her husband's surprise, fell in with this suggestion at once, and the following evening saw her installed in solitude and tranquility. The little hotel was still almost empty, for the rush of summer tourists had not yet begun, and all day she sat out on the beach with the sense of a struggle over. She need not fight the terror any more; dimly it seemed to her that its malignancy had been relaxed. Had she in some way yielded to it and done its secret bidding? At any rate no return of its nightly visitations had occurred, and she slept long and dreamlessly, and woke to another day of quiet.

Every morning there was a line for her from Dick, with good news of himself and the children, but he and they alike seemed somehow remote, like memories of a very distant time. Something had driven in between her and them, and she saw them as if through glass. But equally did the memory of the face of Roger Wyburn, as seen on the master's canvas or hanging close in front of her against the crumbling sand-cliff, become blurred and indistinct, and no return of her nightly terrors visited her. This truce from all emotion reacted not on her mind alone, lulling her with a sense of soothed security, but on her body also, and she began to weary of this day-long inactivity.

The village lay on the lip of a stretch of land reclaimed from the sea. To the north the level marsh, now beginning to glow with the pale bloom of the sea-lavender, stretched away featureless till it lost itself in distance, but to the south a spur of hill came down to the shore ending in a wooded promontory. Gradually, as her physical health increased, she began to wonder what lay beyond this ridge which cut short the view, and one afternoon she walked across the intervening level and strolled up its wooded slopes The day was close and windless, the invigorating sea-breeze which till now had spiced the hate with freshness had died, and she looked forward to finding a current of air stirring when she had topped the hill. To the south a mass of dark cloud lay along the horizon, but there was no imminent threat of storm. The slope was easily surmounted, and presently she stood at the top and found herself on the edge of a tableland of wooded pasture, and following the path, which ran not far from the edge of the cliff, she came out into more open country. Empty fields, where a few sheep were grazing, mounted gradually upwards. Wooden stiles made a communication in the hedges that bounded them. And there, not a mile in front of her, she saw a wood, with trees growing slantingly away from the push of the prevalent sea winds, crowning the upward slope, and over the top of it peered a grey church tower.

For the moment, as the awful and familiar scene identified itself, Hester's heart stood still: the next a wave of courage and resolution poured in upon her. Here, at last was the scene of that prefatory dream, and here was she presented with the opportunity of fathoming and dispelling it. Instantly her mind was made up, and under the strange twilight of the shrouded sky, she walked swiftly on through the fields she had so often traversed in sleep, and up to the wood, beyond which he was waiting for her. She closed her ears against the clanging bell of terror, which now she could silence for ever, and unfalteringly entered that dark tunnel of wood. Soon in front of her the trees began to thin, and through them, now close at hand, she saw the church tower. In a few yards farther she came out of the belt of trees, and round her were the monuments of a graveyard long disused. The cliff was broken off close to the church tower: between it and the edge there was no more of the body of the church than a broken arch, thick hung with ivy. Round this she passed and saw below the ruin of fallen masonry, and the level sands strewn with headstones and disjected rubble, and at the edge of the cliff were graves already cracked and toppling. But there was no one here, none waited for her, and the churchyard where she had so often pictured him was as empty as the fields she had just traversed.

A huge elation filled her; her courage had been rewarded, and all the terrors of the past became to her meaningless phantoms. But there was no time to linger, for now the storm threatened, and on the horizon a blink of lightning was followed by a crackling peal. Just as she turned to go her eye fell on a tombstone that was, balanced on the very edge of the cliff, and she read on it that here lay the body of Roger Wyburn.

Fear, the catalepsy of nightmare, rooted her for the moment to the spot; she stared in stricken amazement at the moss-grown letters; almost she expected to see that fell terror of a face rise and hover over his resting-place. Then the fear which had frozen her lent her wings, and with hurrying feet she sped through the arched pathway in the wood and out into the fields. Not one backward glance did she give till she had come to the edge of the ridge above the village, and, turning, saw the pastures she had traversed empty of any living presence. None had followed; but the sheep, apprehensive of the coming storm, had ceased to feed, and were huddling under shelter of the stunted hedges.

Her first idea, in the panic of her mind, was to leave the place at once, but the last train for London had left an hour before, and besides, where was the use of flight if it was the spirit of a man long dead from which she fled? The distance from the place where his bones lay did not afford her safety; that must be sought for within. But she longed for Dick's sheltering and confident presence; he was arriving in any case to-morrow, but there were long dark hours before to-morrow, and who could say what the perils and dangers of the coming night might be? If he started this evening instead of to-morrow morning, he could motor down here in four hours, and would be with her by ten o'clock or eleven. She wrote an urgent telegram: 'Come at once,' she said. 'Don't delay.'

The storm which had flickered on the south now came quickly up, and soon after it burst in appalling violence. For preface there were but a few large drops that splashed and dried on the roadway as she came back from the post-office, and just as she reached the hotel again the roar of the approaching rain sounded, and the sluices of heaven were opened. Through the deluge flared the fire of the lightning, the thunder crashed and echoed overhead, and presently the street of the village was a torrent of sandy turbulent water, and sitting there in the dark one picture leapt floating before her eyes, that of the tombstone of Roger Wyburn, already tottering to its fall at the edge of the cliff of the church tower. In such rains as these, acres of the cliffs were loosened; she seemed to hear the whisper of the sliding sand that would precipitate those perished sepulchres and what lay within to the beach below.

By eight o'clock the storm was subsiding, and as she dined she was handed a telegram from Dick, saying that he had already started and sent this off en route. By half-past ten, therefore, if all was well, he would be here, and somehow he would stand between her and her fear. Strange how a few days ago both it and the thought of him had become distant and dim to her; now the one was as vivid as the other, and she counted the minutes to his arrival. Soon the rain ceased altogether, and looking out of the curtained window of her sitting-room where she sat watching the slow circle of the hands of the clock, she saw a tawny moon rising over the sea. Before it had climbed to the zenith, before her clock had twice told the hour again, Dick would be with her.

It had just struck ten when there came a knock at her door, and the page-boy entered with the message that a gentleman had come for her. Her heart leaped at the news; she had not expected Dick for half an hour yet, and now the lonely vigil was over. She ran downstairs, and there was the figure standing on the step outside. His face was turned away from her; no doubt he was giving some order to his chauffeur. He was outlined against the white moonlight, and in contrast with that, the gas-jet in the entrance just above his head gave his hair a warm, reddish tinge. She ran across the hall to him.

'Ah, my darling, you've come,' she said. 'It was good of you. How quick you've been!' Just as she laid her hand on his shoulder he turned. His arm was thrown out round her, and she looked into a face with eyes close set, and a mouth smiling on one side, the other, thick and gathered together as by some physical deformity, sneered and lusted.

The nightmare was on her; she could neither run nor scream, and supporting her dragging steps, he went forth with her into the night.

Half an hour later Dick arrived. To his amazement he heard that a man had called for his wife not long before, and that she had gone out with him. He seemed to be a stranger here, for the boy who had taken his message to her had never seen him before, and presently surprise began to deepen into alarm; enquiries were made outside the hotel, and it appeared that a witness or two had seen the lady whom they knew to be staying there walking, hatless, along the top of the beach with a man whose arm was linked in hers. Neither of them knew him, but one had seen his face and could describe it.

The direction of the search thus became narrowed down, and though with a lantern to supplement the moonlight they came upon footprints which might have been hers, there were no marks of any who walked beside her. But they followed these until they came to an end, a mile away, in a great landslide of sand, which had fallen from the old churchyard on the cliff, and had brought down with it half the tower and a gravestone, with the body that had lain below.

The gravestone was that of Roger Wyburn, and his body lay by it, untouched by corruption or decay, though two hundred years had elapsed since it was interred there. For a week afterwards the work of searching the landslide went on, assisted by the high tides that gradually washed it away. But no further discovery was made.

THE GUIDE

Ramsey Campbell

An elderly man buys a rare M.R. James guidebook detailing an area near him. To his surprise, he finds a number of strange notations scrawled inside pointing to an obscure, secluded location. He decides he must find it to see what secrets it hides. This story is a tribute to the great M.R. James, so it's no surprise that something dark and malicious awaits him.

The used bookshops seemed to be just as useless. In the first, Kew felt as if he had committed a gaffe by asking for the wrong James or even by asking for a book. The woman who was minding the next bookshop, her lap draped in black knitting so voluminous that she appeared to be mending a skirt she had on, assured him that the bookseller would find him something in the storeroom. 'He's got lots of books in the back,' she confided to Kew, and as he leaned on his stick and leafed through an annual he'd read seventy years ago, she kept up a commentary: 'Fond of books, are you? I've read some books, books I'd call books. Make you sneeze, though, some of these old books. Break your toes, some of these books, if you're not careful. I don't know what people want with such big books. It's like having a stone slab on top of you, reading one of those books...' As Kew sidled toward the door she said ominously, 'He wouldn't want you going before he found you your books.'

'My family will be wondering what's become of me,' Kew offered, and fled.

Holidaymakers were driving away from the beach, along the narrow street of shops and small houses encrusted with pebbles and seashells. Some of the shops were already closing. He made for the newsagent's, in the hope that though all the horror books had looked too disgusting to touch, something more like literature might have found its way unnoticed onto one of the shelves, and then he realized that what he'd taken for a booklover's front room, unusually full of books, was in fact a shop. The sill inside the window was crowded with potted plants and cacti. Beyond them an antique till gleamed on a desk, and closer to the window, poking out of the end of a shelf, was a book by M. R. James.

The door admitted him readily and tunefully. He limped quickly to the shelf, and sighed. The book was indeed by James: Montague Rhodes James, O. M., Litt. D., F. B. A., F. S. A., Provost of Eton. It was a guide to Suffolk and Norfolk.

The shopkeeper appeared through the bead curtain of the doorway behind the desk. 'That's a lovely book, my dear,' she croaked smokily, pointing with her cigarette, 'and cheap.'

Kew glanced at the price penciled on thc flyleaf. Not bad for a fiver, he had to admit, and only today he'd been complaining that although this was James country there wasn't a single book of his to be seen. He leafed through the guide, and the first page he came to bore a drawing of a bench end, carved with a doglike figure from whose grin a severed head dangled by the hair. 'I'll chance it,' he murmured, and dug his wallet out of the pocket of his purple cardigan.

The shopkeeper must have been too polite or too eager for a sale to mention that it was closing time, for as soon as he was on the pavement he heard her bolt the door. As he made his way to the path down to the beach, a wind from the sea fluttered the brightly striped paper in which she'd wrapped the volume. Laura and her husband Frank were shaking towels and rolling them up while their eight-year-olds kicked sand at each other. 'Stop that, you two, or else,' Laura cried.

'I did say you should drop me and go on somewhere,' Kew said as he reached them.

'We wouldn't dream of leaving you by yourself, Teddy,' Frank said, brushing sand from his bristling gingery torso.

'He means we'd rather stay with you,' Laura said, yanking at her swimsuit top, which Kew could see she hadn't been wearing.

'Of course that's what I meant, old feller,' Frank shouted as if Kew were deaf.

They were trying to do their best for him, insisting that he come with them on this holiday — the first he'd taken since Laura's mother had died — but why couldn't they accept that he wanted to be by himself? 'Grand-dad's bought a present,' Bruno shouted.

'Is it for us?' Virginia demanded.

'I'm afraid it isn't the kind of book you would like.'

'We would if it's horrible,' she assured him. 'Mum and dad don't mind.'

'It's a book about this part of the country. I rather think you'd be bored.'

She shook back her hair, making her earrings jangle, and screwed up her face. 'I already am.'

'If you make faces like that no boys will be wanting you tonight at the disco,' Frank said, and gathered up the towels and the beach toys, trotted to the car which he'd parked six inches short of a garden fence near the top of the path, hoisted his armful with one hand while he unlocked the hatchback with the other, dumped his burden in and pushed the family one by one into the car. 'Your granddad's got his leg,' he rumbled when the children complained about having to sit in the back seat, and Kew felt more of a nuisance than ever.

They drove along the tortuous coast road to Cromer, and Kew went up to his room. Soon Laura knocked on his door to ask whether he was coming down for an aperitif. He would have invited her to sit with him so that they could reminisce about her mother, but Frank shouted 'Come on, old feller, give yourself an appetite. We don't want you fading away on us.'

Kew would have had more of an appetite if the children hadn't swapped horrific jokes throughout the meal. 'That's enough, now,' Laura kept saying. Afterwards coffee was served in the lounge, and Kew tried to take refuge in his book.

It was more the M. R. James he remembered nostalgically than he would have dared hope. Comic and macabre images lay low amid the graceful sentences. Here was 'that mysterious being Sir John Shorne', Rector of North Marston, who 'was invoked against ague; but his only known act was to conjure the devil into a boot, the occasion and sequelae of this being alike unknown.' Here were the St. Albans monks, who bought two of St. Margaret's fingers; but who, Kew wondered, were the Crouched Friars, who had 'one little house, at Great Whelnetham'? Then there were 'the three kings or young knights who are out hunting and pass a churchyard, where they meet three terrible corpses, hideous with the ravages of death, who say to them, 'As we are, so will you be'' — a popular subject for decorating churches, apparently.

Other references were factual, or at least were presented as such: not only a rector named Blastus Godly, but a merman caught at Orford in the thirteenth century, who 'could not be induced to take an interest in the services of the church, nor indeed to speak.' Kew's grunt of amusement at this attracted the children, who had finished reading the horror comics they'd persuaded their father to buy them. 'Can we see?' Virginia said.

Kew showed them the sketch of the bench-end with the severed head, and thought of ingratiating himself further with them by pointing out a passage referring to the tradition that St. Erasmus had had his entrails wound out of him on a windlass, the kind of thing their parents tried half-heartedly to prevent them from watching on videocassette. Rebuking himself silently, he leafed in search of more acceptably macabre anecdotes, and then he stared. 'Granddad,' Bruno said as if Kew needed to be told, 'someone's been writing in your book.'

A sentence at the end of the penultimate chapter — 'It is almost always worth while to halt and look into a Norfolk church' — had been ringed in grayish ink, and a line as shaky as the circumscription led to a scribbled paragraph that filled the lower half of the page. 'I hope they knocked a few quid off the price for that, old feller,' Frank said. 'If they didn't I'd take it back.'

'Remember when you smacked me,' Laura said to Kew, 'for

drawing in one of mummy's books?'

Frank gave him a conspiratorial look which Kew found so disturbing that he could feel himself losing control, unable to restrain himself from telling Laura that Virginia shouldn't be dressed so provocatively, that the children should be in bed instead of staying up for the disco, that he was glad Laura's mother wasn't here to see how they were developing... He made his excuses and rushed himself up to his room.

He should sleep before the dull sounds of the disco made that impossible, but he couldn't resist poring over the scribbled paragraph. After a few minutes he succeeded in deciphering the first phrase, which was underlined. 'Best left out,' it said.

If the annotation described something better than the book included, Kew would like to know what it was. Studying the phrase had given him a headache, which the disco was liable to worsen. He got ready for bed and lay in the dark, improvising a kind of silent lullaby out of the names of places he'd read in the guidebook:

> *'Great Snoring and Creeling St. Mary, Bradfield Combust and Breckles and Snape; Herringfleet, Rattlesden, Chipley and Weeting; Bungay and Blickling and Diss...'*

Almost asleep, too much so to be troubled by the draught that he could hear rustling paper near his bed, he wondered if the scribbled phrase could mean that the omission had been advisable. In that case, why note it at such length?

He slept, and dreamed of walking from church to church, the length and breadth of East Anglia, no longer needing his stick. He found the church he was looking for, though he couldn't have said what his criteria were, and lay down beneath the ribbed vault that somehow reminded him of himself. Laura and the children came to visit him, and he sat up. 'As I am, so will you be,' he said in a voice whose unfamiliarity dismayed him. They hadn't come to visit but to view him, he thought, terrified of doing so himself. It seemed he had no choice, for his body was audibly withering, a process which dragged his head down to show him what had become of him. Barely in time, his cry wakened him.

If the dream meant anything, it confirmed that he needed time by himself. He lay willing his heartbeat to slacken its pace; his eardrums felt close to bursting. He slept uneasily, and woke at dawn. When he limped to the toilet, his leg almost let him down. He hawked, splashed cold water on his face, massaged his hands for several minutes before opening the book. If he couldn't reread James's ghost stories, then viewing a location that had suggested one of them might be as much of an experience.

The book fell open at the scribbled page, and he saw that the line beneath the phrase he'd read last night wasn't underlining after all. It led from the next word, which was 'map', across the page and onto the fore-edge. Rubbing together his fingers and thumb, which felt dusty, he opened the book where the line ended, at a map of Norfolk.

The line led like the first thread of a cobweb to a blotch on the Norfolk coast, where the map identified nothing in particular, showing only beach and fields for miles. The next scribbled phrase, however, was easily read: 'churchyard on the cliff — my old parish.' It sounded irresistibly Jamesian, and not to his family's taste at all.

In the hotel lounge before breakfast he read on: 'There was a man so versed in the black arts that he was able to bide his time until the elements should open his grave...' Either Kew was becoming used to the scrawl or it grew increasingly legible as it progressed. He might have read more if the family hadn't come looking for him. 'We're going to give granddad a good day out today, aren't we?' Frank declared.

'We said so,' Bruno muttered.

Virginia frowned reprovingly at him. 'You have to say where we're going,' she told her grandfather with a faintly martyred air.

'How about to breakfast?' At the table he said to the children 'I expect you'd like to go to Hunstanton, wouldn't you? I understand there are dodgems and roller coasters and all sorts of other things to make you sick.'

'Yes, yes, yes,' the children began to chant, until Laura shushed them, 'That doesn't sound like you, daddy,' she said.

'You can drop me off on your way. I've found somewhere I want to walk to, that wouldn't have anything to offer you youngsters.'

'I used to like walking with you and mummy,' Laura said, and turned on her son. 'That's disgusting, Bruno. Stop doing that with your egg.'

Kew thought of inviting her to walk to the church with him, but he'd seen how intent Frank and the children had become when she'd hinted at accompanying him. 'Maybe we'll have time for a stroll another day,' he said.

He sat obediently in the front seat of the car, and clutched his book and his stick while Frank drove eastward along the coast road. Whenever he spoke, Frank and Laura answered him so competitively that before long he shut up. As the road swung away from the coast, the towns and villages grew fewer. A steam train paced the car for a few hundred yards as if it were ushering them into James's era. A sea wind rustled across the flat land, under a sky from which gulls sailed down like flakes of the unbroken cloud. On the side of the road toward the coast, the stooped grass looked pale with salt and sand.

Apart from the occasional fishmonger's stall at the roadside, the miles between the dwindling villages were deserted. By the time the car arrived at the stretch of road that bordered the unnamed area, which the blotch of grayish ink marked on the map, Bruno and Virginia had begun to yawn at the monotonousness of the landscape. Where a signpost pointed inland along a road, an inn stood by itself, and beyond it Kew saw an unsignposted footpath that led toward the sea. 'This'll do me. Let me out here,' he said.

'Thirsty, old feller? This one's on me.'

Kew felt both dismayed by the idea of being distracted from the loneliness of the setting and ashamed of his feelings. 'They'll be open in a few minutes,' Laura said.

'Boring, boring,' the children started chanting, and Kew took the opportunity to climb out and close the door firmly. 'Don't spoil the children's day on my account,' he said, 'or mine will be spoiled as well.'

Now he'd made it sound as if they were ruining his holiday. He patted Laura's cheek awkwardly, and then Virginia's, and leaned back from the open window. 'Five o'clock here suit you?' Frank said. 'If we're late, there's always the pub.'

Kew agreed, and watched the car race away. The children waved without turning their heads, but Laura kept him in sight as long as she could. Just as the car reached the first bend, Kew wanted to wave his stick urgently, to call out to Frank that he'd changed his mind. Six hours out here seemed a more generous helping of solitude than even he needed. Then the car was gone, and he told himself that the family deserved a break from him.

He sat on a rustic bench outside the building striped with timber, and turned to the scribbled page while he waited for the door to be unlocked. He found he was able to read straight on to the end, not least because the ink appeared darker. 'There was a man so versed in the black arts that he was able to bide his time until the elements should open his grave; only the passage of so many years, and the stresses to which the falling away of the land subjected the grave, twisted not only the coffin almost beyond recognition but also what laired within. Imagine, if you will, a spider in human form with only four limbs, a spider both enraged and made ungainly by the loss, especially since the remaining limbs are by no means evenly distributed. If anything other than simple malevolence let him walk, it was the knowledge that whoever died of the sight of him would be bound to him.'

Kew shivered and grinned at himself. So he could still derive a frisson from that kind of writing, all the more pleasurable when he remembered that James had never believed in his ghosts. Was it really possible that Kew was holding in his hands an unpublished episode by James? He didn't know what else to think. He gazed along the path through the swaying grass and wondered what it led to that had produced the description he'd just read, until the sound of bolts being slid back made him jump.

The landlord, a hairy bespectacled man whose ruddiness and girth suggested that he enjoyed his beer, looked out at Kew and then at the book. 'Bit out of your way if you're walking, aren't you?' he said, so heartily that it served as a welcome. 'Come in and wet your whistle, my lad.'

A bar bristling with decorated handles and thick as a castle parapet marked off a quarter of the L-shaped room, beyond which were a few small tables draped with cloths, and a staircase guarded by a visitors' book. The landlord hauled on the nearest handle and gave Kew a pint of murky beer. 'I was driven here,' Kew explained. 'I'm just about to start walking.'

'Are you not using that book?'

'Why, do you know it?'

'I know all of that man's work that's set around this countryside. He had the touch, and no mistake.' The landlord pulled himself a pint and drank half of it in one gulp. 'But he didn't find anything round here that he wanted to write about.'

Kew thought of showing the landlord the annotation but wasn't quite sure of himself. 'Do you know if he ever came this way?'

'I should say so. He signed the book.'

Excitement made Kew grip the handle of his tankard. 'Could I see?'

'Certainly, if I can dig it out. Were you thinking of eating?' When Kew said that he better had, the landlord served him bread and cheese before unlocking a cupboard beside the stairs. Kew glanced at the handwritten paragraph to remind himself what the writing looked like, and then watched the landlord pull out visitor's book after visitor's book and scan the dates. Eventually he brought a volume to Kew's table. 'Here he is.'

Kew saw the date first: 1890. 'He hadn't written any of his stories then, had he?'

'Not one.'

Kew ran his gaze down the column of faded signatures, and almost didn't see the name he was searching for. As he came back to it he saw why he had passed over it: the signature bore no resemblance to the handwriting in the guidebook. He sighed, and then sucked in a breath. The signature directly beneath James's was in that handwriting.

Was the signature 'A. Fellows'? He touched it with his fingertip, and tried to rub the cobwebby feel of it off his finger with his thumb. 'Who was this, do you know?'

'Whoever came after Monty James.'

The landlord seemed to be trying not to grin, and Kew gazed at him until he went on. 'You'd think these East Anglians would be proud to have James write about their countryside,' the landlord said, 'but they don't like to talk about his kind of stories. Maybe they believe in that kind of thing more than he did. The chap who ran this place was on his deathbed when he told my father about that signature. It seems nobody saw who made it. It's like one of Monty's own yarns.'

'Have you any idea where James had been that day?'

'Some old ruin on the cliff,' the landlord said, and seemed to wish he had been less specific.

'Along the path outside?'

'If it was, there's even less there now, and you'll have noticed that he didn't think it had any place in his book.'

The annotator had believed otherwise, and Kew thought that was a mystery worth investigating. He finished his lunch and drained his tankard, and was at the door when the landlord said 'I wouldn't stray too far from the road if I were you. Remember we're open till three.'

This felt so like the protectiveness Kew had escaped earlier that he made straight for the path. Didn't anyone think he was capable of taking care of himself? He'd fought in the war against Hitler, he'd been a partner in an accountancy firm, he'd run every year in the London marathon until his leg had crippled him; he'd tended Laura's mother during her last years and had confined himself to places where he could wheel her in her chair, and after all that, he wasn't to be trusted to go off the road by himself? James had followed the path, and it didn't seem to have done him any harm. Kew stuffed the book under one arm and tramped toward the sea, cutting at the ragged grassy edges of the path with his stick.

The fields of pale grass stretched into the distance on both sides of him. The low cloud, featureless except for the infrequent swerving gull, glared dully above him. After twenty minutes' walking he felt he had scarcely moved, until he glanced back and found that the inn was out of sight. He was alone, as far as he could see, though the grass of the fields came up to his shoulder now. A chilly wind rustled through the fields, and he limped fast to keep warm, faster when he saw a building ahead.

At least, he thought it was a building until he was able to see through its broken windows. It was the front wall of a cottage, all that remained of the house. As he came abreast of it he saw other cottages further on, and a backward look showed him foundations under the grass. He'd been walking through a ruined village without realizing. One building, however, appeared still to be intact: the church, ahead at the edge of the ruins.

The church was squat and blackened, with narrow windows and a rudimentary tower. Kew had to admit that it didn't look very distinguished — hardly worth singling out for the guidebook — though wasn't there a large gargoyle above one of the windows that overlooked the wide gray sea? In any case, the sight of the church, alone on the cliff top amid the fringe of nodding grass, seemed worth the walk. He threw his shoulders back and breathed deep of the sea air, and strode toward the church.

He needn't have been quite so vigorous; there was nobody to show off for. He had to laugh at himself, for in his haste he dug his stick into a hole in the overgrown pavement and almost overbalanced. Rather than risk tearing the paper jacket by trying to hold onto the guidebook, he let the book fall on the grass, where it fell open at the scribbled page.

He frowned at the handwriting as he stooped carefully, gripping the stick, and wondered if exposure to sunlight had affected the ink. The first lines appeared blurred, so much so that he couldn't read the words 'best left out' at all. Perhaps the dead light was affecting his eyes, because now he peered toward the church he saw that there was no gargoyle. He could only assume that the wind had pushed forward the withered shrub, which he glimpsed swaying out of sight around the corner closest to the sea, and a trick of perspective had made it look as if it were protruding from high up on the wall.

The church door was ajar. As Kew limped in the direction of the cliff edge, to see how stable the foundations of the building were, he discerned pews and an altar in the gloomy interior, and a figure in black moving back and forth in front of the glimmering altar. Could the church still be in use? Perhaps the priest was another sightseer.

Kew picked his way alongside the building, over illegibly weathered gravestones whose cracks looked cemented with moss, to the jagged brink, and then he shoved the book under the arm that held the stick and grabbed the cold church wall to support himself. Apart from the slabs he'd walked on, the graveyard had vanished; it must have fallen to the beach as the centuries passed. The church itself stood at the very edge of the sheer cliff now, its exposed foundations sprouting weeds that rustled in the sandy wind. But it wasn't the precariousness of the building that had made Kew feel suddenly shaky, in need of support; it was that there was no shrub beside the church, nothing like the distorted shrunken brownish shape he'd glimpsed as it withdrew from sight. Beside that corner of the church, the cliff fell steeply to the beach.

He clutched the wall, bruising his fingertips, while he tried to persuade himself that the shrub and the portion of ground on which it stood had just lost their hold on the cliff, and then he shoved himself away from the wall, away from the crumbling edge. As he did so, he heard a scrabbling above him, on the roof.

A chunk of moss, too large to have been dislodged by a bird, dropped on the grass in front of him. He clapped his free hand to his chest, which felt as if his heart were beating its way to the surface, and fled to the entrance to the church.

The priest was still by the altar. Kew could see the blotch of darkness that was his robe, and the whitish glint of his collar. Thoughts were falling over one another in Kew's head: the guidebook was a late edition, and so the scribbled annotation must have been made decades later than the signature at the inn, yet the handwriting hadn't aged at all, and couldn't the words in the visitor's book which Kew had taken for a signature have been 'A Follower'? The only thought he was able to grasp was how far he would have to run across the deserted land from the church to the inn — too far for him to be able to keep up the pace for more than a few minutes. He dodged into the gloomy church, his stick knocking against a pew, and heard a larger movement overhead. 'Please,' he gasped, stumbling down the aisle into the dimness.

He hardly knew what he was saying or doing, but where else could he go for help except to the priest? He wished he could see the man's face, though rather less fervently once the priest spoke. 'It brought you,' he said.

It wasn't just his words but also his voice that disturbed Kew. Perhaps it was an echo that made it sound so hollow, but why was its tone so eager? 'You mean the book,' Kew stammered.

'We mean what you read.'

Kew was almost at the altar now. As his eyes adjusted, he saw that what he'd taken to be dimness draping the pews and the altar was a mass of dust and cobwebs. More than the tone and timber of the voice, its forced quality was beginning to unnerve him. 'Your friend James thought it, but he didn't write it,' the voice said. 'We inspired him, and then I had to write it for him.'

If James had used the handwritten paragraph in one of his tales and identified the setting as he tended to, Kew thought with the clarity of utter panic, more people would have visited this church. He was backing toward the door when he heard something clamber down from the roof and land just outside the doorway with a sound like the fall of a bundle of sticks and leather. 'James nearly saw, but he didn't believe,' said the figure by the altar, and stepped into the light that seeped through a pinched grimy window. 'But you will,' it said out of the hole that was most of its face.

Kew closed his eyes tight. His panic had isolated a single thought at the center of him: that those who died of seeing would be bound to what they saw. He felt the guidebook slip out of his hands, he heard its echoes clatter back and forth between the walls, and then it gave way to another sound, of something that scuttled lopsidedly into the church and halted to wait for him. He heard the priest's feet, bare of more than clothing, begin to drag across the floor toward him. He turned, frantically tapping the pews with his stick, and shuffled in the direction of the door. Beyond it was the path, the inn, and his family at five o'clock, further than his mind could grasp. If he had to die, please let it not be here! What terrified him most, as he swung the stick in front of him and prayed that it would ward off any contact, was what might be done to him to try and make him look.

A GHOSTLY CREW

Introducing our Authors

W. H. Barrett (1881–1974)

W. H. (Jack) Barrett finished his working days as gardener to the Archdeacon of Norwich and in the three collections of his writings (including the seminal 'Tales from the Fens') he captures an all but forgotten world of East Anglian folk customs, myth and ancient lore. His anecdotes – many overheard at the Ship Inn at Brandon Creek – give clear insights into another time when myth and magic were an accepted part of country life. 'Witches at Halloween' is surely one of his most memorable.

E. F. Benson (1867–1940)

Edward Frederic Benson was one of the three decidedly eccentric brothers – all of which contributed considerably to the ghost story tradition. Resident for a time in Lamb House Rye, the home of Henry James at one period too, Benson wrote many successful novels such as the Mapp and Lucia series. His ghost stories have a deliciously nasty flavour which has undoubtedly contributed to their enduring popularity. The horrific climax of his tale 'The Mask' is probably inspired by the crumbling cliffs of Dunwich while 'The Tale of an Empty House' is clearly set in Blakeney and the cottage in question is the still-standing watch-house on the far-off shingle bank.

Noel Boston (1910–1966)

Noel Boston's 'Yesterday Knocks' is a rare, and often terrifying, collection of five short stories by another writer and clergyman resident in East Anglia – where his relatives still persist. His knowledge of the esoteric was considerable including his claims to knowing the whereabouts of the Holy Grail itself. A close relative of Noel Boston still lives in a particularly secluded area of Norfolk and continues in the family tradition as country parson.

Ramsay Campbell

Ramsay Campbell is a highly successful award-winning author of both novels and short stories, some of which are undoubtedly influenced by M.R. James and more significantly H.P. Lovecraft. His dense and evocative prose style makes both his horror and ghostly fiction memorable and resonant. Try as you may, finding the location of Campbell's grim tale 'The Guide' along the North Norfolk coast is not easy: but perhaps that's all for the best.

Celia Dale (1912–2011)

Celia Dale was an award-winning author of eleven novels and the occasional short story and a reviewer too who also worked as the secretary to Rumer Godden. 'Hetty Pegler's Christmas' – her contribution to the December 1974 edition of *Cambridgshire and Peterborough Life* – is a highly original tale with a decidedly chilling twist.

Abraham Fleming (1552–1607)

Abraham Fleming was a clergyman who wrote extensively in many fields. After studying at Porterhouse, Cambridge he became famous at an early age for his translations from the Latin and during his career he went on to translate, write or contribute to over 50 significant works including in 1577 'A Strange and Terrible Wunder'. This classic account of a recorded visit by East Anglia's devil dog - a creature said also to be the inspiration for Conan Doyle's Baskevillian terror - is essential reading prior to your next visit to the Suffolk town of Bungay!

Arthur Gray 'Ingulfus' (1852–1940)

Arthur Gray's books are generally either about Shakesperean studies or Cambridge history and it is only under the pseudonym of Ingulfus that he wrote fiction in the form of his classic 'Tedious Brief Tales of Granta and Gramarye' – a true classic of the ghostly genre. These antiquarian and chilling stories are set in Jesus College, where Gray was master and were initially published as periodicals. First editions of this rare and splendidly illustrated work are collector's items indeed.

James Humphreys

Himself a native of the Fens, James Humphreys's crime novels 'Sleeping Partner' and 'Riptide' are both set in Eastern England and his first collection of macabre short stories 'The Mincer' contains several decidedly ghostly encounters. His tale 'The Lantern Men' is a chilling modern take on an ages-old belief.

M R James (1862–1936)

Montague Rhodes James is arguably Britain's finest writer of ghostly fiction. Although an academic who regarded his fictional work as mere trifles, James' three collections of ghost stories, rich in suggestive indefinitness and antiquarian mystery, are as popular today as ever and have inspired generations of writers. Popularised further by the horror movie 'Night of the Demon' and the BBC's classic series 'Ghost Stories for Christmas', James' work has never been out of print.

R. H. Malden (1879–1951)

Richard Henry Malden was a contemporary and friend of M.R. James. He had a distinguished career in the church and 'Nine Ghosts' (1943 Arnold) was his only collection of stories; in the introduction to which he acknowledged his debt to the master. Several East Anglian locations can easily be spotted in his work: Blakeney Point once more appearing as the fearful Stivinghoe Bank.

Gladys Mitchell (1900–1983)

Gladys Mitchell is the author of 66 detective novels including the memorable Mrs Bradley investigations. However she had a definite fondness for the supernatural too and her books 'When Last I Died' and the extremely rare 'Wraiths and Changelings' with its tale of ghost hunting on the Norfolk Broads certainly bring with them a remarkable - and often chilling - sense of things best left unexplained. It's opening chapter is a delight in its evocation of a memorable - and amusing - party on All Hallows Eve. We include a chapter from early in the book when our intrepid ghost hunters encounter 'The Bure at Night', as a taster for what is to come.

R. H. Mottram (1883–1971)

Ralph Hale Mottram was a clerk at a Norwich bank who published works on a broad range of subjects and is best remembered for his 'Spanish Farm' trilogy. His tale 'The Headless Hound' is a rare excursion into local folklore as he captures the spirit of the infamous Black Shuck. He is buried at Rosary Cemetery, Norwich, a site he decided upon as a four year old child!

E. G. Swain (1861–1938)

Edmund Gill Swain was an antiquarian and long time friend of M.R. James. His stories of Mr. Batchel – rector of Stoneground – are undoubtedly set in his real parish of Stanground near King's Lynn a place very different from what it once was. Although lacking the fearful quality of James' fiction the gentle humour and occasional chills of his tales make them both enjoyable and decidedly distinctive.

H. R. Wakefield. (1888–1964)

Herbert Russell Wakefield was the son of an Anglican minister who eventually became Bishop of Birmingham. His collection of ghost stories 'They Return at Evening' was published to considerable acclaim in 1928 and his many subsequent collections were equally celebrated; although much of his later work is more formulaic than his earlier – and very chilling – stories. 'The Thirteenth Hole at Duncaster' – set 'in a remote hamlet on the Norfolk Coast' – has decidedly Jamesian overtones.

Piers Warren

Piers Warren is a wildlife filmmaker and author of a number of fiction and non fiction books. He lives on the North Norfolk coast the setting for his highly acclaimed novel 'Black Shuck – The Devil's Dog' (Shortlisted for the 2012 East Anglian Literature Award) which continues the exploits of this fearsome animal up to the present day. His tale for our selection is a decidedly nasty, and previously unpublished, prequel to his novel.

Wayne Adrian Drew

Wayne Adrian Drew is a writer, producer and director who has regularly contributed articles on supernatural film and fiction, to magazines such as *Fear* and *MixMag*, as well as producing many Arts programmes for the BBC. During his years working in the film industry for Lord Attenborough, he edited the BFI dossier on film maker David Cronenberg and was consultant editor on 10 editions of the *BFI Film and Television Handbook*. Adrian has also written 26 plays that have all been produced in London, some nationally and one Off-Broadway and these include biographical dramas about M.R. James ('The Laws of Shadows'), Edgar Allen Poe ('Uncommon Spring') and most recently H.P. Lovecraft ('To Dare to Dream') that will receive its premiere in 2016. As such, he is the ideal anthologist and contributor. He now lives in London and in a 16th Century home in central Norfolk that has not one, but two ghosts, and is the setting for his chilling drama 'All Hallows': a play that argues ghost stories are symbolic representatios of cultural paranoia at different phases in history. His admiration for M.R.James and his contemporaries is boundless and the Latin inscription at the head of his New Year's Eve ghostly tale, Shadows on the Fens, comes from one of James' most famous tales.